Breaking the Silence

Breaking the Silence

Book 2 in the
***Within the Walls* trilogy**

by Stephanie Bennett

Wild Flower Press, Inc.
Leland, North Carolina

Breaking the Silence
Book 2 in the Within the Walls trilogy

Published by Wild Flower Press, Inc.
P.O. Box 2532
Leland, NC 28451

Web site: www.wildflowerpress.biz

ISBN-10: 0-9618852-5-4

ISBN-13: 978-0-9618852-5-0

Printed in the United States of America

ACKNOWLEGEMENTS

Two friends who worked on the cover are simply beyond compare. What would I do without you, Chris Jefferies and Terry Craig? I never want to find out. You are so dear to me!

Further, I can't put my name on this book without acknowledging the support and encouragement of a few other friends, Ann Cadaret, Eric Goodman, Wayne Jacobsen, and Terry Craig. Your input and early reading of the manuscript have helped beyond measure. Many others have offered a kind word, a willingness to share the book, or have been faithful to review it. And so, to all my friends and family: I love you and thank you, especially for letting your love for me flow in so much more than words.

Inspiration for this project comes from many directions, one of which that rarely gets mentioned is from my colleagues and friends in the Media Ecology Association, particularly Lance Strate, who has modeled creativity, leadership, and integrity in our intellectual pursuit of meaning.

This book series started in my imagination in 1995 when I was confronted with the challenges of functioning within a corrupt system where people were treated as objects—cogs in a wheel—to work for the vast and elaborate vision of one person. Initially, I entitled the book The Vision, but found that dehumanization takes place on many levels and many contexts, not just in the heart of a single individual. It is corporate. It is systemic. It is the world. My eyes were opened to see that the destructive forces of nature are not just found within the hurricanes and tsunamis around the globe; they are within each of us. It was a difficult lesson, but for it I am thankful and acknowledge the many people who contributed to my education, especially those who taught me how to steer clear of institutional evil.

In addition, and most importantly, I want to thank my husband for his liberality, loyalty, and support. These qualities are not immediately apparent in the hearts of every man, but I find them to be some of the most attractive features a man can exhibit. Without the freedom he has given me to expand my wings, this project would have stayed in the cocoon stage forever, scrunched up inside my head, lifeless. Instead, Emilya's story has become something that is alive, soaring through my spirit with joy into the hands of a reading public. Thanks, dear.

April, 2071

My feet are flying down the mountain path! Stumbling now and again over small rocks and broken branches, I am running faster than I ever could have imagined. Birch trees pass by me as though they are on wheels. What just a bit earlier in the day seemed like a great idea to head out and hunt down my stalled car on this impeccably beautiful day, suddenly changed into chaos as a huge, golden-hued cat leapt from rock-to-rock behind me. After all that has transpired, I never imagined my demise would involve being ravaged by a wild animal.

I am breathless and don't know how much longer I can last at this pace! Heck—I was never much of an athlete, but after the last few weeks of learning to survive out here, my body is a bit more agile and capable of extreme stress. I risk a quick look behind me to keep my eye on the cat, and all at once I see stars. Something takes me down; I am unconscious. Here I am, in some sort of incredulous out-of-body experience, watching myself as I lay motionless underneath a large, scratchy spruce tree.

Fading in and out of consciousness, I see myself encircled in terror. It's not just one, but six hungry-looking mountain cats. There will be no one coming to save me this time; they don't even know I left! Any hope of getting back to the Lab is dashed.

No doubt, my father will be searching for me. Liam may be quiet and stand-offish, but even in this short span of time he has shown himself to be a fierce man when it comes to tangling with the forest. Surely mother will be the first one to become aware that I am missing, and she'll let him know. Either he or one of the other men in the community will eventually find me, bury me—at least what is left of me—and then there will be no one concerned in the least with trying set things right at the Lab.

I begin to weep; it is uncontrollable.

I should never have tried to leave FRANCO. Although they are regularly annoying, this community of outliers includes several members of my family who I thought died decades ago. Although I was told they perished in a skiing accident when I was six, they are alive and well in this remote mountain range. Besides that, I'm just starting to scratch the surface of understanding what Grand'Mere meant when she first told me that her secret writings regarding "FRANCO" weren't about a man, but a people who exist to share life together outside the walls of society. When I first heard the acronym—For Revelation And Nurturing—Community Optimization—I was shocked. All my projections about Grand'Mere having a secret love named FRANCO were totally wrong. That first day I had absolutely no idea what it meant, but now even the crazy concept of community optimization is beginning to make sense.

The very last thing I remember seeing is a vague line of deep green swirling above my head. Suddenly, as if someone pulled a dark shade over a wide open window, I open my eyes, look hazily about and see that the surroundings are familiar.

A few sticks of straw from what passes for a mattress at Grand'Mere's earth shelter are pricking me, pushing into my left shoulder blade. I turn to shake myself awake and see the same inscription on the wall that was there the day I first arrived at this backward mountain camp and have stared at every night since then.

> In that desolate land and lone,
> Where the Big Horn and Yellowstone
> Roar down their mountain path,
> By their fires the Sioux Chiefs
> Muttered their woes and griefs

And the menace of their wrath.
"Revenge!" cried Rain-in-the-Face,
"Revenge upon all the race
Of the White Chief with yellow hair!"
And the mountains dark and high
From their crags re-echoed the cry
Of his anger and despair—
Henry Wadsworth Longfellow

Oh Henry, Henry. I wonder what you were really like. Russa says you're one of her favorite poets, but you sound so vengeful and cantankerous. Huh—I bet you had your reasons.

The fact that my mother and father have been living here in these low mountains of Pennsylvania for over twenty years without even telling me, well –that makes me pretty cantankerous too. But revenge? Nah. Not my style. But I do wonder what sort of revenge you were writing about, Mr. Longfellow. Without access to my deep archives I haven't a clue, although I am starting to understand the echo of these mountains. Their cry is loud and clear—a lonely wail, especially when night falls. (And by now that Rain-in-the-Face passage is embedded in my brain!)

In the meantime, I continue to deal with these crazy night terrors. My face is wet from real tears and a bit of sweat. This numbers five times that I have had the same ugly dream about mountain cats; a nightmare, really.

Still, I tell no one. They don't need to know the extent of my emotional unraveling. I've got to somehow keep it together in spite of the deactivated state of my technical support system.

I hear Grand'Mere is stirring at the other end of her narrow quarters. The feeling of betrayal is still fairly raw, but it's impossible to be truly angry with a woman of her character and elegance. She raised me with soft words and countless kindnesses, and—for Strength's sake—I know Marissa and Liam were the ones who put her up to the deception!

This morning is like every other since I've arrived here in this hidden community they call FRANCO. I'm accustomed to micro-sleeping and would never stay in bed this long back at my flat, but here I sit, barely able to see what I'm scribbling in this paltry candlelight. I am stuck within these granite walls. I am stuck; so stuck.

Out of the open end of Grand'Mere's sparse residence juts a small wooden structure where the hearth is located. The table covered with a faded rose-patterned oilcloth takes up most of the room where she is probably at this very moment making tea. It's early, even for her. I wonder if she heard my flailing.

The cot I sleep on is tucked within the stone wall that separates my grandmother's sleeping space from my own. Clearly, this room was her pantry before I came. All the jars of beans, tomatoes and pickles that lined the walls are now piled up on either side of the hearth. My space is definitely not more than four feet wide and actually is more like a crevice than a room, but at least it gives me a modicum of privacy. I feel relatively safe, but some days I feel sort of like an animal—like a lion or tiger in its lair.

The dim moonlight of the pre-dawn stillness makes everything beyond my lap look black. In an hour or so the shadows will appear.

A strange anxiety slowly ripples through my body this morning, and my mind is weary for want of the pristine clarity that was so basic to my existence.

Back at the Lab and in my own flat on Addison Avenue, I never had to deal with shadows. Everything was clear. Choices were few; decisions were easy. What's happening now is inconceivable to me. All my tek is gone. My car—gone. My identity—gone! Or at least it that's what it feels like. Thankfully, I do still have my nail flap. That was safely attached to my finger when they found me. And my P/Z 1000 is intact, but without diamond dust there's no way to maintain any sort of stable connection with the Lab, my deep archives, or anyone back home!

One fleeting message—a befuddling paradox—probably got through from the residual diamond dust left around the surface of my nail flap. It was sketchy, difficult to read, and its meaning even harder to discern. It came through almost as soon as I arrived here and I've not been able to make sense of it since. That first day was a blur anyway. Dusk had settled in and I was finally by myself again resting on this lumpy cot when I saw the virtual tickertape running along my prefrontal cortex. My head was swirling with so much new information that I could barely think straight, but the message was there. It was short and simple, but utterly unclear:

XrO is ready to go. We're monitoring progress. Let sleeping dogs lie. Do not go in until I give you the word. I repeat: Do not apprise.

What? It made no sense; still doesn't. I couldn't re-read it because the connection broke almost immediately, but it was greatly disturbing. Was it meant for me? It was most definitely from the Lab because the source code always comes first, and I saw that clearly, but was the message meant for me? Was it about me? Whatever it was, it's really unnerving.

Oh, how I hate being out of the loop! It's bad enough the Lab pushed me into a forced leave of absence, but whatever is going on in that communiqué feels sinister. Strength—I must remember not to project my uncertainty onto the situation. Without my digital attendant it is so easy to stress out. I've got to stay strong! Perhaps it was just a stray message that had nothing to do with me and was sent by accident. Oh I hope so; I hope that is the case!

In the midst of all this continual inward uproar, one of the things that's most troubling is that no one understands me. Well, maybe Russa does, a little. The rest of them are celebrating my arrival—acting as if it is the most significant event in the history of FRANCO, but they are oblivious to all that I've lost. What's worse is that in spite of their obvious good intentions to make me feel comfortable, they don't seem to care a lick about my losses, especially the tek. They act as if our neuro-digital enhancements are superfluous, and I find that maddening!

It's . . . it's quite as if my parents—and the entire community—are from another planet. But they're not. What's worse is they're family, my family. I mean, finally, family. I'm here; they're here; but . . . where are we? They say we're just a two and a half hours drive outside of the New Jersey shoreline but it feels like another universe! My head has not stopped swirling. I feel as though I am smack in the very center of a waterspout of confusion.

It might not be so bad except that I have so very much time to think; just me and my brain in Grand'Mere's cozy little earth-shelter—UGH—I want my P/Z 1000! Life without my brain-interface is soooooooooo slow. Never would I have imagined how sluggish and painstaking every little step could be without connection to the network or my Deep Archives. Heck, my D.A. is my go-to place for anything I need to remember. It's all stashed there, and now. . . Strength—I can't get to any of it.

With all this time to ponder, I will admit that my role as virtual vacation developer at Travelite Global did get a little complicated in the last few months, but everything else was so much less demanding than it is here. In fact, I don't know how to deal with all of these . . . these—what should I call them—inconveniences? That's to say nothing of the larger issues that loom ahead. What if the Lab is actually monitoring me? If that message was indeed about me, maybe they've located my car and started to track me. Oh dear. What will they do to my parents if they discover FRANCO? On top of it all, my own allegiances are unclear. I wonder about my own responsibility in all this. Maybe I have a duty to expose FRANCO. They're not hurting anybody, but I'm quite sure ADMIN would see them as dissidents. Ugh. I don't know.

The only thing that seems right to do is something that never made a speck of sense before this year, and that's writing. The log I kept last winter literally kept me sane, and now, writing everything down in my log is just about the only thing productive that I am doing with my time, so . . . so . . . although it's not terribly efficient, that's what I plan to do. Now that I've been here in FRANCO for a little while, I have once again taken up this endeavor and I'm determined to add my observations to it to my log every day. Writing by candle light is the most tedious thing I can think of, but at least it helps to lessen the boredom, especially on dream-rocked nights like this.

The funniest thing is I am finding that there's something I genuinely like about the writing too. Although I'm not quite sure what it is, the quaint practice of lettering is strangely comforting. I'm hoping it will continue to help keep my mental faculties sharp because frankly everywhere I turn I find some crazy challenge to overcome, whether it's what to eat, how to clean my clothes, or even what to say to people who pass by me and say, "Hi Emilya, how are you?" Ughhhhhh. What should I say . . . fine? All this attention is so tedious.

Some days I even find myself struggling about how to think. Perhaps the worst is dealing with people who have not learned to separate the individual regions of their brain into proper sequestered sections. They haven't a clue as how to control their emotions, nor do they seem to have any desire to learn. It's boggling, simply boggling, and just . . . well, it's not one of those small, nettling challenges; it's grueling.

It's doubtful that any of them can see through my charade, but this morning I must admit it to myself: my own emotions are a little out of control.

Although I've been denying all of their many observations about my 'melancholic expression' and 'sullen demeanor,' and this issue with my tone and that, I must admit, I am sad today—really sad. There isn't anything that's motivating me to get off this cot. It's not very comfortable, but—Strength—it's more comfortable than walking around with a smile painted across my face.

I hate it because . . . because, well, they've all been so encouraging, trying to help me make sense of this . . . this . . . life of sweeping complexities, but I am unable to truly embrace it! It seems so primitive. It is primitive! The earth-shelters are beyond rustic—the walls barely keep out the elements. Most of the residents here sleep in the dark, narrow crags of this rocky terrain, with barely enough real roof overhead to provide privacy. I don't like it, and I continue to be confused at my parents' willingness to cope with it all. What's worse, they seem to like it this way!

I don't know. Maybe I'm sad mostly because I miss my flat. I miss my own space and the steady order of each day. I really don't know. Heck, I should be happy. It's just that the sleek walls and controlled temperatures of my home back on Addison Avenue seem so remote and irretrievable. It's . . . it's disheartening to think about how I shall ever get back there, though I do find a modicum of relief knowing that civilization is a mere two-to-three hour jaunt down the mountain and back through the old roads. That little bit of knowledge is indeed a quiet comfort. One day, I will find my way back.

I'm not sure how I'll get there, but I must devise a way out. In the meantime, I guess I've just got to wait it out. The right time to leave will present itself.

There's no way I can stay forever.

Chapter 1

Day 25—The Moment

"You keep talking about our community as them, Emilya. Don't you think it's about time to include yourself?

I must say, mother's words took me by surprise. It's only been a few weeks of being here at FRANCO. She expects too much.

I'm noticing, too, that she has such a way of cutting to the chase. She blurts things out, insensitively and in no uncertain terms. It can be really aggravating. The funny thing is, in spite of everything else that bothers me about this woman, I can't help but notice that her directness is almost the only thing I actually like about her. Well—wait—that's not right to say; she is my mother. I probably shouldn't even write that down being that someone may find this log someday, but the thing is she acts as though she actually has sway in my life.

It's as if she thinks that the fact that she gave birth to me should garner the respect that other mothers have from their daughters, but—come on—really? I have not even known this woman for the past twenty-three years; she left me before I even had a chance to get to know her. Grand'Mere, having raised me, always made sure that whatever she told me about my mother was positive but I was left filling in all the blanks! Frankly, what I see is far different than what I remember.

Marissa's feckless effort to be simple and sweet is outshined by a bombastic personality that is immediately evident upon seeing her face. With eyebrows that are so dark and pronounced her face seems to be a footnote, except for her smile which—when she laughs—is as wide as two of mine! But then there's this undercurrent of melancholia that pops up only once in a while, as if it's a misplaced comma in the middle of a run on sentence. I see it in the fleeting, wistful look that appears whenever we broach the subject of my childhood.

To be sure, in spite of the ongoing internal outrage that continues to nip at the outer edges of every fiber of my being there are actually things about Marissa that well, aren't . . . terrible. After all, she is my mother. She has this sort of quirky sense of humor that catches me unexpectedly from time to time. She has actually made me laugh on a couple of occasions, and even though I mostly don't get her jokes (which are really more like puns), my mother's overly expressive facial gestures and ultra-animated voice fill whatever space she enters with laughter and lively conversation. It's definitely comical to watch. Knowing that I come from her is especially ironic for Marissa and I are absolutely nothing alike.

There's one other thing I've observed that is a bit of an anomaly. It's her warmth. There this magnetism coming from her that, well—I guess it's hard not to notice—people buzz around her like she is the queen bee. In that sense, I guess, well . . . I guess one could say she is mildly endearing. My father, on the other hand, is another case entirely. He and I have not had more than two (short) conversations since I've arrived, and neither one was especially inviting or gratifying.

The first time we spoke was the day he arrived back at FRANCO with a deer strapped to his toboggan. I suppose the contraption works better in the winter when snow and ice help it glide along the hillside, but using it to drag a deer across overgrown grass and granite seems highly ineffective. It made me think of my own clumsy entrance into the community just a few days prior.

Liam was ruddy and shiny-faced that day. The jacket he wore was grossly oversized—and ugly, too. It draped over him with overlapping red and black blocks that matched up in an awkward patchwork pattern that—oh—didn't fit at all with the way I imagined him. One pocket was ripped almost the whole way down with a matted gray lining coming out of the seam. The other was mostly intact and had dirt-encrusted gloves sticking out of it.

With perspiration dripping from his forehead, my father's rustic appearance was far different than I thought he should look. I'm sure he didn't recognize me either; how could he?

Marissa ran to him quickly that day, and with one hand flailing toward me and the other firmly planted on her chest she seemed to dive into his arms and whispered something quickly in his ear. Both the rope he was holding and his jaw dropped simultaneously, and he stood very still without a word.

Grand'Mere's arm circled my shoulder with an ease that I remembered from my childhood. She was always lavish with her affection.

Liam opened his arms and began walking intently in my direction. His penetrating eyes seemed to draw me with an invisible string. Grand'Mere tightened her hold on me for a moment and then gave me a gentle nudge forward; before I knew it Liam and I were in an inescapable embrace. The hug was hearty, but quite surreal. This is my father?

He stepped back, held my face in his hands and tears welled up in his deeply set, chestnut-colored eyes. I don't remember his eyes being so intense, nor did I recognize any of his facial features. On top of that, I didn't quite know how to respond when he pulled me toward him again because the only thing he seemed able to utter was, "my girl . . . my little girl."

What happened next was extremely strange. This lumberjack-of-a-father stroked my hair and then glanced at the deer, muttered something about having to tend to it quickly, and he was gone. Simply gone. Then, when he came by Grand'Mere's kitchen later that afternoon our conversation was stilted and just plain weird.

The next day I was groggy waking up. As I propped myself up on the small, cloth-covered mat in Grand'Mere's closet-sized crevice that passes for my bedroom, the first thing I saw was Liam's face. My brawny tower-of-a-father was peering in through the archway from her kitchen area and wore a big broad smile. Holding a large twined bag filled with some sort of fruit, he lifted it toward the ceiling and muttered something like, "For you." We did speak briefly again that morning, but our words remained choppy, our conversation awkward. He's so quiet.

From then on and this entire past few weeks a cloudy veil seemed to drape over every attempt at communication. Obviously, there are unspeakable secrets in the chasm that exists between us, but I couldn't bring myself to ask him for answers, and he seemed unable to question me, either.

All that to say—yes—we've definitely got some blocks in our relationship, but I am hopeful that we will work through them. The biggest issue, I guess, is that I still feel as though I can't trust either of them. My parents are odd birds. The world was theirs and they gave it away. Who does that?

Back at the Lab they had it all: reputation, clout, money, vision, creative freedom; heck, what more could they want? So you close your eyes to a few things that don't set right, but to up and leave the civilized world? That's so wrong. It's so odd. And to leave me with Grand'Mere? More than odd; it is outright crazy. Maybe it would serve them right to be discovered by ADMIN. I wish I could find a way to activate my tek.

They have no clue, by the way, that the prefrontal cortex has become as integral to everyday operations as it has in the last quarter century. For Strength's sake, the PFC was barely in the mix of our neuro-centric existence twenty five years ago! All these years have passed and they have not been privy to the incredible amount of helpful findings cognitive brain scientists have discovered about the the golden-gray mass. As a branch of brain research, neuro-plasticity has come a long way. Frankly, it's hard to believe that my parents are not on top of it.

I'm still not sure about the dimensions or intensity of Liam's state of mind, but Marissa's oddity is multidimensional. If she's said it once, she's said it twenty times: "the old days." The old days, the old days. STRENGTH, she's always talking about the old days. I think the phrase is engraved on her prefrontal!

Her weirdness is so pronounced that it strikes me almost as a personality disorder. It's hard to put my finger on it, more often than not, it seems that the anomalies resident in her are most evident in her speaking style. Perhaps that's all it is because when she speaks, I always seem to come away with the feeling that she means more than she's saying. Although I knew that Mother received all her early education in London's best boarding schools—I knew that, but it has been so long since I spent time with her or even thought about my childhood that I totally forgot about her accent. Her soft British lilt is actually quite elegant, but every time she opens her mouth it still takes me a bit by surprise.

This is lovely and that is delightful and all of her t's and d's aaarh purrfectly pronounced. It's not just that, either! It's her choice of words that often leave me scratching my head. Mother uses the strangest phrases and seems to twist words— words that easily have double meaning, and I know she's doing it on purpose!

For instance, a week ago she was responding to Grand'Mere's query about the dinner menu for the weekly Friday night gathering around Stone Camp. Instead of just saying "I'll bring the potatoes," which she was scheduled to make, she went on and on about the proper regiment of foods and how important it is to eat "vegge" and herbs in the right order and combinations. She insisted that roasted potatoes would be better with the freshly harvested oh-re-GAN-o and the white asparagus she picked earlier in the day. Then she switched to no potatoes and back again, and in her own inimitable Britishspeake reminded us that "it would be brilliant to match the venison with parsleyed potatoes this week, because all the herbs are in and quite lovely."

What? UGH. She exasperates me so! Make up your mind, mother.

It is clear that her emphasis on the menu quite befuddled Grand'Mere, as well, especially as she left us with an odd exhortation about what human beings really need to survive. She very carefully emphasized the word "human." It's as if she labored over it, stringing it out for much longer than a mere two syllables should take. Just as the last sound came out of her mouth she turned and looked at me with crazy, bulging eyes. Grand'Mere shrugged her shoulders while Marissa walked away shaking her head.

UGH. She definitely makes me a little off kilter.

_____

moni

_____

Oh my Strength! Another shard of a message—part of a word: moni.

Moni. . . ? WHAT IS IT? Where is this broken, distorted message coming from? This is gonna drive me crazy! Okay, okay. It must be part of that original message. Let's see. What was it again?

_____

XrO is ready to go.

_____

"XrO is ready to go." Yes, it said XrO. Uhhhh. No clue.

What was the rest about "monitoring?" Oh yeah:

_____

We're monitoring progress. Let sleeping dogs lie. Do not go in until I give you the word. I repeat: Do not apprise.

_____

Uhhhhhh. What could it mean and WHY am I still seeing glitches? Everything is off kilter! There's no way to activate my P/Z and there is no logical reason I would still be able to receive anything from anyone, even a shred. What the heck!?!

Uhhhhhhhhh. I've got to pull myself together.

Alright, alright. Breathe. Back to Marissa's weirdness. There is something—something about this woman who birthed me. If nothing else, she's definitely intriguing.

I'm learning things about her that I never knew. For instance, just the other day Grand'Mere told me that when Marissa assumed her family's role at the Lab she quickly advanced the early particle accelerator software to bend electromagnetic waves in such way that they could interact safely with the human brain. She managed all that in just the first two years directing the Lab. That's the legacy she left me. I always knew that my configuration of the P/Z 1000 had a direct link to her research—everyone knew it—but what I did not know is why, actually how, she could leave it all and go so . . . so primitive.

Eventually, I'd like to tap into that brain of hers and find out where these advances in technology have led her, at least in terms of her thinking about them. But of course, since she and Liam left their post, much has advanced without them. They never experienced the brilliance of communicating with a colleague via brain waves. I can hardly believe they've missed so much. It would be nice to have an unencumbered conversation with them about what's really happening in the world. Unfortunately, however, they are openly reticent about discussing anything having to do with Alessandro, the Lab, or their previous life. They have buried all of it in the fabricated avalanche that supposedly took their lives back in 2047.

In any case, I still cannot possibly trust that all of what they might say is even true. Can you blame me? After all that they put me through growing up, I really doubt that I could ever trust them fully again.

So this morning, although I was forthcoming in telling her how much I really do appreciate the community, I was also completely honest about how I miss the seamless communication culture that I left. Using the human brain as our main interface we no longer have to deal with the messiness of outside elements, bandwidth issues, limitations in natural resources, or the predictable faultiness of the human condition. How can anyone argue against that?

What did she do? Marissa responded with a curt, accusatory question.

"Is the efficiency of clear and clean lines of communication worth choking off the fragile acoustic layer of space that defines our very breath? How about the efficacy of our relationships? What about touch, my darling girl? What about the importance of true presence? Is communication efficiency worth trading that off?"

My Strength! All these questions. I swear, she acts as if she knows it all!

I think it's mother's insistence that I "come up to speed" that grates against me most. What does she mean by that? Come up to speed? I mean, I'm living in an earth-sheltered house—the most primitive type of dwelling known to humans; I haven't complained once about missing my P/Z, (not even a mumble!) and I have embraced both she and my father kindly in spite of the fact that . . . they left me! If she could just leave things alone once in a while and let me figure it out for myself I would be much obliged.

Yet, yet . . . in spite of her irritating ways, I was about to respond to her cavalcade of questions in a most conciliatory fashion; yes, in the precise manner in which Grand'Mere raised me, explaining that perhaps an actual trade-off was not the only option. At that very moment, however, my attention completely lapsed. There, not thirty feet away, carrying some sort of gardening tool around to the back of my mother's cavern and toting a rickety, wooden cart was the most extraordinary man I have ever laid eyes on. As I glanced toward him Marissa followed my eyes, grabbed my arm and without a word pranced us over to the patch of soil where Belvedere Florencia was headed.

"I'm so glad you came by Viddie." She started right in with that bouncy voice. I swear she sounded like a British Scarlett O'Hara surrounded by a bevy of eligible bachelors.

"I just don't know how I'd plant in time if you weren't here to help me get that stubb'urn spring ground prepared. Now Belvedere—young man—have you had a chance to get to know my Emilya?"

Mother's lilting voice made this spectacle seem somehow less obtrusive than it was, but nonetheless, I wanted to crawl under the huge granite rock a few feet away. Her eyes flashed like fire between us, never missing a beat as she continued to prattle on about peas and potatoes and green beans and all the other vegetables that she intended to grow in her expansive garden this season.

There was no time to ponder her words this morning, however, for there before me stood a disturbingly attractive man staring at me full in the face. Our eyes locked ever-so-briefly, but in that nano-second-of-a-moment he absolutely took my breath away. No exaggeration—Belvedere Florencia is just . . . well, I hardly know how to describe him, but I swear he looks like a fictional super-hero of one sort or the other, and I'm definitely not dreaming.

All those old-timey television shows that Grand'Mere loaded into my recreational files as a child are still securely situated in my default memory, and I am amazed at how much he reminds me of some sort of mix between Old Spain's Estevio Gonsuzia and the Welsh guy in Braveheart. The hair is the same color, just a little longer and curlier—he's got soft waves, really. His blue-grey eyes are deeply-set and, my-oh-my—well—he pretty much is the most handsome man I have ever laid eyes on.

In one quick moment Marissa was gone, muttering something about going back to the nursery to fetch the seedlings that were nearly ready to be planted. Her voice was fuzzy in my ear and I don't even remember her final instructions— something about the gate. She scooped up the handle of the wagon Belevedere had been toting and scampered away. Clickity-clack, clickity-clack; the sound of that wagon tumbling over the rocky landscape seemed unnervingly loud as we stood looking at each other. Although I hadn't budged an inch, I felt strangely off balance.

At first, our infinitely awkward encounter seemed it would never end. Leaning up against the granite ridge separating Grand'Mere's immediate residence from Marissa's, Viddie just stood there looking at me. Like an inanimate icon in one of my software packages, he seemed to be waiting for me to create some sort of story. His tattered t-shirt was unevenly ripped under the armpits and the neckline was torn into a jagged V-shape. I tried really hard not to stare, but it was to no avail. A few dark, wavy hairs jutted out of the opening of that shirt and . . . uh . . . well, I was a bit out of my element.

For a second it seemed as though he might have been a figment of my own imagination instead of the ruggedly handsome son of Fiorella and Carlos Florencia, about whom I had heard so much; but then, before I could reel in my awful, gawking self, he leaned toward me with a funny half smile and winked rather boldly.

With that, I just about fell backwards, stumbling on a rocky patch of earth beneath my feet. Caught completely off guard, I couldn't even muster a few polite words, but as he reached out to steady me, we laughed at the silliness of it all and that helped relieve a bit of the tension.

What I was expecting I still do not know, but as the moment lingered there was yet a word to be uttered by either of us. It seemed like an unbearable amount of time that we stood there, but was probably just about all of ten seconds, if that. Shuffling my embarrassment aside, I fixated on the faded blueness of his shirt and noticed the red embroidered lettering over the right hand pocket; it read "Father & Son Landscaping."

Then there was the business with the garden tool. The hoe Viddie held in his right hand stood erect between us. He fixed his eyes on me quite directly and continued to just stand there, smiling. My own eyes were absolutely glued to the round curvature of his mouth. It was hard not to stare at his tender, ample lips. Frankly, I have never seen a man with lips like this before. So there I was, stuck, right there—suspended somewhere between then and now—staring directly at this man's mouth after my mother all but flung me face-first in front of him.

Thankfully, our voiceless encounter soon came to an end. Before I had a chance to think through my response to all of this, Viddie laughed out loud, breaking the silence with a quick unsolicited lesson on the correct way to ready the ground for Marissa's garden. He placed my clumsy hands around the middle of the hoe and simulated the proper action: up and down, chop-chop-chop, push quickly forward, pull back. Did I care even one iota about how to properly use a garden hoe? Not at all, but I was all in.

Five seconds prior I couldn't take my eyes off him, but now I couldn't even look at him! My heart was pounding so hard that I thought he might hear it! I didn't have a clue about where in the world to put everything that I was feeling—still don't. What is this thing going on inside my chest? Whatever it is, it's the most uncomfortable and delightful thing I've ever known!

When Viddie laid the hoe against the huge slab of gray rock behind us, his hand brushed against my shoulder. I could almost swear it was intentional—at least his smile said it was so. Speaking of his smile—wow—that whimsical, crooked little smile filled me with sheer delight this morning.

Seconds before mother returned, Viddie looked down at my hand and then gently took it into his, looking more closely at the amethyst ring. The deep purple stone glistened in the sunlight. The tiny diamonds encircling it accentuated its brilliance. At that precise moment I thought my heart might actually stop, but what he said was even more surprising than the shock of his hand holding mine.

"This is really a miracle, Emi. Do you know how many times I sat late into the night listening to the story of this ring?"

Still having trouble finding my voice, a slight shoulder shrug told him that I did not know anything about 'the story of the ring.' In fact, Viddie's words made no sense at all. I could barely hear him. It was as if every corpuscle in my body decided to separate itself from my brain or the blood stopped travelling through my veins.

I was completely and utterly undone.

Never before have my feelings been ignited this way. I don't think I even knew that emotions could ignite! There were no walls between us—no time to prepare what I should say. I didn't even have a moment to edit my response; it was pure reaction. The feeling was extremely uncomfortable, but then again, it simultaneously felt like liquid gold pouring effusively out of the center of my chest.

Where once the comfortable distance between Jude, Zeejay, or Alessandro gave me time to prepare a proper response, today there were no layers—nothing to hide behind. I felt so naked.

Absolutely naked.

Viddie gave my hand a slight squeeze and then let it go, explaining more about the ring.

"Grand'Mere kept telling us that it was you who was meant to have it. You were the legacy. Again and again, she'd remind us that it was meant for you—Emilya Hoffman Bowes Brown—always your full name. And then right after she'd say: 'nothing is impossible', and remind us that we needed to keep the faith. And now, here it is, on your beautiful hand. Tell me that's not a miracle."

Beautiful hand? Whew—I am blown away by this guy! My response didn't give me away, though—at least I hope not. "Grand'Mere? You call her Grand'Mere, too?" My vocal chords managed to eke out a few words.

His smile enveloped me as he nodded slowly. "We all do, Emi. In fact, her nickname is Madremia. She's like a mother to all of us."

Viddie's smooth voice is so manly. It's deep—bassy—and seems to have its own gravitational pull; I wanted to wrap myself around him and never let go.

All these feelings were crazy; they made my head swim.

At that precise swirling moment mother reappeared with her cart of seedlings firmly in tow. Tiny crates of tomato and green pepper plants wobbled on the rickety wooden wagon. I don't think I was ever happier to see her, but then again, I didn't get a chance to question him further about the story . . . or the idea that miracles had anything at all to do with my coming to FRANCO.

All day since then I've been thinking about the lunacy of how I feel, and the thing about it is this: By the second week I was here, a lovely woman named Russa who has been such a help to me since I arrived gave me the lowdown on everyone in FRANCO, so I knew in advance that he was only twenty-two. But she said he was "a cutie." Huh! Right. What an odd description for a man like that! It seemed a bit funny that this forty year old lady should describe him that way, but indeed, his looks are off-the-charts! There's a dimple in the middle of his chin, and eyes that are impossible to ignore. The fact is, this . . . this boy-man did not seem too young this morning and whatever he is or is not, he is far more than cute—even if he is seven years my junior!

I truly do not know what to think about this encounter, except that my feelings need to be seriously reigned in, and I must find a way to do that without my P/Z 1000. Thinking about Viddie must logically progress; I must convince my own neural system to override this emotional tornado that has formed within me, but how? It seems the more I try to stop thinking about him, the more my thoughts swirl and expand.

Back to his age again, I mean, is he really too young for me? It's clear that Belvedere Florencia is much younger than I am—too young, really, to consider anything . . . together, but— ah, he sure doesn't seem it.

In spite of the years that span between us, somehow this morning Viddie Florencia and I shared head space—or maybe it was heart space; I really am not sure, but I know this one thing: it is not something I have ever experienced before. Surely, I've read about it—this type of romantic notion is threaded throughout the reams of postmodern fantasy that I familiarized myself with in Early Ed—it's the steady theme of four hundred years of modernism. It's the old-fashioned love story genre, of course. But . . . we all know that the 'love story' is just a genre; it is definitely not grounded in reality. There's nothing tangible or logical about it, just some crazy hormones kicking up, I'm sure. Nevertheless, wherever it is coming from, it feels like a powder keg of energy that is concentrated somewhere deep inside me—deeper than any place I've ever known before and it is all jam-packed entirely in one little, slightly lingering look.

I know he felt it too.

Chapter 2

Day 32—The Weight

My skin feels rough today and in need of some good old fashioned glycer-rub.

Between the mosquitoes and constant exposure to the air up here, I'm not sure what bothers me more. If I had known I would be away from my flat this long I surely would've packed a bag and brought along a tube of my best skin cream. Thankfully, I do have my hairbrush. Ughh. So many things exasperate me lately. It's been more than a month here and I am really missing the privacy of my own shower and toiletries.

On top of that, the guilt I feel for even thinking about leaving my family is weighing like a fifty pound dumbbell glued to my chest. They're so sweet—especially Grand'Mere—but this isn't my home! I can hardly breathe thinking about how I must face Marissa and the others to tell them that I need to go home.

"We are your home, Leeya." I could almost hear them say it as I rehearsed the scene in my mind.

Their voices boom in tandem inside my head even without an activated P/Z1000.

From one of them to the next, I imagine their list of reasons for me to stay will bubble forth like the water that tumbles over the rocks just beyond Rubble Ridge. And, in my mind's eye, I can see them cajoling me into staying, each in their own signature style: Mother with her frenetic gesticulations and stream-of-consciousness brand of speech; Father, ensconced in his chronically letdown look of apprehension mingled with the wordless wonder of seeing me all grown up; Russa, with her delightful demeanor marred by a slightly furrowed brow and melancholic sigh of disappointment; but Grand'Mere—Ah, age-old beauty with eyes that twinkle brightly whether the sun is shining or not. (She'd understand, wouldn't she?)

Who knows what Liam might say, but he's not really one that I'm terribly concerned about. I keep thinking, though, about the first moment I saw him; I didn't recognize my father at all. Although deeply intense, his chestnut eyes are small, belying his rather tall, husky frame. And I still think about the hug we shared that first day. He held me tightly—so tightly my shoulders hurt. But there wasn't the same type of warmth coming from him that oozed from mother and Grand'Mere . . . and still in all these weeks I still have not had a real conversation with him. Marissa tells me to give him time. She says he opens himself slowly, like one of these box turtles that are all around the woods. It takes a while for him to poke his head out of his shell. She boasts about his inner strength and generous heart, but all I can see is that hard shell. I'm not bothered, really. As far as I'm concerned our relationship can stay where it's at. It's tepid, at best, and that suits me just fine. Liam is keeping me at as much distance as I am keeping him. Frankly, I can't imagine him really caring what I do after all this time apart.

The only one I'm ambivalent about is Belvedere. Would he say anything at all? Would he care? What would he do? How would he handle the news? Surely whatever is going on between us is far too vague to be of any consequence to him. And, actually, there really is nothing going on; nothing to speak of, that is.

Each of the others would have plenty to say about my plan to return to the Lab, and the more I consider it, the more certain I am that each would disapprove, and I wonder: would they even allow me to go? Now that's a crazy thought.

Truth be told, there are actually days when the need to go home does not present itself as intensely as when I first arrived, but . . . I'm so conflicted. There are viable reasons to stay—my family, for one. But the reasons to leave are much more compelling. This message fragment that keeps presenting itself on my inner wall is one of them. It's SO annoying! I can't tell if it's for me or about me, and what's worse—it pops up at the absolute strangest times. Once, in the middle of the night, then five days later while I was out walking with Russa, another time when Grand'Mere was teaching me how to can wax beans –all unexpected moments. The other day it crossed my prefrontal like tickertape:

---

moni . . . moni

Akkk—what does it mean? This morning it happened again just before my first sip of tea and for a fleeting moment I thought perhaps all this is a dream. The letter in the attic, the forced "vacation" from work, the unceasing vacuum—maybe I really have lost my sanity!!!! Uh—What a frightful thought. Even worse, what if the Lab has me under surveillance? What if they have created a virtual environment to test my loyalty? With the creative graphics and tek available at the Lab, it's a definite possibility. Thankfully, it's not probable.

In any case, imagining all the different ways I could broach the subject this morning, I find myself mentally listing the reasons for leaving and pitting them against reasons I should stay. I need to really think this through. I think a list might help. I'll analyze each reason and cross things out as I resolve them.

Let's see here. I've got to start with the looming, unresolved issues back at the Lab.

Firstly, when I think of the Xtreme software (the development of which I am primarily responsible) that has become our society's cash cow, I cringe.

Secondly, the whole basis of the product rests on the premise that the environment is corrupt, and to survive we must communicate primarily within the sequestered quarters of our amygdala—the inner walls—and then use our Plutonian Z-1000 as the non-invasive platform to connect with each other within the walls of each other's homes; phew, the whole system has to be adjusted. Talk about a bug in the program!

Just thinking about it makes me tremble. My Strength, the issues to untangle in everyday communication will be like trying to get the knots out of a mass of gold chains all meshed together in one big pile. This is to say nothing of the issues enmeshed in the world at large. I mean, the ramifications are mind boggling! What will happen when the world discovers that such insular communication practices are not necessary? Not only that, what will people do when they find they can venture out into the wild without fear of being overtaken by toxicity. Oh dear—what might it all mean to the global travel business? My head spins when I think about it. There are thirty million people living along the east coast of North America; how will they react when they realize that they are able to travel beyond the established borders of civilization and attempt to connect face-to-face with lost relatives along the European population strip? That fact alone is likely to create utter chaos.

UGH. It's all too much to fathom. There's so much to be concerned about!

Grand'Mere just poked her head into my space and asked if I wanted some cereal with the first strawberries. Unbelievable—all the food they have around here.

"No thank you," I told her. "I am fine."

I must have looked a bit tired because she knelt at the foot of the mat and took my shoes off, without even asking me.

"Let me just rub those tootsies a bit for you, *mi amor.* You still look so tired."

I squirmed back a bit, definitely not thrilled to have my feet called tootsies, but Grand'Mere is hard to resist.

"When I left you were heartier—much heartier—and although I still don't figure you for more than an inch over 5' 7", you look frail to me my darling. I'm afraid you've succumbed to the sparse foodstuffs of ADMIN'S regiment; we've got to plump you up a bit!"

"Grand'Mere! They'll be no more talk of making me plump, please. I am already at the highest acceptable weight for women my age. The 110 pounds I carry is the maximum allowance. If I go over, I'll get taxed!"

"Oh dear," she said with a chuckle, patting her abdomen. "My goodness, by now I would be a pauper if I hadn't come to FRANCO. What a world it's come to, child; what a world."

She left the room and headed to the hearth to brew me a cup of tea. I must say—all this attention is going to take some getting used to.

Back to my deeper concerns.

I am a bit confounded when I think about the Principles and what it might mean to let such an elegant vision of the world slip away. Our tri-fold banner of progress, perfection and productivity has long inspired me—given me a reason to live; how can I possibly forget the glory of the Principles?

Even if this were to become my permanent home, there is little here in the way of mission and purpose. For all the concentration and intensity of effort put forth here, there are no real principles to speak of. I mean, every Friday evening Stone Camp becomes a sing-a-long featuring ancient hymns as the centerpiece and conversation peppered with stories of days gone by, but a strategic plan to bring about a better world? They don't have it. It's not here. Forget strategy; they don't have any sort of plan at all. At least, I've heard nothing of it so far.

Oh no, there's a gross little bug crawling much too close for comfort. I hate this! It's one thing to have to manage life here without connection to my Ongoing Life Sustaining Membrane, but creepy little insects, too? Ugggghhhh. Zero OLSM means zero connectivity to the outside world, but I think I hate these bugs equally as much as being without my tek!

Finally, there are important facts that ADMIN must be made aware of—number one, the earth is replenishing; there is less danger than previously supposed. They must be told. Others must be told. I mean, there's beauty and fresh air and provision out here!

Oh—there is so much to think about, so much that my head hurts. Fact is, some days my head feels about ready to burst! So, my list is shoring up to look like this:

- The Lab needs me
- Global citizenship is not only a privilege it is a responsibility
- Misinformation about the planet (people deserve to be told that the earth's natural resources have been renewed!)
- I miss my cognitive enhancements (P/Z, I need you!)
- The Principles . . . the Principles!
- Restoring face-to-face travel with others throughout the globe. Now wouldn't that be a gas!

The list is hefty, but it definitely seemed more cumbersome before I wrote it down.

There is a way that . . .

Hmmm. Someone's just come into Grand'Mere's front room. More later.

It was a round little face that appeared from the other side of hearth. Her freckly cheeks were aglow. Two eyeballs beamed back at me and were as wide as saucers.

"Knock, knock! Hello in there; Miss Emilya? Hello there, hello! Watcha doin'?"

"Liberty? Liberty Martin, right?"

"That's me, alrighty! Daddy and Mommy named me Liberty so that my name would echo throughout all of Holly Mountain whenever anyone called for me. Do you like it? I like it, but I like the name Emilya better. Emilya is a fine name for a writer, a very fine name. You're a lucky ducky. Do you know that? But I'm a lucky ducky too, cuz I've never known a writer before and—wow-wee—now you're here!!! Did you always know you wanted to be a writer, Miss Emilya? When you were my age did you carry that book around everywhere you went? Can you show me how you do it? I'd like to be a writer one day too!"

I couldn't help smiling. It's hard to remember what it was like to be ten.

"Ho—ha, wait a brisk minute little tiger," I said. "There are too many questions for me to answer all at once. Why don't you answer one for me first, and then I'll try to answer yours. Tell me, how do you milk a goat?"

Miss freckle face started giggling and had a difficult time believing that I didn't know how to milk a goat, let alone that I had never seen one till less than a month ago. When I finally was able to pin down an answer, she explained her skill as something she always knew how to do. (What?!?!) Nevertheless, the little charmer took her leave and went back to the goats after ten minutes of nonstop babble. Quite an inquisitive little girl, and a sweet one, at that. Our banter is always . . . oh, I don't know; it's always just on the edge of rationality. Never having been around children before, it's kind of funny to see the world through her eyes. My Strength, the girl can talk!

Now that she's gone I can resume thinking deeply about my options in regard to home.

In spite of the fact that I am genuinely happy to see my family again, I am not going to kid myself. I've been fine on my own, just fine. It's been twenty three years since I've seen Marissa and Liam, and twelve since I've seen Grand'Mere, and I don't think it's conceited to say that I've done pretty well without them so far. It's clear they've done just fine without me, too. Logically, there doesn't seem to be anything stopping me from going home, so the question in my mind right now is not should I? but, when?

Yet, yet, in spite of the overwhelming desire to return to civilization, there are several things that I simply cannot imagine and I must plan accordingly.

First, I cannot picture saying goodbye to so many people who care for me, especially Russa. It's surprising (even to me) that in such a short period of time friendship could come to mean so much. Where has this come from? I'm not sure. The thing is—she is more than a friend; some days she is my teacher; other days I feel as though she's my mother—much more so than Marissa!

Ever since the second day I arrived at this humble mountain hideaway Russa has made it a point to be kind to me. She has come by Grand'Mere's to inquire about my comfort every single day. I wake up, and there she is, poking her face into the hovel where I lay my head, dragging me out of my morphean daze with her wide, toothy smile and the overwhelming aroma of a blueberry muffin or pecan scone. (I feel a smile emerging on my face even just thinking about it.)

She's always holding that fantastic walking stick that Earl made her out of an old walnut tree branch. He said the tree was uprooted in a terrible Nor'easter a few years back, but what that man did to it is quite remarkable. Its burnished wood and intricate carvings are set in a lovely vine motif with tendrils intertwining all the way up to the handle. It's a true work of art, and although I can detect no malady that would cause her to limp, the thing is so much a part of her that I swear—If I didn't know better, I'd think she was born with it!

I haven't been at FRANCO long enough to know what sort of fruit Russa might bake into her luscious little cakes when the wild blueberries are out of season, but I have heard stories about the apple muffins that appear in August; I am sure they are exquisite Having subsisted mainly on provisio bars and a weekly portion of hydroponic vegetables, I am surely looking forward to it, that is, of course, if I'm still here by August.

Some days I can't imagine that I haven't always known Russa. I have never had a sister, and certainly not a friend like her. It's strange, but knowing her has made me realize that most all my colleagues are men. I haven't had a girlfriend since I was a teenager! This . . . this friendship has opened up places in my heart that I never knew were there, and it's . . . it's a nice feeling. However delightful it is, I simply cannot let my emotions sway me. Once I get back to my flat I'll renew my P/Z and get my brain health back into tip-top shape again. For now, I have no choice but to grapple with a vast mélange of conflicting feelings and just . . . just . . . well, I'm making the best of it.

It feels strange not having lipstick on each day. That's the least of my concerns, of course, but when the notion of going home pops into my head I can't help thinking about my creature comforts. And my hair—ugh—it's such a mop lately. The only way I'm able to wear it these days is up in a ponytail. I'm glad I had an extra hairclip in my bag the day I drove off in my car last March. My hair doesn't seem as dark as it was back home either. Must be all these hours in the sun each day.

The other conundrum is figuring out what to do with whatever is (or is not) happening with Viddie Florencia. This is something to consider. I will miss him when I go, but frankly, the only real thing we have together is a gaggle of stolen looks telegraphed in each other's direction, several shared lessons in gardening, and—I'm hard-pressed to admit it—my own over-active imagination.

It's true. When I see him, overwhelming feelings of desire continue to radiate from some place deep inside of me. Naturally, that place must be my brain but it sure doesn't seem that way. Instead it feels almost like a flock of birds landed in my gut and they've escaped in sudden flight, wings fluttering and soaring straight into the sky, aiming, it seems, for the sun itself.

On Friday evenings at Stone Camp he sits directly across from me. Even though there are probably twenty-five feet between us, I have no trouble noticing the edges of his lips and how they curl up when he looks at me with those deep blue eyes. Other times I've seen him chopping wood or tending the gardens and all I want to do is run to him and . . . and . . . be near him. I want him to look at me!

I'd never tell anyone this, but it is really frightening not to be in complete command of my emotions. Frankly, it would be much easier to neatly fold up each feeble feeling in its own tight little packet, stick each one in oversized duffel and throw that bag as far down the mountain as the wind might take it. But then—oh, then—in the very next moment, I never want to stop feeling every last particle of emotion.

As yet, our most significant conversation is still the day when mother dragged me into his personal space, but eye contact across the campfire does seem to be increasing weekly. Russa thinks that there is lots of potential between the two of us, but —ha!—well, that remains to be seen.

Anyway, in spite of Viddie and the great wealth of treasure that my friendship with Russa has become, I simply cannot get Addison Avenue out of my mind. It's where I belong.

Lately, these thoughts have been consuming more and more of my time—much more than what I am jotting down in this notebook. It's worse when the residual connection comes into play because it makes me think the LAB is looking for me. Like yesterday, yet again a little blip raced across my brain. Clearly it was not my own thought and only one word kept coming through on my interior wall:

———

monitor . . . monitor.

———

For the life of me I can't figure out what that's all about, but surely it's some sort of leftover data from a Lab communique.

And the thing is, it's not that I actually miss Jude and Zeejay, nor do I have even an iota of desire to stand before Alessandro's wall and allow myself to be intimidated by his condescending tone. Oh no. I am quite happy to be free from the apparent manipulation of that place, but . . . but . . . Jude and Zeejay are the closest I've got to brothers and, Paty, Rake, and Dr. Marc, Rolly—all of them—I can hardly help thinking about them and, well . . . I'm reasonably certain that the Lab can't do without me forever; can they? I mean, how far do they think they can take the latest line in Xtreme vacation packages without my input? But then again, if it's really true that the earth is not as noxious as we've been told, how long will they need by virtual vacation packages?

The more days that go by, the more I am concerned that they will forget me.

8 P.M. (same day)

My writing was interrupted earlier today by Marissa.

Uuuuuuhhh.

Mother came in to ask Grand'Mere about the hybridization process she that she and Fiorella are working on. She wanted to know how much the difference in molecular weight mattered when they were trying to marry the blackberry and raspberry bushes without doubling the number of seeds. Their conversation was funny, as usual. I find it a little bit ironic that Mother still defers to Grand'Mere when it comes to her knowledge of physics and science, in general. Their conversations are quite comical, but more than that, bewildering.

Marissa: "Mother, do you have the thingamajig?"

Grand'Mere: "Marissa, what on earth are you talking about? I have a number of things in storage here. What thing are you looking for?"

Marissa breathed deeply and with an exasperated sigh she looked at me directly, set her hands akimbo, and stormed out.

Grand'Mere shook her head and folded her arms, calling out to my mother. "Marissa! Why are you so impatient today?"

Grand'Mere motioned to me with a quick glance as if to say, "Go after her," while she hunted around for something in the bin.

I called to her, and before she was even ten feet away from the cave she turned around and with hands situated one on each hip, she looked at me squarely. Mother's eyes were filled with smoldering fire. Her typically lilting accent was harsh and her sarcastic tone presented precisely the opposite emotion that her polite choice of words gave off.

"What do you want, Miss Leeya? May I help you with something?"

"Mother! What is going on with you? Grand'Mere wants you to come back and . . ."

She cut me off right in the middle of a sentence. "Emilya," her tone softened marginally but her words still struck me as curt. "Your father is driving me bonkers. He is tired of waiting for you to come around and reckons that you might never do so, and quite frankly, I don't see why you are holding back from us, either. I have no comprehension on the mattah."

Marissa's eyes looked downright googly; I was taken aback by her candor and even a bit scared by her intensity. No comprehension on the matter? I'll say! She has very little comprehension of any of it.

My voice was calm, but the tumble that was going on inside me was a different story.

"Mother, what is it that you expect of me? And why are you so emotional? I didn't do anything to you!"

Marissa's upper lip curled up toward her nose. Her eyebrows seemed like they raised three inches. She began shaking her head with quick little darting moves in both directions, and when she spoke she all but spit out the next statement in emphatic, flawless syllables.

"An oh-ccasional visit would be nice."

I just could not believe that she was being so dramatic! My own emotions were starting to percolate and I found myself projecting them on her with uncommon liberty.

"Why is it that you expect me to come to you? I don't know what to say to him, Marissa. If he's got something to say to me, he'll come to Grand'Mere's. Besides, he's obviously too busy. The man is out hunting more than he is here."

"The man? The man, Emilya? The man is your father— your one and only father—and I should think that you owe him a little respect, to say nothing of gratitude!"

For the first time in as long as I can remember I felt tears well up in my eyes; bitter, burning tears that were just on the verge of spilling over. I was so spitting mad at her that I didn't even recognize myself! How could my emotions be so wickedly out of control? One more minute and I knew my anger would completely unravel.

The night back in March when I cried on my car sofa after I got stuck in the snow—ugh—what a terrible ordeal, but it wasn't the same as today; I felt desperate and was afraid. Then, I cried about the cougars chasing me, but that was in my sleep; it was just a dream. Today is totally different. The feelings that welled up inside me seemed to come from a place I never even knew was there. My heart was pounding in what seemed a cross between outrage and . . . and defeat.

I am unwilling to inveigh against my parents for leaving me and yet neither do I intend to become their adoring child. I can't. It's impossible. I just can't.

My eyelids fluttered as I closed them and breathed deeply, trying to work through the familiar steps of neuro-emotional segregation without any digital enhancements.

It wasn't working. On the edge of a tiny breath that escaped on my vocal chords, I expelled one word. All I could manage was her name.

"Marissa."

It was as if she was totally oblivious to the fact that I was fuming. She grabbed both my forearms and shook me.

"Your father is out there foraging for food and hunting for protein for all of us, Emilya. Are you so dense that you do not see how integral he is to the survival of this community? He is not just a man who does so much around here, he is the singular, sole, heart of this community. If not for his tireless care and passion to make life together a beautiful thing we would have nothing. Do you hear me? Are you so hard-hearted and myopic in your self-absorbed vision of life that you do not even realize the pain you are putting us through?"

This woman has the ability to get under my skin like no one else on this planet.

Again, tears threatened my composure. I am unaccustomed to dealing with tears; they just are not part of my personal repertoire, so it took everything in me to keep from breaking down in a flood of them. I felt the pressure building.

"I am listening, Emilya. What do you have to say for yourself?" Mother's eyes were piercing.

The knot I felt in my stomach when we started talking twisted; I swallowed hard and felt my chest begin to contract. I considered smacking her across the jaw.

Deep, heaving breaths wreaked havoc on my ability to think straight. It is probably best because speaking would have brought me to the place of no return, but she would not stop with her badgering tone. In one unutterable moment of disdain I remained decisively silent while googly, bulging eyes kept their insistent focus on my face.

I pushed away from her and ran back to the relative safety of Grand'Mere's cavern.

She did not come after me.

Chapter 3

Day 46—The Break

Some days I can hardly contain all there is to take in. My eyes observe such marvelous sights here—small scampering creatures, luminous skies, vast mountains and lakes—all carrying such a weight of beauty and a depth that I couldn't even have imagined within the walls of my life back at the Lab. I must be crazy to think about leaving.

Mother and I patched up our little scuttle, but it took me going over there to smooth everything out. Clearly, she is not altogether there, and on top of that, it is evident that she has little—if any—comprehension of what it feels like to be six and nine and TWELVE without a mother or a father. Grand'Mere's words stung me at first, but I know she's right. "Give them a chance," she said. "They've paid a price too."

When I hear Grand'Mere's sweet voice and feel her gentle hug I'm reminded of days gone by when she would sit down on my bed and tell me stories. Hour after hour she'd recount the tales of her own upbringing, sharing the books she loved as a child. I remember always looking forward to the evening because I could count on being with her at my bedside, and it was the warmest, most wonderful feeling. There's just no way she could be part of a virtual package. No way. I touched her hand and heard her voice and it gave me strength to approach Marissa and Liam.

Stepping into their small earth shelter with a bit of tentative angst, I saw they were busy patching blankets with small swatches of deer hide, sewing them into a quilt that was a mishmash of duck down, cotton, embroidery, and twine. The disparate pieces looked strange, but neither of them seemed to notice. Then, as if they were being directed by an invisible conductor, they looked up simultaneously when I walked through the opening to their outer room; they glanced at each other with a single beat, and then looked back at me, each wearing a broad, glowing smile. I didn't even have a chance to say a word before Liam and Marissa were surrounding me with hugs and words of affection. I swallowed hard and let them cling to me.

No one ever accused me of being self-absorbed or myopic before, but I realized it would do no good to hash over the details of our little spat, so I just continued on as if it never happened.

"Darling, it would be lovely if you stayed for a spot of tea. Won't you?" Mother's soft voice was inviting, but her wide eyebrows and imploring expression made me laugh aloud.

"Oh—well, Yes, I suppose so, Marissa. What are you brewing today?"

Mother's glee was nearly tangible. She clasped her hands and turned to Liam to ask him to stoke the fire and then took my hands. Undoubtedly she prefers her various chamomile flowers for tea, but I was hoping for something new. Instead of a response, mother completely ignored my question and began a surprising and effusive litany of affection.

"Oh darling, darling. We have missed you so. We have so longed for this day—for our reunion. We knew it would be difficult, so many challenges—but we always believed you would join us. Look, we've have set up this very special section of the shelter over here for you. You've got your own table and cot and fluffy duck down pillow, and look—your father has built this room divider to give you privacy. Isn't it lovely? It's just for you, darling."

I closed my eyes and offered a faint smile. What am I to say to her? I know she wants to hear the same from me, but I find it hard to believe they have truly missed me when all these years have passed, and they want me to stay in their shelter? I don't think so! Liam placed a cup of steamy sweet chamomile in my hands and lightly kissed my cheek. Hmmm. The aroma was lovely. Blueberry, I think.

Truth be told, I am feeling increasingly at home here, but it still doesn't take away the fact that I know I'm not truly a part of them. I want to trust Marissa, perhaps even tell her about the strange fragmented messages that I keep getting, but what if there are more secrets she's kept from me? What if this whole encounter is part of a plan that is even more convoluted than the story they've told me? My only real home is the Lab—the colleagues, the work, the mission. In so many ways I feel more loyal to them than my parents. But oh dear—all these thoughts keep haranguing me. My mental state just keeps flip-flopping from one place to the next! Today, I am thinking quite much about my little flat on Addison Avenue. It's not the most luxurious place, but it's safe, it's familiar, and . . . it's mine!

So—I don't know—I still don't have answers, but today I just feel just slightly lighter than I have in recent days. It's the strangest development, really. I mean, I don't have much patience for Marissa's outbursts and effusive affection, but being around her does seem to create new places for me to explore in my thoughts. And it's not just my mother. During the short time of shared life here, deep in this mountainous province of eastern Pennsylvania, I do feel more at home than I have, well—actually—more than during my entire life leading up to it. It was wonderful being raised by Grand'Mere; she taught me so much and I know she loved me, but after my parents disappeared I never really felt at home—even there. Here, as each day passes, my eyes gain greater focus; and, in spite of the doubts, bit by bit I'm finding clarity about my surroundings and all the events that have transpired to get me here.

Recently, in fact, it has occurred to me that there may be something more to the human condition than how well I do at work or the certainty of death. There's something oddly nostalgic about living in such close quarters, sharing chores, working together to make a life that is rich in laughter and affection but lacking in every sort of convenience or nicety that one might imagine. Its appeal is unexpected. I didn't see it before even though I worked closely with my team at the Lab, but I must admit, I am seeing it now.

The implications of these two starkly different lifestyles are not completely clear to me, nor am I sure of what any of it means, but there are marked differences and they are worth noting. For starters, this community works together like a well-oiled machine. It's a vibrant, really vibrant village. They make soap and medicines and hybrid lanterns; summer crops get them through the winters; every square inch of renewable resources is used to the fullest, and where there is a problem, they join forces and work on a solution, together.

I must say, though, in spite of all they do to get by here, FRANCO is sorely lacking in creature comforts. I long for my silky-soft bed sheets and fluffy towels. I miss my wall panels and the ability to virtually visit any place I want to in the world with just the tweak of my P/Z 1000 and the thought to do it! The misty warmth of my Xtreme Caribbean Ocean package with its soft, rollicking breakers hitting the shore and images of palm trees waving in the breeze—ah, what I wouldn't give for some safe, virtual fun right about now.

In spite of that, there are some appealing aspects of life here on the mountain. I am breathing more deeply than I ever have; I am feeling things more fully than I ever have, filled increasingly with a growing sense of wonder and awe at the beauty of this planet, and yet I wonder—why didn't I notice any of this back home?

The funny thing is, this place is the land of dichotomies! In spite of the low-key atmosphere, there's so much happening here each day sometimes I can hardly get to my writing, but I know if I don't try to keep up with it I'll be sorry later. There are no enhancements that might help me store my memories and I want to be able to revisit these interesting, cherishable days once I get back to civilization.

This week it is especially apparent to me just how far FRANCO is removed from civilization. It might only be a couple of hours drive back to reality, but they are light years away mentally. Heck, their thought process isn't even remotely like what I am accustomed to. We had three straight days of rain and then a cold snap. Instead of freaking out, everyone pulled together and spent time doing what they call, "rainy day things." Grand'Mere, L.J., Liberty and her parents—everyone gathered each day to play games, sing songs, cook together; they just rearranged their normal routines as if staying on task didn't even matter! It's so strange, but even stranger that it works for them. Their attitudes all reflected a certain joy about the rain, or at least an acceptance of it. Fiorella and Carlos were actually glad about the precipitation because they maintain the rain barrels that collect wash water for bathing.

That's the other thing: There's a noticeable sense of pride they all take in doing what they do well, but no one really looks at any of their stuff as their own. From what I can tell, it seems that the sense of property here is nonexistent. So much of their daily life is drawn from collective effort.

They all share their lives most generously here, but the shared life is definitely non-communistic because although everyone contributes what they have to the common good, they all do so freely. Each continues to enjoy the freedom to do as they please and there is no one single commander or parson dictating what must be done, when, etc. It's a really interesting thing they've got going here. And when things get messed up it's like they're okay with conflict. "Just talk about it," that's what I hear and see going on all the time.

L.J. manages the well that's situated 'round back from his humble trailer, making sure it's clean; Grand'Mere cans food for the long winters, Liberty and her family maintain the small goat herd for milk and cheese, and everyone's got something growing in a small garden patch. Typically it's a selection of herbs and garlic or a few tomatoes, but it's funny, Marissa has the largest garden of everyone here. I never would have pegged my mother for that job, and she loves it! I would think she'd be working on inventions and systems to make life easier here rather than spending so much time nurturing little seedlings and pruning plants. But no; her large garden feeds Grand'Mere's massive canning effort which nourishes the entire community.

Every time Russa and I head up to Rubble Ridge I walk by Marissa's garden and Roos points out okra, kale, broccoli, tomatoes, string beans, onions, chamomile, coriander, parsley, Bibb lettuce (both red and green), and a great variety of other delicious vegetables, some of which are only coming up now. She has everything! The foodstuff aside, it seems that her main contribution involves organizing the seasonal plantings and harvests, and keeping the soil ready for use.

All that to say, while I do detect a respect for each person's uniqueness they don't really have the sense that anything they have is explicitly their own, and . . . and that bothers me a bit. I mean, their lives are so integrated. They depend on one another. It's far too unpredictable for me, that's for sure, but it seems to work for them. Speaking of which, that's another thing that's been bothering me. I've been missing the predictability of my life back home. Here, there's no telling what will happen from day to day. On any given day anything could happen. Life here is far too uncertain . . . and wild! We are truly in the wild.

I guess it bothers me a lot.

Back home there is the comfortable, steady rhythm of efficiency and along with it comes much more than a modicum of control; not like this, crazy life! Out here in the open we are vulnerable to so many hazards. The camp could be attacked by bears or other real animals—even snakes. I saw one slither past me last week in the woods! UGHHHhhhhhhhhh. On top of that—heck—we could all freeze to death in the winter. I'll be sure to be gone before that!

Some nights I already feel cold and it's just June.

Worse yet, we could be discovered by the land monitors. So far as I know FRANCO has never been detected by a land monitor, but I know they're out there. ADMIN keeps a close watch on all of the populated regions of the country, making sure there is enough food and water production for everyone. Surely the last forty years have made number crunching much easier, what with the Devastation wiping out the entire population east of Pennsylvania. These foothills are just off their radar screen so it's likely they'll all be fine, but . . . but I keep thinking about it, going back and forth, rehearsing the ways I'll break the news to them all that I'm leaving, and I don't know how I'll do it, but I will. It's coming soon, that I know.

In the meantime, I am here, and in spite of the ongoing adjustments in breathing and dealing with this molasses-paced lifestyle, it has not taken long for me to feel like a different person—utterly different—and that difference is . . .well, I think, well . . . part of me thinks it may actually be something good.

What it comes down to is—I can't really explain it—but I find I am forced to look carefully at each step I make here. One misstep and it can throw my whole day off. For instance, if I draw water from the well and forget to raise the turnstile, we could lose the whole bucket and be without drinking water until they build a new one.

Learning to observe what is going on around me more carefully is making me . . . oh, I don't know. In any case, because of it I feel—I feel like someone else; like someone I might have been, had I been born here. Sometimes I feel like I have a shadow, but really . . . it's just me—an encumbered me.

It sounds a bit bizzaro, but it's almost like I feel my shadow; I hear my voice and there's an echo, and then, then . . .

there's me. I'm, I don't know—it's a crazy kind of new awareness. Yes, that's it. I am aware of myself in a very different way.

This peculiarity is not evident in anyone else here. I've been watching Viddie and Alessa and this preoccupation with where they are is just not there. In fact, I don't see it in Marissa, Liam, Grand'Mere, Russa—any of them. Fact is, I see clearly the opposite in them. They are so . . . free? Yes, that's it. They are free-spirited, like people from a classic movie or novel—something that's fiction.

Once, while watching Fiorella run in circles after a rat with her iron skillet I couldn't help but think of that small screen actress, Lucille Ball. Grand'Mere screened all those files from last century into my rec folder and I remember the carefree, sometimes zany, free spirit that she played with Ricky Ricardo—wow, that really brings me back! There was this scene where she and a coworker were trying to package candy from a conveyor belt. The belt went haywire and sped up. It started going so fast that she started popping the chocolates in her mouth until she couldn't even speak. Grand'Mere and I laughed so hard at those screen scenes when we viewed them together.

It's that same sensibility here. Free, funny, unpretentious—like they don't even take their treacherous situation seriously. I don't know. In some ways it's just plain fun to watch them, almost mesmerizing. Other times I feel lonely and I am just acutely aware that I am not like them.

The strangest part of this free-spiritedness is that I would also call them disciplined. ?!?!?!

It's so strange. These particular cognitive phenomena are mostly intangible but I have become acutely aware of them because I am so . . . well, like I said—different. Everything about me is methodical and measured. I don't like not knowing what the day will bring. I don't like exploring, and some days this adventuresome business really drives me half out of my skin. Liberty comes skipping my way asking to play hide and seek in the fields; Fiorella comes calling to give me a lesson in goat milking; Russa urges me to take my shoes off and run with her in the grass; I balk at all of these requests, but not because I don't like these dear people. It's only because I don't like anything that's not clearly laid out. I like knowing precisely what to expect. This . . . this living without definitive structure and order. It's much the same sort of thing that almost drove me mad back home.

But these thoughts didn't come out of nowhere. They were prompted by Russa, who asked me a question a couple of days ago that stirred my thinking.

I'm not sure why she asked, but she did. It seemed like a simple question, but it took me a while to figure it out.

"Lee, do you feel different now that you are here?"

Oh my! What was I to say? I still haven't answered her directly, but the fact of the matter is, I do feel different. I feel seen here. And I . . . I . . . I feel here. I mean . . . I just feel. It's almost like I've had a rebirth (but then again, not quite). I feel so many things that I have not felt before, and most days it's overwhelming!

The most significant difference about all this is that in spite of the difficulties I'm having dealing with my gangling array of feelings, it somehow seems like my life matters in ways that it never did before. And it's crazy because there is pretty much nothing I contribute here; very little, for sure. I mean, what I do, they don't want. FRANCO has no use for my expertise. In fact, they want as little technology as possible. They don't need the enhanced OLSM technologies or the neuro-segmenting magnets that I find such satisfaction in creating. They are fine—just fine—with this ultra-simple, almost primitive existence. It's so frustrating sometimes! Back home, my life was integrally associated with the whole of life! That's why "crazy" is the only word I can muster for what's happening here. Even if it's not officially crazy, it surely is counter-intuitive.

Besides everyone at FRANCO thinks differently than I do, there's not a one who reminds me of anyone from my world, so it continues to feel quite foreign here.

For instance: soul? What exactly is that? Some days I think I get it; In fact, I've even started using the word now and again, but . . . then again, not really; it seems like a word one would use in a script, a show, or . . . a fantasy tale. Is there even such a thing as a soul, a person beneath the skin, under the bones, someone at the very core that is more than just flesh and blood?

When I hear them saying things like "the very core of my soul" sometimes an uncomfortable sort of evanescent consciousness threads its way through every cell in my body and I want to scream, "WHAT ARE YOU PEOPLE TALKING ABOUT?" Other times, their words and their ways pierce me; they pierce me deeply. They grab a place inside me that is so unfamiliar and so foreign; the only thing I can do with it is sit still and soak up what they say. Is that my soul speaking? I don't know. Perhaps, it is. It's all so confusing.

I've been able to piece together a few things that have been said that let me know that most of them are theists. It's hard to believe, but it's true. My family all believe in God. It's a subject I really don't want to even broach, because it is so antithetical to everything I believe. I don't quite know how they could be so brilliantly intelligent and still believe in an intangible, invisible, super creator of the universe, but they do. It's like they forgot that God belongs in the fairy tale file with Santa Claus, Clark Kent, and the Easter Bunny. I really cannot go there, but I know they believe even though they don't say much about it.

My first clue was the letter I found in my Deep Archive. When mother talked about prayer I first thought she was crazy, but then when I arrived Grand'Mere told me outright that my presence at FRANCO was somehow connected to carrying the torch, remembering from whence I came, walking—that's right, it all came back to me—walking in the anointing with the strength and grace of the ancient Jewess, Deborah.

Then the news that my name was to be Holly—a symbol of the lovely red berry of Christmas. Sheesh. Glad that didn't happen.

Unfortunately, I've noticed that this archaic belief in God seems not to have spared dear Viddie. He called me a miracle. They all believe. Uhhhhhh. I feel so out of place.

Well, whatever their failings and idiosyncrasies, none of these folks are conformists. As much as they are alike in their disdain for the mechanized, each has his or her own story to tell about their "escape from the machine." That's what they call my world, the machine. They speak of it as though it has a life of its own, but really they are just talking about the way we function back home. I mean, yes, it's a distanced existence within carefully constructed walls, but it is much safer, cleaner, and predictable. How can they possibly refuse it?

Their stories of "renewal and revelation" are told and retold with zeal and passion as we sit around the Friday night circle at Stone Camp. Although each of them has vastly different backgrounds, the theme is always the same: Renewal and revelation. Nurturing and community. It's as if their stories narrate their entire existence up here in the mountains. Sure they work hard at maintaining a clean water supply and a lovely variety of food, but it's the stories that they keep coming back to!

They are most zealous in rehearsing their individual accounts of "leaving the machine," and they clearly don't approve of our efficient use of brain space. It's never been said directly, but I get the distinct impression each time they happily choose a primitive means of communication over tek. I really don't get it. The use of invisible, embedded media—it's cleaner and it's more efficient; there's less opportunity for what we want to communicate to get junked up or misunderstood by human limitations, and . . . well, the OLSM is just a tool, right?

In any case, I am realizing that in spite of these marked differences, there are indeed a few things I have in common with them, one of which is that I do have my own story. And being here—in their midst—makes my own crazy story seem just a touch more normal, which is kind of ironic, isn't it? Anyway, that's why I've taken to bringing this journal with me just about everywhere I go. I've got the little knapsack that L.J. the guitarist gave me the other day. Strength—I don't know what I like better, the man's guitar playing or the kindly demeanor of his time-worn face. At first, the patch covering his bad eye made me think of the Lab's Pirate Adventures on the Caribbean vacation package—the one we put together back in '65—but now when I look at him I don't even see it. He's such a thoughtful old man. And this sack he gave me fits so snuggly around my shoulders; it gives me a little bit of a sense that there are some things that I can call mine. It's nice and light, too— just the pen, the art book, my hairbrush and the sparse personal hygiene items that I still had with me from my car. I really like carrying my stuff with me.

So, all is well—I guess—though some days I feel a little blue, like today. I'm not quite sure why, but all this newness, this, this dealing with feelings I can't control and the uncertainty of what each day will bring—ugh . . . I feel detached from myself and it makes me feel, well . . . just a bit low.

Without my P/Z 1000, the gravitational center of my brain is off kilter. Just a bit, but it's enough to make me feel off some days. And that, of course, taxes the center of emotional activity in there, as well. It's like a vicious circle. The very neural plasticity that makes OLSM operate so seamlessly, works against my cognitive health when I don't have the tek. The pathways weaken. I lose stuff.

It's been a couple of weeks since the last fuzzy message trekked across my prefrontal. As scary and weird as those blips were, at least they were a reminder that there is another life, another world where I have a life and a purpose.

However, the worst thing about my loss of tek is this topsy-turvy head-trip I keep dealing with concerning my feelings! Instead of the crystal clear control I've always been able to maintain, my emotions are regularly bleeding over through the amygdala, affecting the decision-making expertise of my prefrontal lobe. I feel it. I can actually feel it! The clarity and distinction that I've always depended upon to keep me in control is fading, and I, well, I don't like it, but then I do, sometimes. Uggggggggggh.

Maybe if I keep writing about it I will be able to conquer the complexity of it all without my enhancements. It's such a strange tension. That rush of affection welling up inside of me unexpectedly as I see a flock of bluebirds take flight—I like that. Intellectually, I know it is overkill; it's just too much gush. I also know that human beings do not do well with unchecked emotions—it's a proven fact! But without my tek I am reverting; I feel like I am slipping into a primitive mindset and if I don't reconnect with my world soon I might just forget everything that is true and real and wise.

Just yesterday I thought more deeply about this whole thing when I experienced a daydream that was so vivid that I got lost in it for a few minutes. This was a first for me, and while Roos says daydreaming is a completely normal experience in healthy, reflective, human beings, I am not so sure. Here's what happened:

Leaning lazily against Grand'Mere's granite portico, I felt the sun fall gently on my face. It was such a delightful warmth that I closed my eyes to enjoy it more fully when all of a sudden Viddie jumped directly in front of me, his chest pressing intimately against mine. His eyes, smoky and blue as the May sky seemed to draw me right into himself.

Those eyes spoke to me without any words at all, bidding me to come to some secret place, the likes of which I had never encountered, neither at FRANCO nor back home within the walls. All of a sudden the once gentle rays of the sun felt like lasers, beaming into my every pore. I was burning up and quickly shook myself out of the reverie.

This day was a first. It was the first day among many that I began to dream about a man . . . while I was awake yet! Up until then the entrenched habit of micro-sleeping didn't really foster much in the way of dream life, and daydreaming was something none of us had any head space for at the Lab. Now this daydreaming was happening regularly and I simply did not know what to do with everything that my (seemingly) overactive subconscious was throwing my way.

Yesterday, after my chores I went for a walk and stopped to speak with Russa as she was weeding. When I told her about the daydreams she stood up and brushed the dirt off her knees, slowly removing the gloves she uses to garden. "Lee, this is the beginning. You must give yourself to these imaginings and not be afraid. They are not vain. You are beginning to feel things deeply, and that is a wonderful thing."

She took my hand in hers and spoke with such gentleness. "I am glad you told me; it is important to share what is in our hearts, my friend."

Russa's kind eyes were probing; her smile, so comforting. In spite of the fact that I really didn't want to, I found myself agreeing with her, reminding myself that my life was here now, with everyone in FRANCO.

"I can't stop thinking about him, Russa."

"And what, pray tell, is the problem with that, my friend?" Her playful question and deliberate tone coaxed me to continue.

"I don't know. I just know I don't like this feeling, Roos, I don't like it. I almost feel sick; it's not an ugly feeling, just one that has got me spinning. It's something I'm not able to control and that scares me. I mean, what is he feeling? What is he thinking? I just never know. If I had my P/Z I could maybe hack my way in there, but without it I have absolutely no way of knowing what he is thinking. He just looks at me and when he does it seems like his entire body is looking at me, like he's drawing me by some—I know it sounds crazy—but by some mesmerizing invisible power."

Russa smiled and took the opportunity to remind me that she never saw Viddie do as much gardening work for Grand'Mere or Marissa as she had seen this particular season.

"Usually, once he's plowed, he's off to the next yard to help, but he always seems to find something else to do around your mother's place. Lee. I think that tells us something, hmmm?"

It was hard not to smile.

Her openness made me feel a bit braver. Perhaps I could disclose a tad more about just how much Belevedere Florenica was consuming my thoughts.

I went for it.

"It's not just the images that stream into my days, Roos. It's pictures of the two of us together that fill my head at night, too! And the thing is this: never before have I ever dreamed of a man—any man—or have I felt so off-kilter when I saw one, but every time I see this man I am floored, totally floored. There's something about him, Roos . . . it's like, well, I know it sounds impossible, but it's as if he's been fused to the very fabric of my being, like he's under my skin or something. When I see him I just want to vanish inside his kiss."

My hand popped over my lips unconsciously, like some straight-shouldered sentinel ordered my mouth shut. I immediately regretted my poor judgment in telling her something so private. Immediately Russa flashed me that big, toothy smile of hers and quelled my feelings of remorse.

I hung my head.

"Looks like you have it bad, Lee. I don't think there's any turning back now. Viddie Viddie Viddie—everything Viddie. Yup. I've seen it before. You've got it bad, for sure."

She laughed aloud and I gave her a friendly shove. Russa was teasing the heck out of me, but her welcoming chuckle and soft eyes let me know that she meant no harm.

"I think you've got to let him know how you feel, Leeya."

"Impossible," I told her. "I won't do it. I don't even want to recognize these feelings, let alone tell him."

Russa didn't respond, but walked behind me and began French braiding my hair. It was getting pretty warm out there yesterday, so I welcomed the help. As soon as she finished braiding, her words came easily. She sounded like an old-fashioned school teacher listing the ways I might approach my Viddie quandary.

"Okay, so you won't actually say anything, but perhaps you could start with a little positive nonverbal energy."

"Huh? What do you mean?"

The woman had a definite plan.

"For starters, you need to change the way you slink away from the group any time he shows up. I mean, it's one thing to clam up and quite another to disappear. You're not even giving it a chance."

Hmmm; I do shrink back from him, but I'm not even sure why.

Leave it to Roos to call me out, though. She finished braiding my hair, walked around and just stood there in front of me, folding her arms, cocking her head, with a silly expression on her face waiting patiently for a response.

"Gosh, I don't know why I do it, Roos. I don't know. You're right though; I'm not myself around him, and it's not that I want him to ignore me, but I ... Oh Russa."

I looked away, but she persisted with a gentle nudge to my arm.

"Go ahead. Tell me what you're thinking. Why are you shrinking back from this conversation? Why are you pushing yourself away from the possibility of happiness when you obviously feel something very real here?"

Wow. Did I feel cornered at that exact moment, but ... well, I also felt safe enough with her to continue my thought process.

"Men are ... well ... just men. Even my dalliance with Alessandro was more perfunctory than anything else. I never let him anywhere near my heart, Russa. That was off limits, for sure. But virtual romance, well ... it's more like a play date; it's like a game or a ... tryout. Yeah, that's it; it's a very safe place to try a person out to see if you're compatible.

"But Viddie, Viddie is ... entirely different. He is something else ... he is someone to reckon with. What exactly it is about him that draws me, I'm not entirely sure. I've seen other fine looking men before, though none quite as extraordinary as he. And what to do about him? I have no idea."

"Alessandro was your old boss, right?" Russa's question interrupted the heavy flow of energy I had been concentrating on Belvedere. It threw me for a loop and it also betrayed her perspective.

"He is my boss, Roos. He is still my boss. I'm away from home; just on leave, remember? I may not answer to him directly at the moment, but one day I'll be back there and I have no doubt that he'll still be at the helm and all will return to the well-oiled operation that it was before I left, but ... but ... yes;

Alessandro and I . . . we shared some . . . virtual space . . . several times, in fact. We, well; we went on vacation together."

Russa raised her softly rounded eyebrows and cocked her head. I continued my confession.

"Yes. Alessandro joined me in the Hawaiian Islands and we experienced the XtremeTropics together before the software was ever released to the public. We . . . christened it under the Wailua Rainbow waterfalls in Kauai and we . . ."

Russa interrupted me abruptly. "Lee, I don't need to know the details; I love you. Some things—c'mon . . . some things are meant to be kept private." She squeezed my forearm slightly and continued. "No matter what you experienced with your boss, you've got to keep this in mind: Alessandro is not all men. There are some men who want more than what their vain imaginings can conjure up. There are actually some who are tender and genuinely care for one girl, one special girl."

I detected a slight glisten in her eyes as she spoke.

"You sound like you know this from experience, Roos. Am I right? Was . . . was there ever anyone in your life who was that to you?"

Her faraway smile belied her words while she stuck strictly to speaking in generalities.

"Men and women are made for each other, Emilya. It's right and it's good that you have these feelings for Belvedere Florencia, and clearly he has feelings for you. Why on earth do you deny your feelings as if emotions are invalid or criminal? I really don't understand that."

Once again I hung my head low and rubbed my empty index finger with vexed longing.

Chapter 4

Day 52—The Light

"What's that melody you're humming? I like it."

Russa and I settled into our daily jaunt with a first stop at Rubble Ridge, just outside Stone Camp's closest perimeter. She loves to pick flowers and I like to settle in on my favorite grey slab of granite to jot down notes in my art book, making observations about the vast open spaces and lovely air of these real mountains. One day I'll use these details to create even better virtual vacation packages at the Lab.

Always the highpoint of my day, our walk has nearly become a ritual, only missing here and there for various unexpected things that crop up. This morning, as my friend was humming a sweet little tune, I put my book down to listen more closely.

"I recognize that melody, Roos. What is it?"

She called back from the midst of the buttercups and daffodils, her silky auburn hair shimmering in the late spring sun. What a picture Russa is this morning, her favorite cotton dress with the faded purple and orange wild flowers populating her long, flowing skirt. I love seeing the happiness emanate from her; it's like she's a bottle of a delightful fragrance that pours out over the rest of us.

"Oh, it's an old—really old—song; it's the one that L.J. plays all the time. I'm sure you recognize it because of him."

"Hmmm. No, I don't remember it at all, Russa. Are you sure?

"Yes, definitely. He plays it in between every other song he plays; it's his fave. It's that old-timey Celtic song from the middle of last century; I can't get it out of my head this morning. Did you ever see the parts of a buttercup close up, Lee? C'mere, Have a look."

"Ah, you are right! That's where I've heard it!" I said, brushing the wild cucumber vines away from the small protrusions of granite coming up through the wide swatch of daffodils, "and no; I've never seen a buttercup up close."

"Oh then you must," she explained with a smile spreading across her face like sunshine. Holding the tiny yellow flower under her chin she seemed to glow with childlike exuberance.

"See? Look—this is how the legend goes: Hold it under your chin. If you're a happy person its yellow hue will appear on the skin. Here, you try."

As I copied her buttercup theory she reminded me that L.J. has played the tune at every Friday night circle since I've been at FRANCO.

"It's his "go-to" song, you know—what he plays when he's just sitting there by himself. In between our call-outs, in between meals, in between his forest outings with Liam. The man fingerpicks it constantly, but hardly ever with the words, at least anymore."

The sun was shining brightly and I squinted as Russa continued to explain the origin of the music. She climbed one rock higher than the one I was on and made a little place for herself between two smaller boulders that jutted out of the speckled granite. It reminded me a bit of my office chair.

As I looked up, she steadied herself with one hand and with the other held half-a-dozen daffodils that she had been gathering along the crags.

"Okay, happy person, you're right; I have heard him play that melody before, but never with the words. Why not? Doesn't he remember them anymore?"

"Ah, he's up there in years, Leeya, but I think he remembers the words, just fine. It's just that he and Sierra used to sing it together when they were young. The words are winsome. Once I heard him speaking with Blake and your father. He was reminiscing about his youth and mentioned that they used to sing together—this song was their favorite."

"Oh, that's sweet. So, do you know the words? What's it about?"

Russa squinted for a moment, but not because of the sun. It's taken me a while, but now I understand when she furrows her brow like that she is calling something up from her memory. It's really quite a cool thing to see, because that type of recall is pretty much a lost art where I come from. I kind of get a charge out of seeing raw memory in action.

"Yeah . . . yes, I do. I think so" she replied. "It's really meant to be sung in harmony, but I'll sing as much of it as I remember if you like."

I just about leapt to my feet. "Will you, really? Yes, please! Go for it, oh bold one."

She laughed and agreed easily. "Okay, here goes:

> And when at last I find you,
> Your song will fill the air.
> Sing it loud so I can hear you.
> Make it easy to be near you.
> For the things you do endear you to me,
> Aw . . .
> You know I will.
> Love you forever, and forever . . .
> Love you will all my heart.
> Love you whenever we're together,
> Love you when we're a part.
> La la la la la . . . [1]

"UH . . . that's all I remember, Lee."

"Oh Roos," I said, clutching her forearm as she helped me up to the flat rock further up the ridge. "I don't think I've ever heard anything as beautiful as that. And I didn't know you could sing! Your voice is lovely—truly. "

Her face turned a light shade of pink and she began slowly shaking her head in disagreement.

"It is a pretty song, Leeya, but I am no singer—not by anyone's standard. I do enjoy music and L. J. so generously fills our lives with it. These old folk songs from a century or so ago, well, very often they are just the help I need to remember the things that matter most."

Well, what strikes me most is the melody. It's captivating. The idea behind the song sounds a little too naïve for my sensibilities, but it is quite sweet—in a childlike sort of way. In any case, I made her sing it again and again all afternoon and by the time the day was through I knew all the words and could join her. As long as I sang the melody, Roos kicked into a beautiful harmony, and we spent at least an hour perfecting it. Over and over, our voices blended until we were hoarse.

"Lennon and McCartney, that was the duo!" she exclaimed. "Now it's coming back to me; they were from Europe, not sure where; maybe Ireland? They were part of a band that supposedly revolutionized twentieth century pop culture."

We harmonized for hours and sang L.J.'s go-to song until our throats were parched, and then—we sang it some more.

> Love you forever and for-ev-er;
> Love you with all my heart.
> Love you whenever we're together;
> Love you when we're a part.
> And when at last I find you . . .

Russa broke off from singing mid-verse and turned to me with such intense eyes that I could hardly believe we had been so lighthearted only a moment before.

"What is it?" I asked her immediately.

She shook her head and seemed to take on a rather solemn look.

"Russa?" I shook her arm lightly. "What happened? Your countenance. . . . What are you thinking?"

Her soft green eyes were kind and full of intensity as she looked at me squarely.

"I never had a sister, Lee. My parents vanished after the Devastation; I don't even remember what they look like. The truth is, you're the nearest thing to a sister that I've ever known." Her eyes got glassy as she spoke and her now familiar winsome smile continued to winnow its way into my heart.

Until today I never realized she suffered so. While I was rather surprised to hear her emote so openly, I couldn't help but feel for her.

Listening to Russa's story it almost seemed as though there could be good reason to allow myself to indulge in the same sort of emotive excess, but if I do, I am afraid that my strong hold on reason will weaken and I might give in to the weakness of letting my feelings take precedence over logic. Yet, as she spoke, with each passing moment my heart felt as though it was literally enlarging in my chest.

Although I normally would have called her back to a sound and rational analysis of her past, today I simply tried to encourage her to get beyond all that messy emotion, and I felt my own insides start to melt. Instead of words, I simply smiled and gave her hand a little squeeze.

With that, her lighthearted demeanor returned, just like a cloud passing quickly through the big blue mountainous sky.

I thought I might take a chance and share the weirdness of the glitch with Russa, tell her about the strange message I received back when I first arrived, and maybe ask her advice. Before I could muster the courage, she broke into my thoughts with sentimental gushing and a melodic voice that seemed just a bit over-the-top for my liking.

"It's so much fun to just to walk, talk, sing and laugh together, Lee, isn't it? I don't remember ever experiencing this before, even as a child. I know you feel it too." Russa gave me one of the daffodils as she finished that statement, to which I responded in kind with a knowing smile and a nod. It seemed harsh to try to give her a lesson in emotive self-management, so I accepted the flower and cleared my throat, attempting to politely change the subject.

"Roos, you never did tell me what brought you to FRANCO or what it is that keeps you here. I also can't help wondering if you ever think about leaving. I mean, there's a whole world out there that is just brimming over with possibilities. There's all that tek that you are missing, a very stable, predictable daily life that is largely free from confrontation and conflict, and a whole flurry of inventions just waiting for us to create them! Do you ever wonder what you'd do in the civilized world?"

Russa's peaceful smile turned to laughter, erupting into a sort of maniacal chuckle that was quite out of character. She tossed the rest of the daffodils up into the air with a somewhat vehement flip. "You are REALLY something else Leeya Hoffman-Bowes, something else!"

"What?" I smiled quizzically. "It's just a question. Have you? Have you ever thought about leaving?"

Russa's response was not at all what I expected. She spoke quickly and with unexpected verve. "More and more I am noticing that this friendship with you is having a significant effect on me; you've become like a sister to me Leeya, but I guess it's just not the same for you. I mean, we are from the same planet, but I keep forgetting we are worlds apart."

"And just what is that supposed to mean, Roos?"

"It's supposed to mean that you have been here nearly two months; you have enjoyed the hospitality of everyone at FRANCO, you have entered into the festivities, you have visibly demonstrated the newfound joy you are experiencing with real friends, real family, to say nothing of real food, yet you still cannot open your heart to any of us."

What? What is she talking about? That seemed to come out of nowhere, and then she just rattled on with her diatribe.

"It's sad—and it makes me even sadder to know that I value our friendship so highly but it's not the same for you. You keep yourself shielded . . . hidden away. It's as if you truly do not realize that life is precious, and its meaning is far beyond work, productivity and perfection."

My head swirled. I wasn't sure how to respond to this version of Russa, but I knew what she said could not be ignored, so I attempted a careful response.

"Don't you think you may be over-reacting a bit, Roos? You are my friend. You know I care about you. Why would you think it necessary to accuse me of hiding myself? It's not intentional, this . . . this supposedly closed off attitude of mine; it's just the only way I know how to be. You know, this just proves my point, actually. We simply cannot afford to allow the emotional center of our brains to engage in the drama of everyday relationships this way or our communication process gets muddied and we fall into confusion. Human beings are not made for chaos, Roos. It's not like I want to shield myself from you or anyone else. It's something I have to do if I want to stay strong and engaged in the world."

Her passionate reply was immediate and full of unseemly emotion.

"Answer me this: what does it mean to be engaged in the world if we are not engaged in each other's lives, Leeya? We were made for love. Love is infinitely more important than communicating efficiently and . . . and . . . and friendship is a type of love—a pure love—one that wants the best for the other and doesn't think firstly about oneself. Don't you see it? Oh no, my dear, I don't think you see it at all."

Our feet dragged in the dirt as we walked slowly back to camp, the song having long evaporated into the once-effusive and fragrant mountain air. Although the sun was still shining, the fog over our conversation rolled in and hung heavily over our entire walk back, covering everything beautiful as we traipsed the long trail back to Stone Camp. It's strange, but what started out as a splendid day in the mountainous sunshine, now seemed desperately dull—even dreary. I got back to Grand'Mere's and took out this journal, trying to make sense of what just happened, which is where I sit right now.

The Principles are so deeply ingrained into my thinking that I have to keep reminding myself that the current take on what is a proper way to live is not universal. Pride, Progress, and Perfection—man, they sound so right to my ears, but I'm watching FRANCO live out an entirely different set of values. I would say that they do not care about perfection at all! In fact, in the midst of our little . . . misunderstanding this afternoon I told Russa that it's like they let an entirely different set of P's rule their lives.

Instead of pride and progress they're always talking about living lives of purpose and preparedness; oh, and we mustn't forget proclamation. Proclaiming 'the truth'—which they do all the time—is so, so important.

> Stand up; proclaim the goodness of the day.
> Stand up; proclaim the things for which we're grateful.
> Stand up; proclaim liberty and justice for all!

It's sort of amusing to watch, but in some ways quite elegant. They call out to each other at Friday night circle and pretty much tell each other what to say. Grand'Mere tells me that if they don't proclaim what is true, and beautiful, and worthy of praise, they find themselves giving in to frustration and fear. It's what she calls "minding the Light."

Without proclamation, it seems they risk dipping into depression, probably because there are so many challenges to life in FRANCO. It's such an odd practice, but perhaps it's part of what helps them thrive.

Now, neither Grand'Mere, Roos, nor Marissa has ever mentioned the fourth "p," but I have seen it up close. In fact, I see it every day. They plod. << Grin>>

It's definitely not part of their official mission, but I can hardly believe how these precious people plod. I mean, half a day can go by without any sense of urgency or productivity. While they do accomplish a great deal overall, some days they'll just lay it all aside and sing . . . or dance!

And the funny thing is that there's not-a-one that produces shoddy work or is lax about doing their own share of work in the community; If anything, the opposite is true. I mean, each has a particular talent and skill that they bring to FRANCO, but instead of pride I see something entirely different. It's . . . well, it's that humility thing again. Everyone has this sort of self-effacing way about them; even Liam, whose quiet repose has never really stopped making me nervous. Even he has an understated, but obvious humility about him.

The other anomaly is that everybody's personalities are vastly different from each other; they're not pressed into a mold. They are individuals, in the truest sense of the word, but they don't seem to have much pride in personal achievement—I just don't see it here. It's so weird!

Not even in their achievement of living a hugely successful alternative lifestyle; nope—they are just . . . humble people. I mean, the high level of skills of most of these folks is incredible. Salvatore Salingwa was a medical doctor in his twenties and thirties. Darren was a botanist; I guess he still is.

Blake was a Navy Seal when the government was still strictly the United States. Others, of course like my parents and grandmother, are physicists.

Holt Buckster, the former Midwestern rancher and FRANCO'S key financier doesn't walk around likes he's Mr. Important, nor does anyone treat him that way. Everyone treats him just the same way they treat Alton or Carlos. Hux is what they call him; I'm not exactly sure why. He's got this wide, breezy smile that sort of comes out of nowhere and nearly forces you to stop and say hello.

Harold-in-the—I don't remember his last name, something about a camper—whose wife was a seamstress, is in charge of all the tanning in the community. He's got every manner of deer hide stretched out behind his camper. I don't know how they learned to tan deer hide, but that's what they both did until Elyse died a couple years back. He's in charge of making all the boots, shoes, belts, and hats, and does quite a job keeping everybody outfitted.

FRANCO's also got a couple of former civil engineers . . .

Oh, wait. Someone's here. It's Viddie's sister!

"Hello?"

"Hi . . . uh, Alessa. Sure, come in. No, no . . . not a problem; I was just jotting down some thoughts."

"How are you, Miss Emilya? How are you faring? I brought you some of my mother's best morning cookies. They're called biscotti, flavored with walnuts. I hope you'll enjoy them."

"Thank you, so much, Alessa. That was kind of you; come, sit down—here, there's room on the edge of the bed."

Her shyly modest demeanor makes me want to pull my hair out. I want to say, "Speak up! Speak up, Alessa. I can't hear you." But that would be rude, so I just lean in a little bit when she starts talking about the jam.

"Mother likes to bake something fresh every morning, but she leaves the jam to your grandmother. Grand'Mere makes the finest preserves in FRANCO. Shall I fetch you some from her cupboard?"

"So kind of you, Alessa. And kind of you to bring these. I think you must just be a kind person. Yes, why yes, I'd love some, thank you."

Alessa's entire face flushed a fair shade of pink and she shook her head as she rose to grab a jar of the jam.

"She's got peach, mulberry, apricot, apple, pepper, and blueberry up here, Miss Emilya. Which shall I bring you?"

For all they don't have up here in these mountains they sure to have a bucketload of jam and tea. It makes me chuckle.

"Uh . . . let me see. I'm not quite sure, Alessa. What do you recommend? There are too many too choose; I have options anxiety."

Soft footsteps and a quiet smile brought Viddie's twin back into view.

"Here. I think the apricot will be quite nice. It's the rarest. We have buckets and buckets of blueberries each summer, but the apricots are fewer. You'll like this. . ."

Alessa's an interesting character. So quiet. It's a bit unnerving, actually, but—what a very nice gesture this morning.

She's got quite handsome facial features and looks a lot like her mother, just a bit larger boned and slightly less angular. I think she looks more like Carlos than Fiorella. Penetrating dark brown eyes, silky lighter brown curls that bound down just past her shoulders, and a lovely slender mouth—quite a nice picture, but such an oddly quiet personality. We sat there without much to say until it got awkward. She asked if I need anything in particular and made a point to let me know she is happy to help, but then left abruptly.

Let's see. Where was I? Oh, chronicling the people here. Yes, I left off with the engineer.

Then there's also an elderly former pilot, and one neurosurgeon. Jake (the pilot) is almost 80, but still really vital. He and Rooney (one of the mechanics) are constantly tinkering with an old plane engine that they've got stashed somewhere out in a field a good distance from Stone Camp. I've seen it, but not up close. Dr. Charles Gaines (the neurosurgeon) is mentoring Blake in surgery and Dr. Salingwa thinks it's important to leave everyone with a little lesson in the medical arts whenever he's called upon to help someone who's sick.

A goodly number of what we used to call blue collar types are here, as well. Maria and Justin Martin, for instance. When they were younger they worked with their parents in the furniture business and brought lots of skill to the community by helping to construct the tables and chairs we all use here. Their children are cute as the chickadees that play at my feet under the spruce trees. At twelve, Justin is already an important part of the community, tending to the goats and sheep. He's in charge of rounding the animals up once the day's grazing is done. He hangs out with Russa's cousin, Alton, quite a bit; and since Alton makes the cheese here I guess cheese and goats bring them together. Little Liberty is just ten, but helps milk the herd and . . . well, I think she's in charge of following me every time she sees me. Ha—the child is constantly energized.

Of the eighty or so people who live up here in these low mountains of Pennsylvania, there are a number of former construction and metal workers, some plumbers, even a guy who was a trucker before the fossil fuel changeover. Plus, they've got three mechanics; a couple of farmers—and all are valued and accepted without a pecking order. It's a very interesting setup. Although they each take their responsibility very seriously, they often defer to each other; I see it all the time.

Crash! In the middle of my thought a strange blip of light once again reached across my prefrontal cortex, almost as if someone was trying to message me, but there was no source code, no real words—just a blip with a few letters.

X appris . . .

Weird. Nothing to do but ignore it.

Anyway, then there's the specialists—described this way because of the vital services they provide, namely food and water. This, of course, includes Liam, my own dear, disappearing father. He is much appreciated for his hunting expeditions, game trappings, and water routing as highly as is Fiorella, the tiny but vivacious woman who gave birth to Viddie.

And that woman—what a gourmet! Her cooking method is foundationally Italian, but Viddie tells me that she was also trained in the French culinary arts.. What he never told me was where she got her sense of humor. She is just so much fun to be around! She tells these little jokes, really just random phrases, but they often have a double meaning and when she speaks, she speaks quickly. So between the Italian accent and the speed, Fiorella is really fun to watch.

She brought her Aunt Vichenze with her from Italy at the very start of the Devastation and was never able to get her back to her homeland because things got so much worse so quickly. The moratorium on air travel was imposed immediately and has not let up since. Aunt Vee (everyone calls her that) and Grand'Mere spend much time together in the kitchen, knitting, keeping each other company, taking turns keeping the fire going. Nearly every time I see her she starts the same ritual. No 'hello Emilya, how are you?' No words. She just begins slowly shaking her head back and forth with a sort of air of incredulity and without fail repeats the following: "Oh, oh, how much like your mama you look. Bellisima, bellisima." And then invariably she touches my head and rehearses the length, silkiness, beautiful nut-brownness, or some other aspect of my hair. She's a real character, and especially so because her fawning is ridiculous. My hair is a mess. I swear, it's a mop! It needs conditioner so badly, but Aunt Vee thinks I'm some sort of old Hollywood movie star. She's really a crack up.

Anyway, before FRANCO, when Aunt Vee was living with Firoella, she worked in a food manufacturing company in Connecticut. Her stories about her work in the plant making provisio bars just after the explosions are another subject she gets stuck on, but I don't care. At least they distract her from harping on the subject of my appearance.

Fiorella is just as much of a character as her sweetly eccentric Italian aunt. She doesn't seem to know that she cooks everything better than everyone else. I would like to see her take a little credit for the magnificent meals she makes, but she always points to someone else's contribution when she gets praise. Mother called her broccoli cheese casserole 'exquisite' the other night as we took a meal together around Stone Camp.

"Oh, oh, it would be nothing without our dear Alton's labor over the fromagia. His chees-a-ess di most favorite part, yes?"

Oh, no no no. I want to tell her that the cheese is definitely good, but the best part is her special touch. For the life of me I don't know what she does to her casseroles and soups, but they are the tastiest! She's always got some sort of root vegetable that's she's grown, along with the venison hunted by my father, and an array of fresh herbs from mother's garden. But she acts as if it is nothing to think up these culinary delights, like anyone could do it, but no one can cook like her. I just don't get it; this . . . this humble streak—or whatever it is— is evident in every last one of them. I see it at the oddest times and in the strangest ways, but mostly it's in the way they relate to each other, the things they say, their demeanor, their actions, their conversations.

The examples are just countless. If it's not L.J. tipping his hat to the 'fine dancin' while he plays for hours to entertain everyone, or Grand'Mere pointing out Darren's innovative hybridization techniques when one of us complements her latest recipe, it's Harold-in-the-camper emphasizing 'the top-notch job Liam did in the hunt' or 'the fine and diligent tannin' work accomplished by the Martins. Even little Libby is always rushing to praise the supply of milk from mama goats that keeps us all in cheese. There's not a haughty one among them!

It's clearly something they believe to be important, but I find it very strange. Everyone knows humility is a weakness. In the principled life, we are all aware that personal pride is preferable to such archaic notions as humility. It's just . . . backward. I hate to say it, but they really are backward!

Aside from the humility thing, they do have a few other things in common that I've noticed. One is the deep sense of purpose that pervades the camp. It spills over into everything they do. Not that it's set out clearly in any sort of structured rules or policies, but they are just really, really purposeful. The funny thing is, in spite of the difference in past status and education levels, there is just no difference in the way they treat each other; they function so well together, it's almost as if they are a unit, a single unit.

They are exceedingly intentional about planning for the future, maintaining peace—even singing and having fun—they work it into everyday life as if their lives depended upon it. The other thing I like, but still find a bit challenging, is that they cherish time together, and treat it as if it is just as important as their jobs. I have noticed this very thing creeping up inside me every day with Roos; and now that Viddie comes around to chat it's evident with him, as well.

Oh my Strength—there he is now. Viddie's coming up from the ridge.

Chapter 5

Day 62—The Birds

Fiorella and I sat for well over an hour sipping her favorite minty bee balm tea. We chatted lightheartedly about cooking, baking, and her fanciful obsession with growing all sorts of plants; which ones steep best, which ones have the best medicinal properties, etc. It's clear that the leaves of the particular plant we were drinking provide a rich source of satisfaction for the woman, as she is the one who discovered what a nice alternative it is to the chamomile and spearmint that grow wild up here. Fiorella educated me on the bee balm, and I learned that it not only has brightly colored flowers that are lovely to look at, but when dried and steeped, the aroma emits a deeply complex combination of citrus and spice. It's good for the stomach and—as she's so fond of saying—it's good for the soul.

As we were enjoying our second steamy cuppa, Fiorella was right in the midst of explaining how important it is to use an entire stalk of celery—leaves and all—when making soup. Her hands seemed to move even faster than her lips and she was making me laugh as she demonstrated the amount of herbs that are 'just-a-nice' for her savory pasta y fagioli when we heard a loud yelp coming from outside the earth shelter. We shot to our feet and immediately ran toward it.

"Oh no! Noooooo!" Marissa's voice pierced the eight o'clock hour and even though most everyone in FRANCO was already up, FRANCO mornings are typically low key so everyone in the immediate vicinity ran to the sound.

There she was, my mother in a puddle of tears sitting in the midst of her garden. Where once there had been lovely summer squash just about ready for harvest, there were only leaves and broken vines left, scattered across her yard.

"How could this happen?" Mother cried, lifting a lonely, half-bitten zucchini up in the air. "I have tended to this little patch of soil faithfully for nearly three months and now this? Just look at it!"

With her other hand she lifted a mangled eggplant into the air and peered upwards to see seven faces staring down at her, each of us wearing looks that ranged somewhere between befuddlement and surprise. Everyone, that is, but Grand'Mere. My compassionate grandmother was already bending low to reach for mother's hand.

"Come on; get up, my Marissa darling. No need to cry. The rabbits are just plumping themselves up for us. Liam will set out the trap this evening and we'll be enjoying some fricassee by tomorrow at noon." Grand'Mere smiled and brushed the dirt off mother's face.

"In the old days, we would have used pesticide. This could have been averted!" Mother's dismal whine faded into the folds of Grand'Mere's fleshy arms and a collective sigh of relief resonated through the camp as she led her away for some tea and comfort.

"Three months! I've been working on this patch for . . . "

"I know, I know," Grand'Mere replied with kind affirmation as she led her back to the shelter. Grand'Mere truly did behave as Marissa's own mother; that was obvious.

Fiorella ran back to her kitchen to check on the sizzling garlic in her cast iron kettle. Alessa coaxed Liberty back to the goat gate. L.J. hobbled back to his trailer. Everyone returned to what they were doing before mother's drama; everyone except Viddie. He was on his knees inspecting the mesh surrounding the plants and looking at a bulge in the soil.

We were alone.

What happened after the incident with Marissa kind of took me by surprise. Who would have expected a day-long walk in the woods with FRANCO's most captivating and eligible bachelor? It all happened rather quickly and I will recount the details exactly as they took place, but first, I must preface it by saying that the most fascinating part of this trek so far from my little home in Jersey is actually something other than discovering my parents and Grand'Mere are still alive or that a community no one back home knows about exists beyond the outer limits of civilization.

I know I've written about the wonder of discovering the reality of real relationship with others—especially, the joy of friendship—and that's astounding, truly astounding, but even more captivating than friendship is what I sense is growing with Viddie. It's friendship, yes, but of a different sort. It's more than friendship, but as yet, I'm just not sure how much.

The crazy thing is, I never knew I was missing it. I thought I had friends back home, but now that I am experiencing friendship a la FRANCO, my past relationships might better be described as alliances—weak ones at that.

Frankly, there's no other way to say it but admit that I am quite flabbergasted by it all, which brings me back to my day with Viddie.

Just as Marissa and Grand'Mere walked away, he put down the rake he was holding and laid it against the granite bank. He tilted his head, looked at me squarely, and held out his hand. Just like that! He held out his hand.

Before I knew what I was doing, I placed my hand in his and we walked around the low mountain trail, hiked up to the waterfall and wandered along the path of dense trees and foliage known as friendly wood, and there we stayed for the better part of the day.

Much of our walk was of the quiet sort, just observing and enjoying the movement of the birds and the trees and other living things, but as the day went on we took a break from our walking to sit on a small, mossy hill only about half of a mile from Stone Camp. It was a lumpy, funny sort of hill covered with a lavender flower that Viddie said was a weed, but it was oh so pretty. Never having seen anything quite like it I wanted to sit for a while and take a closer look. He found a nearby tree and made a place for us to sit in the grass.

Our conversation was slow, but we were totally engaged. Viddie is a relatively quiet fellow, but knows just how to pose a question that draws me out. And he's adept, too! The way he probes into my background does not seem invasive at all; rather, like a caring older brother. He makes me feel so secure.

First, he asked about my journey here, and wondered how I discovered there was something more than the life I knew back at the Lab. I told him about the documents I found in the black box and how it led to finding Marissa's letter in my Deep Archive. He seemed fascinated, especially about my D.A., and begged me to continue, so I shared a bit more and explained that the D.A. is really just an advanced storage system that makes better use of the brain because of the enhancements we use. Then, in the middle of attempting to answer a question about one of the philosophers mother mentioned in the letter—that Ellul guy—he stopped short, raised his index finger in the air and said, "Wait. Listen."

I didn't hear a thing and when I started to speak again he shushed me.

"Listen. There is a distinct birdsong coming from up ahead. Those are finches, can you hear them?"

I shook my head, 'no.'

"They are either gray singing finches or strawberry finches, Emi, I'm sure of it. Listen—you can tell the difference between them if you listen carefully. Right there—do you hear?"

I did. I did hear something, certainly not as clearly as he heard it, but I could make out a little bit of the melodious refrain. It was lovely. Shaking my head in the affirmative I wondered aloud how he became so knowledgeable about birdsong.

"So, how did you figure out what differentiates them, Viddie?"

"I guess you could just call me resourceful." His wink reminded me of the day we first met by the garden gate when our conversation was so stilted and awkward. I smiled at him and could see that he was being a little flirty.

"No, seriously," he said. "I like to study them. If you listen closely you'll easily notice the wide variety of sounds out here."

"Really? They're that different? C'mon, Viddie," I nudged him playfully, "you seem to know everything about everything, so tell me about the difference between them. What makes these birds so special?"

His side-winding glance was full of mischief but he continued his explanation in a serious tone. "Strawberry finches are rare, Emi, but we've seen them here every year—as far back as I can remember. It's their music that distinguishes them from other birds. It's quite distinctive—listen! There they are again."

"Their song sounds very much like a flute; can you hear them?" His large eyes widened even more than usual as he lightly tapped my nose.

I definitely don't have the ears that he has. I mean there was something out there; I heard them, but surely not as intensely as Viddie. In any case, I could not stop smiling. The day was sheer perfection.

"Let's walk up toward the old resort; it's not that far and it sounds as if they're heading up that way. Look!"

His discovery interrupted our conversation but I hardly noticed because he was pointing to a flock of birds dancing through the sky in close formation, as if some great choreographer had spent hours rehearsing them.

"There they are! Look;" he said pointing toward the treetops.

"I knew they were the finches because if you hear one finch singing they're bound to be a bunch of 'em. These birds are social, you know, really social."

Viddie's boyish delight saturated my heart like the honey his mother pours all over her raisin cakes. He spoke with such simultaneous seriousness and childlike delight about the birds, I couldn't help but join him. "I really do hear them now, Viddie, I do!"

At that he took my hand and started running toward the abandoned lodge; we stumbled and both nearly fell over the exposed root of a giant walnut tree, but he caught me just a moment before I crashed. We regained our balance and the entire rest of our run was engulfed in laughter.

Breathless, we stopped at the edge of some broken-up asphalt and he held his hand to his chest. "This is the place we love to come to every June. When the weather breaks and it's warm enough to swim, a bunch of us head up here as often as we can find time."

His voice was tinged with excitement but he said 'swim' in such a matter-of-fact way; it was clear he had no idea that he was blowing my mind.

"Swim. . . . . In the lake?" My tone was just shy of shouting back at him.

What, was he kidding? He couldn't be serious. Swimming was prohibited almost forty years ago! Everyone knows that the waters are noxious—all of them!

The thought of being immersed in water gave me a sinking feeling; Swimming would clearly be a death sentence.

Reading the concern on my face Viddie squeezed my hand and smiled tenderly; his words were warm and comforting. Speaking slowly, he stared right into my eyes as he held both of my hands in his. "Emi, what I am about to tell you is sure to be upsetting, but I really have to tell it to you straight."

"Of course. I wouldn't want it any other way, Viddie. I think by now you must know I can take it."

"Okay. Well, yes; then here goes: What you are feeling is unfortunately the result of propaganda. The government of this great land was simply not prepared for the aftershocks of the Devastation so they promoted the 'noxious tide' theory as a means to keep the population inside. Their rhetoric was a means of control. I promise you, the waters are just fine."

My mouth hung open, filled only with incredulity. He continued, and spoke with certainty, a certainly that until that moment I had not heard from his lips.

"Don't you worry, my fine lady, everything bounced back after the Devastation and within a few years the waters were not only fine for swimming, but drinking, too."

I was aghast.

"Who told you that, Viddie? And how do you know it's true? How can you be so sure?"

He spoke with continued confidence as he explained it to me further.

"This lake—Grand Lake—is our main water supply, Emi. It's connected to the well we use every day in the middle of Stone Camp. It's a tributary of the Delaware River, which also helps supply the brook where we wash our clothes. Stop and think about the well; it's the very center of our survival. Without the water from the well we would surely die. We've been drinking from it for years, all the years I've lived here. It's one of the main reasons the spot was chosen for the community. Where do you think that well water comes from that we drink every day?"

As he continued, my head started to spin. I hadn't thought about the water before. How had I missed the water supply? I felt like a complete fool! This may take a while to sink in.

My thoughts drifted off to the Xtreme package I created for our customers to virtually visit Alaska. It was such an elegant product. We called it Grand Lake Alaska, but it was a construction of our own imagination, not real.

I was having trouble focusing on what he was saying. 'Dazed' might more aptly describe my state of mind.

His voice rose in elegant articulation as Viddie spread his arms in a large, circular motion to include the water, and it jolted me out of my homeward reverie. I heard him saying, "Yes, yes Grand Lake is grand, but it's just one of the many bodies of water up here that provide fish, irrigation, drinking, bathing, and—fun."

My mind continued to swirl, and with his mention of Grand Lake I felt a strange new twinge of recollection of my life at the Lab. Yes; the clean, clear walls; perfectly pure distilled water; sleek, glass doors; graphite panels and cars— nearly indestructible, all of it so elegant and efficient. Never again would our world be taken down the way it was during the Devastation. We are more prepared now. We all know the precautionary protocols.

———

"Moni, moni. . . X. . . restrictions. . ."

———

Oh no! Right in the middle of our lovely afternoon the message fuzz came bouncing into my brain. Akkkkk! Viddie noticed it, too, because leaned into me and snapped his fingers in front of my face. "Emi. . . Emi, what's up? Where'd you go?"

"I'm . . . I'm just thinking of some software I developed back home, where I work. It's nothing, Viddie. I'm sorry. I'm fine."

Images of my department came gushing through my frontal lobes like the mountain stream we just passed—it was clear as day—but I couldn't recall the exact dimensions of our Alaskan cruise facsimile. Smack; I am forgetting my life back home; the specs and formulae are fading. I can't even remember the colors we chose for our Grand Lake teaser pack either.

It's times like these that really bother me, when I cannot easily access the valuable layered information in my D.A, to say nothing of this bothersome message fragment. Uhhh. This is the part I hate. It's so primitive, so abnormal!

Without the PZ/1000 personal interface my memory is far too fuzzy and I find I am missing so many details—stuff that would easily have been at my disposal if the necessary tools were available to reactivate my communication device. It's like being without a limb!

As we walked past the far side of Mt. Holly, the dilapidated remnants of a sprawling, abandoned ski resort came into clearer view. Cottages in various states of disrepair were scattered throughout the heavily wooded acres. Various types of foliage crept up the largely intact walls, splendidly arrayed over stone chimneys, covering them like a fine green coat.

Surely these cabins were once regal and inviting, but decades of vacancy and decay left them terribly run down. Some didn't have roofs, others were openly exposed to the fresh air through a blown-out wall or window. There seemed no rhyme or reason to the wide variety of decay in this lost world. As we approached, I could picture the lavish outside arena as it might have been at the turn of the century—full of vacationers crunching across the snow to experience the finest in elegant dining. My own Alaskan Xtreme software package included an enormous virtual dining experience. I couldn't help layering my own imagination over the entire scene.

Viddie said the construction may have been 90—even 100—years old; an intriguing bit of history to observe. Behind the cottages, just beyond the farthest one, I saw a glimmer of the body of water Viddie mentioned. It shone brightly through the trees and sparkled in the distance. Quite a pleasant shade of blue.

I had fun explaining to him the way my research team dug up photographs, old vid-clips, and interactive files from the virtual stacks to get a feel for what it's really like in the Alaskan front. He listened with interest and that made me . . . hmmm. It made me happy.

"I can see it in the distance, Viddie. It looks like diamond crystals shimmering. Wow. The archived clips of a lake are nothing like looking at a real lake, Viddie. I . . . I am . . . I can hardly believe what I'm seeing. It's so much grander than what we conceived back at the Lab."

He squeezed my hand, holding it tightly as we traipsed over layers of old leaves and twigs with careful steps. Our feet crunched through a number of different types of debris, some of which appeared sooty, others, out of sturdier material. Then we passed the dismantled playground and concrete slabs that once were tennis courts. I was taking it all in, wondering what the people might have been like back in the day when outdoor sports were all the rage. Then, snapping out of my reverie—it must have been the warm, sunny day that sparked him, or perhaps all the talk about swimming—right in the middle of his explanation of twentieth century recreational practices and old fashioned sports teams, Viddie gave me a friendly punch in the arm and shouted, "Beat-cha to the shore!" and took off like an Olympic runner.

He did beat me there, of course, and before I could stop him, he peeled off his shoes and socks and ran to the edge.

"Viddie, STOP!" I yelled, terrified.

He turned, his smile beaming.

"STOP! Please! Viddie!" My heart was pounding.

I was horrified, and tried to keep him from plunging into the water, but to no avail. Before I knew it, this rugged, intelligent man who was stealing increasingly larger pieces of my heart each moment we were together was thigh deep in the water and yelping about how cold it was.

"Come on in, Emi." He reached his arm toward me. "It's really worth it. Look—the fish are swimming happily enough."

Fish? Oh my Strength.

His eyes sparkled; he was so hard to resist.

Reiterating my concern, I begged him to come out, but who knew that Belvedere Florencia had such a stubborn side?

When he saw that I was no longer screaming he began flapping his hands and spinning around, then all at once thrust his head forward and he dove under the water—under the water completely! Oh, I couldn't take it; I had to turn away.

Just then, he popped up and yelled to me: "Come on, Emi! Would I steer you wrong? It's a beautiful day for swimming. You don't know what you're missing!"

The man just wouldn't give up!

I shook my head fiercely. No way was I going to get any closer to that mess of wet poison.

So, here was the only man I ever wanted to really be with and he was in the water, but I . . . I was terrified. I walked slowly past the grassy knoll a smidge nearer to the pebbly shore.

I don't understand myself, either. Me, the formerly fearless one; the woman afraid of nothing. Oh dear. Welcome to Freaky Experience, Room 101.

It's just so difficult to let go of long-held beliefs, and from my earliest memories I knew I was not allowed to walk barefoot on the earth's floor, and was taught early on I never to go near the water. This was something embedded in all of our earliest education files.

The noxious results of the Devastation left everything outside off-limits. Natural resources were no longer pure enough for consumption. Everything had to be filtered to the max—air, soil, and especially water. To even try to use these resources is criminal. Though jail time no longer exists in a world of 30 million people, if we go against social protocols, we are taxed fiercely by the local authorities. It's that way throughout the world. All the land masses that have People Centers have well established protocols that help keep everyone safe. To see Viddie splashing around gleefully in the water was just . . . well, it was just plain terrifying.

It's equally hard to imagine that my neighbors on Addison Ave and colleagues from the Lab are living, breathing and functioning at this very moment in uncomplicated cluelessness. How could they all remain in such a fog about what's really going on out here just a few miles beyond the city centres? Like me, they were raised to be strictly cautionary about the earth and to take seriously the dangerous place it has become. But here—here, the community embraces the land, partakes of its beauty, and they are not afraid! Yes, yes—I knew some of this before today, but I still couldn't muster enough courage to get my feet wet.

What a day. So much has changed in a mere nine weeks, my experience of finches and flowers and outside air—and now water—just to name a few of them. Never would I have thought that the world could be so beautiful and inviting outside the walls.

We spent the rest of the heather-scented afternoon exploring the vacant cabins and sitting amidst the lilacs that were still in full, luxurious bloom. He brushed the leaves off a portion of the dilapidated old tennis court and stood with his back against the twisted metal fence. Drawing me into his arms, I stood there, just allowing myself to be held by him as he stroked my forehead and hugged me tightly. My emotions were on overload; I could tell because I felt on the verge of tears one moment and the next I was laughing. My mouth hurt from smiling so much; I sure wasn't used to it. Until this moment I can say that nothing here at FRANCO has impacted me as much as my friendship with Russa, but after today's wild events Viddie Florencia moves into position one.

When we first met Viddie told me that I was a miracle. I didn't know what he meant that day, but today I knew he was my miracle. There is something more satisfying to my life today, this 62nd day at FRANCO—something more appealing has taken root in me—something more than the vague experience of knowing someone's affection through an image; it's . . . well it's . . . the difference is incalculable.

Everything changed today. The developments in my relationship with Viddie and the break in my attitude toward community at large are beginning to shape my behavior. I can feel it. This is the day! My very thinking is changing right in the midst of this slow little life I am living out right here in the middle of nowhere. But this new revelation—this revelation of love is not little at all. I am beginning to understand what Russa meant about shielding myself. Well, the gate is down. I am open for business. Hello Belvedere Florencia. If you want me—

I.

Am.

Yours.

Chapter 6

Day 65—The Change

We settled down to a nice cup of raspberry lemon verbena in Russa's impeccably clean and completely weatherized cave dwelling and as she expounded on Ellul's reason for hope in time of abandonment. The rain fell gently against the side of the mountain and I could see a puddle forming just outside of the wooden entryway that juts out of her shelter. A steamy mist rose from our teacups that mirrored the one rising from the ground outside. We like to sit as close to the opening as possible to gain the most natural light, and as I watched the drops hit the heavy black granite I noticed that the sound of the rain was actually quite comforting, and I wondered aloud if there were other people in the world who took philosophy and religion as seriously as she does.

Poking fun at her intensity, I told her she was born in the wrong century. She should've been born in France in the 1900's and married that Jacques Ellul.

She insisted that he had been quite happily married to a woman named Yvonne and that she, herself, could never imagine herself married to a philosopher. We had a nice chuckle, but seriously—they would have been quite a pair. My Strength, the girl is so devoted to his writings!

Russa laughed in that wonderful, inimitable style of hers and prodded me on. "Hey—you are the one who wanted to talk about philosophy, Lee; did you forget that, my friend? I am perfectly content to continue listening to you moon over the young Mr. Florencia."

I couldn't help but laugh either. She's right. For all the weeks that we talked about consciousness and what it means to be human, the subject I keep reverting to in just about every conservation is . . . uh, one extremely comely and fascinating gentleman.

It's true; I'm a little obsessed with Viddie, but I do also want to learn about this great philosopher they all revere—this guy Ellul, from last century. I'm still not sure why Marisa's subversive messages were so loaded with his work and frankly the snippets aren't enough to help me understand him—at all.

Roos knows me well enough to ignore my periodic rants, and she was kind enough to continue telling me about Ellul without cutting Viddie completely out of our conversation over this morning's tea.

"His thought underpins our motivation for being here, Leeya."

Her right hand opened up and swung behind her to signify the whole community, much as it often does when she's telling a story. In fact, she speaks with her hands all the time; I imagine it's from spending so many of her younger years with Fiorella.

Russa's quite captivating to watch, what with all the gestures and pictures she paints with her words. When we gather 'round Stone Camp for Friday night fellowship everyone loves her stories the best. She often gets applause.

Russa continued her explanation as if she was a motivational speaker; In fact, as she barreled on with her very strong opinion on the matter, I was sure she missed her calling, and I told her so.

She just shrugged it off and continued trying to explain the nuanced meaning of Ellul's key term, la technique.

"We all know the human community is valuable, but it erodes when we give up on our most fundamental desires. It ebbs away when we distance ourselves from each other and refuse to get involved in the messy business of close relationship—communication in community. To maintain its significance we have to give it more than just lip service. We've got to live it, Lee!"

I listened intently. It was more than just a polite listen; I was truly interested. She went on to talk about the philosopher with a sort of reverence.

"Ellul was one of the most interesting figures in twentieth century philosophy specifically because he understood that in a technological society people could easily be swept into behavior and lifestyles that are more mechanized than human—without even realizing it. He wrote that for every technological advance, there were unforeseen consequences, and that these consequences ultimately detract from human life, and . . . well, unfortunately, the changes demean the human experience."

"See, now that's what I don't get," I finally piped in. "Let's just look at the advances we've made in technology since the Devastation. These innovations have done nothing but make life livable on this planet. If we had to depend solely on human cellular sufficiency we would have no way to communicate daily with people living hours away and no way to manufacture enough food to sustain all thirty million of us who are still alive along the eastern coastline of North America today. Thirty million plus eighty, if you count you guys up here," I said with a smile.

Russa began chewing on her left lower lip, just like she always does when she's looking for the right words. She mouthed the words, 'eighty-one' and pointed to me; I continued with my unsolicited commentary.

"I just don't see a downside—or, uh . . . consequence, as you put it, Roos. We'd be lost –maybe even extinct—if our technological research and solutions were not put in place."

Here's where it got a little sketchy and weird.

Missing even the hint of a smile and with a tone that seemed rather matter-of-fact, Russa reminded me in no uncertain terms that the members of FRANCO were part of a vast network of others who meet in little pockets around the globe and exist outside city centre perimeters. And then, as if she couldn't help herself, she dipped into what sounded quite a bit like self-defense, saying: "We're not nuts, Lee. Sometimes I think you believe we're just off our rockers."

Russa has a sort of effortless and compelling personal style that I can't quiet put my finger on. She is at once placid and perfectly composed, and the next moment totally intense and excitable, but never have I seen her become defensive.

Some days, her seriousness flips even to the point of being what I would deem childlike. She runs through fields chasing butterflies and sits for hours with Liberty making bead necklaces. I have never known another human being quite like this woman.

It wasn't long before I shrugged my shoulders and gave in.

"Whatever you say, Roos. You seem to know where your people are, yet you haven't communicated for decades. If you say there are other FRANCO-like communities, I'll take your word for it, but I find it very hard to believe that the government knows nothing about it. I mean, there has never been even word one about any dissenters where I come from. The world has gone on without you. But . . . I give. You have too much invested in this to see it any other way, don't you?"

"It's not that we are dissenters, Leeya. See? You don't get it. Were you even listening to me? It's really unfair to try to slap that label on us . . . or me, for that matter. It trivializes our entire effort to maintain true community here. It's true, we are tangled in a mass of motives, not the least being strong reaction to what has happened to our world, but what you don't see is that the reasons we stand together outside the walls of society has mostly to do with a deep respect for society and in particular, human life."

Gulp. She's so serious about this. I didn't dare respond, but let her go on full throttle.

"You're correct in thinking that we don't believe that technology is the panacea for every human ill, but we do see how innovation can help us survive. It's just that we can't find a way to have one without giving up the other."

That was it. I couldn't hold my tongue any longer. "Russa Keelly Jenkins, you don't have to give anything up! Don't you see? We could actually go back there to live at the Jersey Shore and work together to help the rest of the world live in such a way that we can all have both. Innovation and freedom. What we—"

Russa cut me off at the chase: "What we will not abide is the loss of our freedom, Miss Leeya. It is far too precious to let convenience and efficiency have the reigns in determining what is important. Ellul spent a great deal of time teaching about the ramifications of a world driven by technology, and especially the over-arching belief in Technology, big 'T.' Listen. Listen to me again. Over time, the technological solution creates a drift—a moving away from what is intrinsically human and . . . and . . . beautiful. He called this tendency to drift a result of la technique—it's a French term. It doesn't mean technology, per se, rather, it's the tendency to automate human choices until the efficiency gained from them becomes a value in itself, leaving the more significant societal values in the dust. Eventually everything spontaneous gets tangled in the web of automation and freedom to choose no longer exists. And clearly, history has shown that as we move further away from human solutions and human ingenuity, we come to seek a life of unreality, an illusionary life—the illusion of perfection, to be exact, ultimately editing out the very things that insure our freedom. Then, instead of the natural beauty of humanity and all of creation, we're stuck with a poor facsimile of what it means to be alive."

"Now just wait a minute there, Russa. You can't say that and get away with it. Just look at me. I am fully alive! Have I been hurt by tek? No way. And frankly, that theory just doesn't fly in the face of disaster. We simply wouldn't survive without it!"

She shook her head vigorously at my comments and insisted that my line of reasoning was faulty. She reminded me again that I was the one who queried about Ellul.

All I said was that our tek helps us regulate the proper amount of emotion and that in my world we understand our duty to each other, so we happily embrace the OLSM. It keeps us all in line. You would think I wanted her to become a robot or something, but I couldn't even get a word in edgewise.

That's when things began to heat up. She starting quoting Ellul and telling me that I was so damaged that I couldn't even think straight, that I no longer knew what it means to be truly human. Oh my Strength! She opened her own notebook and pointed vigorously to Ellul's words about human emotion which went something like:

"Love, which cannot be regulated, categorized, or analyzed into principles or commandments, takes the place of law. The relationship with others is not one of duty but of love."

Wow, I can't believe I remembered that. At least I think that's the way it went.

"See, Leeya? Do you see how much your own heart has been stifled? So much so that you are not even aware that you are obeying external principles. You are more inclined to follow ideas people have planted in your head instead of following your own heart. I am not accusing you of being a robot my friend, but face it—you have been living in such a deep lack of awareness that you don't even know that people need each other. It's a bit like a stupor!"

How could she say that to me? I've just about run out of patience listening to her contempt for our world and our ways. My insides bubbled like hot lava but I capped the fiery flow without a word.

Russa is indefatigable when it comes to telling a story, spouting off a boatload of beautiful poetry, or remembering lyrics to a song, but she tires so quickly when it comes to talking about technology and human progress. I'm not quite sure why, but it's more than a little aggravating. She cleaned up the dishes in a hurry and said it was time for chores.

The rain stopped and Mother's face appeared at the rocky exterior of the cave . . . I wonder what she wants.

Chapter 7

Day 67—The Opening

    Almost two full days and Russa and I have still not spoken. I don't know what gives. I walked up around the bend about an hour after she didn't show up this morning at Grand'Mere's and didn't find her helping Liberty milk the goats. If she's not there, she's usually with Fiorella setting up the days' baking. Alton told me yesterday that she was taking a quiet retreat from people and not to fret about her absence. I guess she does that periodically. When I walked down the path to the large earth-shelter where the Florencia's live, Fiorella wasn't there either.

    It's a strange day. Even stranger, Viddie was still sleeping when I stopped by.

    "I can't believe you're still snoring." I nudged his calf playfully with my big toe and stood there waiting for his eyes to open.

    Another snore.

    "Viddie," I shook him lightly. "Wake up." As I knelt down I noticed perspiration was beading up all around his forehead and ears. He grumbled a raspy 'hello.'

    "Ohhhh, you're not feeling well; I'm sorry. No wonder you're not up and around."

    He got up onto his elbows, cocked his head and smiled crustily, peering at me through mostly closed eyes. "Heeeyyyy, what's going on?"

Viddie's dark brown locks half-covered his face, but even straggly he looked so . . . so darn good. The man clearly has a handle on handsome.

He cleared his throat and squeezed my hand. "I'm glad you're here but . . . uh . . . this is a first, isn't it? Everything a-okay?"

"Sure. All is well. I just wondered where you were. Russa's not around either. I was just . . . I was missing you both."

The rumbly chuckle that emerged from his throat was mockingly sinister. "Ahh. You missed me. I so like the sound of that," he said, wiping the sleep from his eyes.

Strength, that smile could break a heart, that's for sure—and it was sure doing a number on mine. His perception's not too shabby either. Before I even had a chance to deflect it, he was in my face, repeating the question.

"So, you alright? You look a little pensive."

"I'm . . . I am just fine," I started haltingly, "but I guess; well, there are a few things going on. Nothing pressing."

A tiny smile curled upward across his face as he encouraged me in typical Florencia fashion. From time-to-time I've noticed Carlos giving that same look to Fiorella, especially when she gets all worked up over a missing ingredient in one of her dishes or she can't find her favorite wooden spoon or something of the sort.

"Nothin' I hope you won't let me help you get through."

I looked down but couldn't quite keep the smile from spreading across my face. A rush of blood made my cheeks feel hot; I am sure my skin turned a light shade of fuchsia. My Strength, he is so sincere.

"Um. Alright," I started in with a bit more confidence. "It's Russa. Remember the spat I told you about the other day? Well, I haven't seen her since. It's really weird, Vid. She hasn't come around like she always does and . . . I don't know what to make of it, but it feels like she's avoiding me. I think she's punishing me for disagreeing with her. I did, in fact, disagree with her heartily, but I don't know. I don't know. Anyway, do you think I'm stubborn?"

Viddie sat up straight and looked at me squarely. "Okay. You've got a couple different things going on there, girl. Here's the deal. I can see that this conversation requires my full attention. Let me go wash up and then we'll have a walk up around the ridge. I can do my chores later. We'll talk it all out; I think it may be something that I can help you untangle."

"Thanks, yeah. I'd like that, but . . . but you're not feeling well. Look at you, you're feverish."

He swiped the top of his forehead with the back of his hand. "It broke, Emi; I'm fine. Just give me five and I'll be right out, okay? And, by the way, yes—you are a little stubborn."

I leaned against the outer edge of the Florencia earth-shelter, drinking in the morning light and savoring his words. The sun looked like it was going to be strong; I really should run back and grab the skin ointment Grand'Mere gave me to prevent a burn. Instead, I found myself given over to dreaming.

Standing just outside the stony crevice that separates the inner cave from Fiorella's kitchen, I peered over at the hearth. It was empty and the kettle that is usually simmering over hot rocks was nowhere to be seen. Viddie would be back in a few minutes, so I stepped completely outside and leaned against the porch ledge and stood there waiting—just basking in the warmth of Viddie's availability. He's not just handsome, not just sweet; the man knows me, he's willing to be honest, and he wants to spend time with me. A deep breath let out all the anxiety that had been building up over the last couple days.

Then I got to thinking about what he said . . . or actually, didn't say. Am I stubborn? Hmmm. Am I? Mother's stubborn, but I would never categorize me as stubborn. We are night and day different. What's disturbing is there are now two opinions in accord that don't jive with mine.

Justin was helping his sister carry pails of milk just beyond Stone Camp and I called out to them. Neither had a hand free to wave but their nods and expressions were exuberant as ever. Libby yelled to me with her usual zeal, "Hiiiiiii Miss Leeya, I miss you! May I come by to listen to your poetry later?"

"You know you can, Lib." I called back. "Wait 'til a little later, though—maybe before dinner?"

"Oh goodie! See you then, my blessed poet mentor; I can't wait!" The two of them giggled as they walked off trying to balance the buckets without spilling anything.

Strength, the last thing in the world I need is poetry; Just a bunch of ramblings, for sure, but it's funny how a child's mind perceives things. Libby thinks of my writing as poetry and swears what I write in this book is beautiful, but I certainly have never shared it with her and it's definitely not poetry. But if she wants to call my writing poetry, what's the harm? I don't even bother challenging the idea anymore.

It's really quite a joke, because whenever the little jabberbox comes up to Stone Camp and finds me writing she begs and begs to hear it, so I make up something on the spot that is just, well, abstract and meaningless and—it's so funny—the girl is jazzed and oh-so-sincere.

Viddie scooted past me, back from the outhouse lifting his index finger in the air. "One minute," he shouted with a smile. "Be right with you!"

I nodded in the affirmative.

The quiet smile I'm wearing today seems like it is becoming a permanent fixture on my face. I can hardly help it! I feel a distinct disadvantage when it comes to keeping my cool. Not having much practice at holding back my emotions, I find myself often doing what they call, 'wearing my heart on my sleeve.' I don't like it because . . . uhhhhh . . . it gives me away. Oh P/Z, how much easier it would be to keep cool if I could initialize your search engine and power up. Ugggggggggggggh.

When Viddie returned I noticed the pale blue T-shirt he was wearing was nearly transparent. His jeans were the same tattered pair I've seen him in nearly every day since the day we first met, but they were intact and couldn't have looked better if they were brand new. Hmmmmn. Maybe it's just my perspective.

His rope-twine belt frays at each end and is studded with what seem to be a few lead beads. Of everything that he's wearing, his hat and moccasins are in the best shape. The hat is factory made; I know that because it belonged to L.J. and have heard the entire story—several times. It's something L.J. wore in his younger days. Viddie told me that when he was a boy he ogled the hat every time he saw L.J., always asking if he could try it on. Then one day—his sixteenth birthday—L.J. came over to the Florencia's, lifted the white ten-gallon hat off his own head and plopped it on top of Viddie's. "I hereby declare you a certified honorary Texan, Belevedere Florencia. Along with it comes the transferrin' of the Texas-sized duty of lookin' after the ranch from this old cowboy's gaze to yers. Alrighty then, young'un; Ya got da hat, now you da man!"

I hear that L.J. really hammed up the cowboy thing, and that's just so him. Viddie says the slight Texas drawl is leftover from his youth, but he wasn't really ever a cowboy, he just has fun playing the part. He does that with me, too, playing the part of an elegant Englishman, that is. When I see him it's "milady this, and milady that," always tipping an invisible top hat. He does seem to have a sort of internal people-meter. The man's a charmer. UGH. Now I really sound like one them!

In any case, since then, Viddie's rarely without the hat.

The back pack Viddie brings on our walks carries L.J.'s signature, as well. I can tell by the beads and feathers. It looks a lot like the pouch LJ (sometimes they shorten his initials to "L") has where he keeps his guitar picks and things.

Viddie's shoes are made by someone else in the camp—a man we hardly see who lives in a camper up and around the bend from the Martins. Everyone calls him Harold-in-the-camper. I think I've finally got his name right!

It was fun hearing how this moccasin-making process goes, and especially great hearing Viddie explain it. What happens is, after Liam skins the deer, he brings the hide to the Martin family so Fidelity and Justin can tan it and get the leather ready to make shoes or belts or whatever else they make with it. That's where Harold-in-the-camper's workmanship comes into play. He does such lovely, intricate beading and thread work, depleting Marissa's stash of sewing goods year-by-year. Seems funny that she chose fancy threads and colorful beads to take up space in the trunk of treasure she hauled to FRANCO so many years ago. I would have thought a woman of her intelligence might load up on lab equipment.

All in all, the stuff they produce here is sturdy and nicely designed; somehow, the setup works. Fact is, it's pretty cool the way they've managed, but I can't help but noticing that twenty-plus years of T-shirts and jeans are starting to wear thin, and although everyone here has their own little patch kit, I can't help but wonder what another twenty years might bring. Will they be wearing deer-skin and bear fur? I can't see how this whole set up is going to work for the long-haul, but no one here is asking for my opinion and no one seems quite rattled by the future prospects, the least of which, Mr. Belvedere Emmanuel Florencia.

"So, just what's got your googling eyes going this morning, my fine lady?"

Uggggh; More of that red flush creeping up my neck! Looking down, I know I couldn't conceal my smile. A flirtatious spirit rolled over me like the fog does on a cool, mountain morning. The truth just slipped out: "You know I'm checkin' you out, don't you?"

"Oh yeah," he replied, took my hand, and we were off.

By the time we reached Rubble Ridge I thought for sure we might run into Russa, but she was still nowhere to be seen.

"So what exactly is bugging you today, pretty lady?" Viddie started out our conversation with a direct question.

I settled comfortably onto my favorite mossy ledge and he sat close to me.

"Like I told you, it's Roos. I think I offended her or something. We disagreed about . . . you know, the stuff we're always talking about—LIFE here, there, in general—and it got a little heated, and now I haven't seen hide nor hair of her in almost two whole days!"

"Heated? That doesn't sound like Russa, Emi. She doesn't get offended easily and I doubt she would intentionally try to hurt you by staying away. That's just not her style. Why don't we go investigate and see what she's up to. Maybe we could all go for a swim later today or . . . a walk, at least."

Viddie winked when he mentioned the water. He knows I'm still not keen on the whole swimming thing. Intellectually I understand that the waters are fine, but . . . uh, I don't know. It's still too difficult to enjoy it.

"Wait, Viddie," I said, "I don't want to think about swimming. My brain's on overload right now."

He leaned over and brushed a wayward strand of hair from my forehead.

"What is it, Emi? Tell me what's on your mind."

This man is impossible to resist.

My response came tumbling out. "Okay. I've been hesitant to talk about it because it's my own . . . my own stuff. I don't want to focus on me, Viddie. I don't want our relationship to always be about me and my struggles. I'm a little hesitant to talk about myself; I don't want to wear out your ear."

I stood up and brushed the thin layer of pollen off my shirt and tried to let him know that I was done talking for the day but before I could finish, Viddie stood, wrapped both arms around my waist and drew me close. My head fit snugly between his chin and his chest. He stroked my forehead and kissed it just above my ear, speaking softly as he caressed my face. I felt a crazy tingling sensation up and down my neck and my ears got extremely hot.

I thought my heart might actually stop when he touched my arm and whispered how I had captured his heart. Then, he kissed my temple and forehead with such gentleness I felt like gossamer wings were flitting around my head. I did not want to move an inch, but when I did, I glanced up at him and searched his eyes to see if I could read his face.

Breathe, breathe, breathe.

He cradled my cheeks in his hands and then spoke to me in a gentle, caring tone.

"You are the one that was catapulted into this entirely new world, Emi. Did you ask for it? No. Did you even dream of another world? No. Frankly, I think you are doing well acclimating to this whole new way of life. It can't be easy, my sweet lady, so please don't be afraid of sharing too much of yourself, ever, okay? I am here. I am here for you. I'm with you and I will help you through."

My emotions were stretching past the point of no return. Part of me felt ready to let tears spill over my eyelids and come clean with all that I've been feeling, but another part was just suspicious and afraid. Did he really mean it? Was he really listening to me? I wondered if my thoughts really mattered as much as he declared.

So many completely unvarnished feelings are just oozing out of my skin these days. It's like someone poured some sort of emotional expectorant all over my body and now my feelings just come free-flowing out of every pore. I hadn't intended on talking about my longing for home, but Viddie's eyes welcomed me so.

"I don't want you to laugh, Viddie."

"Laugh? Why would I laugh, pretty lady? I promise; I'm all ears."

He slipped his hand in mine and helped me to a large, level rock and we situated ourselves to sit face-to-face, with legs crossed. He's eyes continued to beckon me.

"Okay—I'm gonna hold you to it, Viddie. Well. Okay. It's just that . . . It's just that, you see, you might not understand this, but I miss my OLSM. Being de-activated . . . makes me feel so acutely powerless. On . . . on . . . on the one hand I like feeling these fiery bolts of lightning between the two of us, but on the other—well, on the other hand it's all so far beyond my control. It's like I'm at the mercy of my emotions, and frankly, I'm just not used to it."

Kind eyes and a warm smile bid me to continue.

"All my adult years I have functioned with the knowledge that my OLSM capacity is nearly as integral to human existence as DNA! It was my fervent belief that without it we could not hope to sustain our communication systems, hence our very existence, but now I see that there are alternative ways of remembering—other ways to catalog all the social and biological knowledge necessary to communicate. I get it. I really do, but . . . but, Viddie, I miss my old life. I miss being able to pull up an interior wall and get the information I need from a quick and easy dip into my Deep Archive."

He leaned in and cupped my face with both hands. Brushing away the hair that had fallen into my eyes, he looked at me with the intensity that matched my own.

"You know," he said, "I'm hearing every single word you say and I do understand, but as long as we're being so perfectly honest with each other, I've got to tell you that I'm having a difficult time concentrating. Your eyes are absolutely captivating, do you know that?"

Melting, melting, melting.

I'm sure my face was flushed.

How can I possibly keep talking when all I want to do is fall into his arms? I just smiled and shook my head.

"We can definitely stop talking now, Vid. I'm sure I've said enough. Let's take a few minutes to stretch and walk farther into the woods, okay?"

"No, no. No—go on, please. I'm sorry. I'll stop distracting you, I promise. I do have so many questions about this, Emi. I want to know every aspect of who you are. The OLSM surely seems important, and I've never experienced what it can do for a person, so I can't fully understand. Tell me, does everyone else at the Lab function the same way? Is everyone dependent on their OLSM for connection and memory? And remind me again what it stands for? I mean, how did the scientists even figure this out? I really want to know— the history and all of it. I want to know all about what makes you tick! Tell me everything."

I lapped up the attention like one of Liberty's baby goats drinking its mother's milk. He really wanted to know?

"Okay. First off, my Ongoing Life-Sustaining Membrane is something that everyone has; well, everyone has it, in theory. You see, everyone's born with the same cranial membrane that lines both spheres of the brain, but what turns the membrane into the OLSM is that it becomes networked to external stimuli, and this enables us to go beyond the limits of human brain power—the P/Z 1000 that I helped develop is just one example of this extension, the primary example, actually, but there are others. With the P/Z we don't have to be tethered to wireless networks to allow them to function. You know, the skin is the one organ other than the brain that stimulates the human emotional center, and it can also activate or sequester our emotions. Because of this, we focused our research on developing a connection apparatus that is built-in and simply requires the correct application of diamond dust to a finger . . . or a toe. But nobody uses toes because, well, it's not terribly convenient."

I chuckled at my own joke and he laughed along with me.

"Yeah, I can just picture it now, Emi. You kicking your shoes off and rubbing your toes every time you want to speak to me! Ha!"

"I know, what a thought, right? Anyway, I much rather have you rub my toes any day!"

Did I say that? Did I really say that? Oh Strength, I am getting weaker and weaker. My ability to hold back my feelings keeps waning. Uhhhhhhhhh. Of course, he picked up on it immediately.

"Hey, that's a deal. I can't think of anything better than rubbing your toes right now. Let's head down to the crossway creek and put our feet in the water. I'll dry them off with my shirt and massage every muscle 'til you're utterly and completely relaxed."

"Viddie. Stop with the water! You're such a tease."

He whistled a funny little melody that sounded just like a bird chirping, and didn't let up on me for a second. "Whew-ee, that's sounds good to me, yes sir-ee—sure does—but I want to hear the rest of this story my lovely lady. No toes until I get the whole picture. C'mon, now. I know there's more about your P/Z and the diamond dust and all. You were just about to tell me a bit about the history?"

"Yeah, yeah, okay. As far as history, there are a couple of things to know. Part of the picture came from early twentieth century research. When scientists realized that the parasympathetic brain disengages from the emotional center of the brain, doctors learned how to better manage pain in terminal patients. The research changed palliative care completely and set the stage for interior computing. Then, of course, major changes occurred between 2020 -2025 when Dr. Weston Marcus discovered that the blood barrier of the brain made it possible to adjust brain chemistry through manipulation of the membrane with other organic substances, in particular, using a derivative of the turmeric root—an herbal concoction called curamin. Everyone knows about the doctor's work; his is a household name, just like they knew Grand'Mere, Marissa and Liam back in the day. Those of us who have had the privilege of working closely with him know him as Dr. Marc. Today he's something of an elder statesman."

"And you've worked with him, Emi? You know him well?

"Oh yeah. In some ways he mentored me. Any free time at the Lab was spent with him for a good couple of years in my early twenties. And let me tell you, he may be elderly but the man is still so vital. His mind is sharp and he is still making discoveries in the research department down the hall from Triple D."

I was really on a roll, but being that Viddie was not raised with this history, it really wasn't common knowledge for him at all, so I found myself getting a bit granular with all the details. He had little understanding of anything pharmaceutical or associated with physical science, so the questions just kept coming. The funniest thing was his queries about curamin. I mean, nobody thinks about curamin anymore, but I explained what I could.

"It's really a very natural substance that comes from the turmeric root. It's a plant in the ginger family. Before the Devastation curamin used to be plentiful and used mainly in Indian cuisine—curries and such. Now we have to manufacture a synthetic version of it, but it works out quite nicely. The stuff is indispensable to our purposes."

"That's so cool, Emi. Now you're almost talking like an herbalist."

That made me smile. It's nice to hear that we have a little something in common besides living on the same mountain. He seemed happy about it too and shed a little light on how they come up with such delectable things to eat.

"You know, there's so much out here in nature that has healing properties and uses far beyond the most obvious ones. I love that. Walnut trees are like that up here. We'd be lost without them. My mother uses walnut flour for her scones and then Darren came up with the perfect mix for skin cream from walnut seed oil and water several years ago. It's really been a treat for the women in FRANCO. And the rhizomes of many plants that we find here up here in the wild help in all kinds of medicinal ways. It's great when you see nature come together with human ingenuity, isn't it? Hmmm. So interesting. So, that's what happened with this curamin stuff. Tell me more. What's the connection between this curamin stuff and the OLSM?"

"Oh, okay. Well, when used at high levels and infused directly into the membrane surrounding the hippocampus, Dr. Marc's team found that it created an exponentially more secure brain blood block. It created thickness, but did not mess with function. He discovered that over time the natural route of neuro-transmitters became altered, so ultimately these pathways could circumvent any particular section of the brain if it was necessary. At first this made an enormous difference in the way brain surgeries were done. The doctors enjoyed an unbelievable success and recovery rate, helping folks with tumors, and all kinds of dementias. Then, however, the bigger breakthrough came. They began to use Dr. Marc's findings to create a safety net—a barrier protecting other areas of the brain from the cellular irregularity that is caused by electromagnetic infiltration. The block also works as a platform for neuro-pathways to communicate with one another during neurogenesis."

"Whoa, whoa, WHOA, Nellie!" Viddie said holding the palm of his hand toward me.

"Just wait a minute to let me be sure I have it right. Don't forget, you're not talking to a physicist here or a neuroscientist. I'm not your father—I'm just a guy who knows dirt. So wait, wait. I need a moment. Tell me again: why is the brain's blood barrier so significant? And . . .what does it have to do with this OLSM thing you mentioned?"

The rush of adrenalin I felt just from talking about the process again was exhilarating. He was open, more open than Roos, so I continued without pause. I'm sure my pace quickened as I outlined the progression of our brain-to-tek ratio protocols.

"It was an amazing discovery, Viddie—a necessary component of my own work with the P/Z 1000. The early discoveries were what my mother and grandmother were involved in. As I studied Dr. Marc's work and paired it with theirs, the pieces seemed to fall into place with hardly a snag! I was running experiments with smaller mammals and I found— my team and I—found that we could use this new interior networking platform to make life easier and more interesting, plus create a way to jumpstart the economy.

We learned that the blood barrier segmentation allows the brain to be used in ways that separate function. By keeping the emotional center of the brain sequestered from the memory section we could access key neurotransmitters, those that help us gain immense entry into brain capacity without harm to the rest of the brain! It has changed the world, Viddie and . . . and I . . . well, I miss being on that cutting edge. I miss having my P/Z and I feel so limited sometimes . . . many times."

"Whew. That's a lot of information, Emi-girl. Man alive, I guess I should really be referring to you as Dr. Hoffman-Bowes. Your mother told me you were brilliant, but I never imagined the depth."

His words took me back a bit. My mother told him? WHAT exactly did Marissa say about me? We got up from the ledge and I weighed my words carefully as we started to walk. I'm sure my response seemed tentative but I was just trying to practice the whole 'being real thing' that I keep hearing about. So, I went for it.

"Uh, when did you speak to Marissa about me, Vid? I mean, Marissa doesn't really know me; I'd appreciate knowing what else she said."

Viddie's eyes were like a magnet, drawing an irresistible, invisible line from my heart to his. As I gained my composure and looked up at him, his response was a gentle squeeze of my hand, but then he cleared his throat and spoke with quick confidence: "Your mother always talks about you, Emi. From the time I was a small child I heard about this fascinating little girl with shining chestnut hair, deep brown eyes and a personality that was equal parts inquisitive and melancholic. Marissa memorized the countless hours you spent together working on science projects and modeling clay, and dazzled us with stories around the campfire; stories of her precocious daughter, 'the wonder child' with the thoughtful, penetrating eyes; the daughter who was 'more beautiful than the sun itself and more brilliant than the fire we stoke.' I knew you were beyond compare before I ever met you."

A huge lump formed in my throat and I closed my eyes as he continued.

"Now that you're here, she speaks of you no less. Why do you think I came by that first day we talked? Marissa and my mother were deeply involved in conversation, and it was all about you—constantly talking about your beauty, your intelligence, your journey, your creativity, your needs, your future, and on and on. If she told me once, she told me twenty times that first couple of weeks: "You've got to come meet her, Viddie. You will love her! And oh—how right she was."

"Twenty times? It took you twenty times before you decided to meet me?" I elbowed him with a feigned look of disappointment, but the intensity of his words pierced me and I couldn't take it anymore. My attempt at a joke helped relieve some it of it, but in truth, I simply could not handle what he was saying. Mother really loved me?

"So that was a setup? That day with the garden hoe—you weren't really preparing her soil? Viddie! You've been playing with me!"

"Yes I have, and it's been fun, hasn't it? Your mother knew we were made for each other and she didn't have to press me hard to come and see for myself, but I was unsure that you'd find me acceptable, what with field hands and no credentials. You're . . . well, you know you're really so far above me."

Viddie stopped walking and took my hand in his to help me over a large protruding root. "Oh lovely and most Inquisitive One, do you know how happy I am to share these moments of my life with you? It means so much to me that you tell me what you're thinking . . . that you trust me with what's important to you, Emi."

Nearly every time I'm with him he says something that takes me aback. At that very moment the songbirds were serenading us and his words hung in my heart like the juicy, ripe strawberries from the large patch on the other side of the Ridge. I stared up at the clouds and breathed in the freshness of FRANCO'S most lovely natural resource—the thickly treed woods and gorgeous mountainous terrain.

My eyes got glassy, so I had to look down. How could this be happening to me? Could it possibly be that I had to step clear out of my life to find this joy?

I could no longer keep from speaking the words I know are true. My eyes met his and I was mesmerized by the light coming from them. He wasn't teasing this time. Viddie really did question his worthiness as a suitor. Oh my. I couldn't let him suffer another moment and stretched out my hand to touch his.

"Viddie, there has never been anyone in my life who affects me the way you have—not even close. I've never shared as much with another living creature. Credentials mean nothing. You are brave and funny and strong and there is nothing about me that is better than you; nothing!

With that, he drew me close and put his finger to my lips, and said, "Do me a favor then; don't ever feel as though you have to hold back with me—with anything—I'm here because I want to be here. I will help you through anything and everything. I am here for you, Emi."

I pulled slightly away, still feeling a bit strange that I had revealed so much. My emotions, jangling like the beads on Libby's countless lanyards, betrayed me. Strength—I'm am really losing my edge. I am riddled with ambivalence. Uhhh, I felt so awkward after all that gushing, also because of the sudden realization that he knew so much about me before we even met. It bothers me primarily because it was mother's version. It's just plain weird that she said so much.

To be rude is to be wrong, so I resisted; but to be truthful isn't always advantageous, so I let him believe I was okay and disclosed my feelings to him in measured spoonfuls.

"That's nice to hear, Viddie, and I believe you; I do. I guess what I'm trying to say is that the issues I have with both Marissa and Liam make me feel extremely hesitant to trust them, and frankly, the fact that they left seems completely incongruent with what you heard growing up. Even aside from the fact that they abandoned me, I often still get the feeling that because my parents left my world, they look down on it and don't really want to hear what it is that I love about it."

"Hmmmm." His response was saturated in the deepest, truest, most exquisitely sultry voice I have ever heard.

One word. One word. "Hmmmm," isn't even a word, but—man—the way it resonated from his body—what a word.

The blue-gray smokiness of his eyes reminded me of one of those days deep in November when the sun is mostly behind the clouds and it's darker than it should be because something is brewing in the atmosphere. We get those days quite often in the fall. I love the hue and, in fact, chose a color called November from the pic-palate for my London sky vacation package. It turned out so well—much more vivid than what I recall from looking at the sky.

There's a turning of the seasons in my heart this week . . . an almost something new. That's what I sensed today when he paused and looked at me ever so purposively. He held out his hand and carefully led me up to the next ridge, boulder by boulder. We settled on a long, gray rock that was large enough for two and comfortably warm from several hours of morning sunshine. Our conversation was rich.

"I'm not sure if you're right about your parents, Emi, but maybe so. I mean, we do generally look at our life here as an escape; it's a necessary departure from a world that is falling apart and doesn't have room for the individual or for community. Not so much me—I never had to escape. I mean, I have lived here all my days—I don't know any other way of life, but I believe the stories and I believe in the mutuality necessary to nurture human community. From all that I hear, it's nearly as if the world is slowly snuffing out the most basic human functions and desires; there's not much room for a more natural, closely-knit community in what's left of our country."

I was glad to hear him speak of America as 'our' country. These mountain people are such extreme separatists; I guess I just assumed he disowned the nation, too. My own assumptions keep tripping me up. Gotta watch that.

"Wait, wait, Viddie. Back up a minute. You make some heavy accusations against the developments in our world that, uh, well . . . just don't seem to jive. How can we have no room for the individual or for community? If you just said 'community,' I could see your point. It's obvious, even to me, that in terms of community FRANCO is heads above the current state of things in America, but railing against the loss of the individual too? How can both be true? I'm afraid you can't have it both ways my friend. The individual rules back at the Lab. Back home, it's all about the expansion and development of the individual."

"Really? Well, maybe so. You know the score there; I surely do not. But the way I figure it, community and individuality go together. The two are intrinsically linked. Knowing who and what you're a part of forms the foundation of every person's sense of self. Without true community the sense of the individual diminishes and over time a person's individuality is reduced to what job they perform or some other external aspect of personhood. It's like the person just becomes more of an object—a thing—and expendable widget instead of a unique, creative, person to be reckoned with."

He makes me smile, this man. Yeah, it's a smile on the inside that I don't remember ever having before; something new and unusual for me.

"You continue to surprise me, Viddie Florencia. Every time I think I've got you pegged you come up with something unexpected. So, how do you know so much about human psychology, eh?"

"Guess you could just call me resourceful." A mischievous little smile curled up around his face. The man's definitely not as quiet as I first thought.

"You see, Emi, I tend to figure things out as I go. Plus . . . I've got a few more surprises up my sleeve that you don't know about, too." He winked with that familiar little signal of affection and began throwing mock oranges across the ledge. They're all over the ground these days; green, wrinkly—gosh, they look like little petrified brains. The squirrels love those ugly things and they're of no use to us.

I didn't respond to his secretive little quip immediately and then he got distracted by a couple of birds making a racket in the birch tree above us. So, I took my art book out of the satchel I was carrying and thought we'd spend some time quietly enjoying the sunshine, but Viddie still had a bit more to say about my mother and about the stories that she, Grand'Mere, Fiorella, and the others shared with him about life outside FRANCO. What was so dear was that he was so careful to keep from degrading my past life. The sensitivity of this man surpasses anything I've ever known. He really floors me. When I looked up again he was brushing the dirt off a few more of the mock oranges that he'd been using for target practice. Gosh, they really do so look like little green brains.

"The stories are lovely, Viddie. I do enjoy hearing all of them: yours, Grand'Mere's—the one about Harold-in-the-Camper's Aunt Adele. It's hard to imagine they can all remember such detail about their lives. Gosh, I can barely remember being fifteen, let alone details. You know, the Friday night circle stories are interesting too: I know they're your main source of entertainment, what without electricity or screens and all, and there too, everyone seems to take such pains to get the details right. It's funny."

His response took a serious tone. "The stories are not fiction, Emi. FRANCO is a choice, and your parents—especially your parents—sacrificed so much to start this community for us, and from what I'm told they really had it rough for many years, really rough."

I nodded in feigned agreement. "I've heard that: yeah. Really rough. I know. I have heard it since the day I arrived, Viddie, but what does that actually mean? It just . . . still gets to me. I mean, why? Why did they have it rough? Doesn't it seem to you that they brought this suffering upon themselves?"

He shook his head with a look of incredulity as I barreled forth with my own interpretation of their sacrifice.

"When I think about the fact that they left me with Grand'Mere and let me think they were dead. . . . I still can't figure out how they are the ones who suffered. Viddie—they left me knowing that they might never see me again—what's that all about?"

His brow furrowed while his tone remained quite stoic.

"It's choices Emi. Everyone's got to make them. Sometimes they are extremely tough choices and they're made for reasons other people can't fully grasp."

He picked up something from between the boulders—a walnut, I think—and pitched it forward toward the woods as he continued to speak. "You know, I really do want to hear all that you are thinking, and I want to help you figure out your parent's motives and all, but I'm not inside their heads. It's the two of them that you should speak with about these things, especially if you want to get to the nub of their reasons for their choices. You gotta know this, though. They are deeply respected members of FRANCO—everyone here looks up to them. I mean, you can trust them, Emi, even if you don't feel especially trusting right now. Give 'em a chance; I think it's time to open a conversation with them about their motivations and . . . well, all the questions you have about your background. They are alive; they are here; and I'm sure they are willing to hash it out."

Hash it out? Who wants to hash it out? Not me, for sure. That's a dead end if I ever saw one. It's bound to end badly. Emotionalism, tears, debates—one hot mess; how productive can that be?

I wanted to come back with my list of reasons for not confronting them, but instead I agreed with him, and I'm not exactly sure why. "You're right, Viddie. I should talk to them more about it. The few conversations we've had about their "plan" have not satisfied me. Mother's tears are too fast and too furious to allow me to take her seriously. The very idea that they left digital breadcrumbs—uh, doesn't cut it either. I just feel such continued disappointment when I look at them. I know some of it must be me, maybe much of it, I'm not sure. But clearly, I can't approach them objectively and that's part of the problem. Seriously, at one time I think I could have—and even now, if I had my OLSM engaged through the P/Z I'd be in control, but today—now—it's clear my emotions are no longer sequestered. They are not tightly bound, not tightly bound at all, and dealing with it is far too emotionally taxing."

I sighed deeply, feeling a little overwhelmed with the entire conversation. Shooting a quick glance my way, he seemed to pick up on my weariness with the discussion of my parents. Without missing a beat he launched back into cognitive brain science. My, my; we came full circle with such a gamut of subjects along the way.

I looked down and rubbed my index finger. It's so hard without the tek. Actually, I lost track of what it was he was saying so he repeated himself when I didn't answer immediately.

"Emi, did you hear me? You never finished telling me how the tek actually works. I mean, it's crazy to me, this idea that everybody in America is tapping into their gray matter and using it as a platform to network communications. How is that possible? Tell me, please; wouldja?"

What a dear. Viddie is the only one who has ever called me "Emi," and never in front of anyone else. I'm not sure what to make of it, but it makes me feel quite special when I'm with him. And now, all this discussion about the things that matter to me. Whether it's a whistle, a wink or a touch of his hand, the man melts my heart.

Our conversation was so gratifying at that moment that I was sorely tempted to tell him about the nagging suspicions I have concerning the Lab and the message fragment I've been receiving. Luckily, my better senses snapped into gear. If this is all a dream I don't want it to start unraveling now! Instead, I took him up on a request for more information.

"More history?" I laughed out loud. "What is that they say—a glutton for punishment? That's you alright. I'm happy you're interested, Viddie, but I don't really know where to start; I've already told you so much about the beginnings. Plus, I'm not an expert in neuroscience. I know just enough about the brain to understand cognition, but the vast layers of knowledge are situated in guys like Dr. Marc. Like I said up at the ledge, it's a complex process that's loaded down with much coding jargon and such. Essentially, it's all about manipulating blood paths in various quadrants of the brain, particularly isolating the auditory thalamus and making sure those pathways are properly firing and connecting with the epidermis. The rest is easy."

"So, if it's easy then tell me about it. I don't think I need a crash course in computer science to understand how our central nervous system works. I mean, I can't imagine there aren't residual effects. And my goodness, all that sequestering of emotions—is there ever any backlash, like the inability to tap in emotionally when necessary? I mean, have you studied that aspect of the tek?"

"Ooohh. Questions and more questions. You really are interested Mr. Florencia, aren't you?"

"You know I am, Emi. Will you tell me more about how is it that you all avoid side effects—you know brain aneurisms and old-fashioned disorders like depression? It would seem to me that manipulating blood paths in various sections of the brain might help us to use our gray matter more efficiently, but it also might mess a person's head up. Surely there must have been some precedents set. Is there a history of what happened early on? I mean, how do you all deal with the risks involved? And I'd love to know how the Lab made the leap from brain research to interiorizing ninety percent of all communication. How did that happen?"

I squeezed his hand and turned to look up at him. The smile on my face was quite pronounced, of that I am sure. What fun to discuss this stuff!

"I do know quite a bit about the early history, Vid, but do you really want to know? I don't want to bore you."

He rolled his eyes and shot back a goofy look.

"Okay, okay. I'll tell you what I know to be fact. Surely, they must have considered the risks, but of course, I was not there in the immediate aftermath of The Devastation. Neither were you. To be sure, the government's actions made it possible for both of us to be here today having this conversation, but certainly it was not without risks. Nothing happens without taking a risk. Frankly, the danger of not doing something to close-in our communication system was a more frightful thought. So . . . like I said, much of the progress was made early in this century when medical doctors were busy doing research on Alzheimer's. It was a disease that ran rampant during Grand'Mere's youth, and it was ripping the life out of people as young as 50."

Viddie's eyes were locked in to my story and his expression was so intense that I had to just pause for a second to take it in. He leaned into me, and was listening intently. I noticed the stubble along his jawline was coming in strong. The man takes my breath away. He jumped in to comment before I had the chance to go on.

"Alzheimer's. This is the disease Harold-in-the-camper's Aunt Adele had when he was still in Kentucky, before the big D, isn't it?"

"Well . . .I guess. Yes; at least that's how it sounds to me, but. . . I don't know anything about Aunt Adele."

"You haven't heard all his stories, Emi, but when gets going the ol' yarns just come a-tumbling out. Like when his Aunt Adele began eating petunias from the flower bed and insisted they were tomatoes, well you should have heard the way he. . ."

I couldn't help cutting in. It's funny that Viddie talks about Harold-in-the-camper's tendency to tell long, flourishy stories, but oh-how-easily he can get going too, and when he does, he can redirect an entire conversation without even realizing it.

"Definitely. Sounds like it to me, Vid. That's a pretty clear giveaway, but actually there were many categories of dementia back in the day, and it wasn't until some breakthrough research in the thirties that we started seeing real help for these folks."

"Yeah—I've heard of it for sure. Actually, I think Aunt Vejenze has a touch of it. Did you ever hear her talk to the rocks?"

"Oh Viddie, no I have not. She doesn't talk to rocks, really? I think you're just making that up. Does she? Does she really?"

His laughter is so totally contagious. Here we are, smack in the middle of an explanation that he asked for and he's on his joke-a-minute kick. Never a dull moment with Viddie Florencia, that's for sure! Then, of course, he also knows just how to bring us back into the conversation.

"Listen, you. I am actually not kidding. Ask Grand'Mere. She'll tell you."

"That I will; that I will. Anyway. Really, Viddie, it was a terrible disease, and I sure hope Aunt Vee doesn't have it because it steals a person's memories and can get real ugly. Thankfully it is no longer prominent, but around the turn of the century it was almost epidemic."

"So, okay. How did they cure it? If it's not rampant anymore, did the cure have something to do with your work at the Lab?"

"Oh, no, no, Not me, not at all. I am one of the benefactors of the research though. No one (at least in the civilized world) has to fear an early death because with Alzheimer's anymore. Remember I mentioned the curamin? It's a common root-based supplement that was part of the initial trials. Once they discovered that ingesting high doses reduces clusters of amyloidosis in the brain, the next thing they learned is that it also proved to reduce brain aneurysms, something that doctors kept finding in people with the disease after they died. This was an amazing discovery and led to the decline of all of the horrible dementias of the past century. Experimentation continued and through it they discovered that this amazing plant-based nutrient did other positive things, like protect brain membranes from natural corruptive influences like aging."

Viddie's jaw hung open and his eyes grew even more intense than they already were.

"I am in awe of you, Emi, absolutely in awe. Now my brain is on overload. That's probably about as much of an education in neuroscience as I can take right for the moment."

Viddie didn't say another word, but his eyes spoke thousands as he once again drew me closer to him. In the next moment I hardly knew what hit me. All at once I was there, my face leaning on his chest as he held me closely. Then I dared to look up at him, and pulling a few more wayward strands of hair away from my face, he kissed my forehead, and held me even closer.

My breath felt hot against his neck. I clung to him and didn't move an inch, bathing in the beauty of feelings I never knew could exist. His arms surrounded me as he held me tightly. Then he whispered something foreign to my ears: "*Mi lasci senza fiato.*"

I have no idea what it means, but it sounds so beautiful. It sounded like . . . like . . . it sounded like the clouds were singing.

Surely, my own eyes sent a thousand questions to him with just one look.

"It's true," he said. "*Mi lasci senza fiato.*"

"What? What does that mean? You know I don't speak Italian."

Viddie's soft laughter was contagious and broke the tension of our sweet embrace. First he started with a little chuckle and then I joined him. Next, it turned into a belly laugh and then he was holding his stomach, bent over and roaring.

"And what are you laughing at, Viddie Florencia?"

His words spilled through in halted breaths. "It's just that . . . that . . . I can't believe I know something that you don't!"

I feigned a punch to his right arm and tried to catch my own breath. "Oh, so you're going to keep this to yourself, are you?"

Once again he held me tightly and melted me with a whispered word of sweetness. "Yes, oh beautiful Inquisitive One. Yes, I am going to keep you guessing just for a little while, most elegant lady. By the way, what is your middle name? Do you have a middle name?"

What am I going to do with this man? What on earth am I going to do?

The blue-sky optimism of the late May sun showered through the billowing lilac tree a few yards away. A gentle breeze carried its delicate petals to where we were standing. The fragrance of lilacs was intoxicating. Truly, I had only seen this in my film files.

I was dumbstruck.

Chapter 8

Day 69—The Thinking

L.J. was strumming his guitar as I made my way back to Stone Camp today. I had a cracked ceramic cup filled with blackberries in one hand and my art book in the other. When I heard the familiar strands of his "go-to" tune I stopped in my tracks. I felt a lump in my throat.

"Whatcha got there fine lady? Is there enough for me?" L.J.'s gruff, elderly voice is totally antithetical to his gentle presence. It always throws me for a loop. I walked over to him with my cup of berries outstretched.

"You may have the whole cup if you like, El. The blackberries are totally ripe and the bushes are loaded with them back in the grove. That's why I'm headed back to Grand'Mere's. I've got to get a bucket or at least something bigger than this."

"Mmmm. I think I'll take you up on that offer, Miss Leeya. Thank you, kindly."

L.J.'s snowy hair flowed down to his shoulders, and always looked tussled. This afternoon's breeziness made it especially so. "Do you think a storm's coming, L.J?" I asked as he savored each of the tiny purple clusters.

"Dunno, milady. You see that wayward cloud out there beyond the ledge? It's got a dark caste behind it. We right well could see a storm later, or . . . it could pass." He chuckled and mumbled something about the unpredictable weather.

At the same moment Libby was walking by and stopped briefly to say hello. She peered into the cup I was holding and plucked up one of the berries before L.J. finished them off.

"YUM! They're ready; I can't wait; it's almost time for jam making! Wanna make some together today, Miss Leeya? Let's go get a whole bucket of 'em! I just love it when Grand'Mere makes her jalapeno jam, and Fiorella makes her lavender spice jam and, and, Russa makes that famous scram jam—triple berry goodness—Mmmm, mmmm, so good! We can cook ourselves up a delicious batch and have it ready for morning muffins! Let's do, Miss Leeya, can we? Please?"

The double sweetness and enthusiasm of Liberty's voice was always a delight to the ears. Although making jam was not something I was eager to do today, it was hard to turn this vivacious little powder keg away.

I nodded and called back. "Yes, yes, my little sanguine surprise. I think we just might be able to fit some cooking into our hectic schedules. We'll have to see if anyone's got an open hearth, okay?"

She chuckled at the thought of my feigned busyness and turned to L.J. asking if he had seen her mother.

Just as soon as Liberty skipped away, Alessa came around the corner with an armful of dry clothes she had just pulled off the line. She was looking for my mother because several of the shirts needed repair, and stopped to talk to L.J. about the dwindling supply of thread. Normally she says so little, so it's especially nice when she finally talks. I could hardly help listening in, and watched the pleasant exchange between the two of them with admiration. That L.J. has quite a way with everyone. He just always knows the right thing to say. I was thinking about that when suddenly Alessa turned and looked at me with a curious expression.

"What? What is it, Less?"

"Oh, I . . .just . . . nothing. Mom and Viddie mentioned you at breakfast. She asked if he'd bring some of her peach scones to you and Grand'Mere. I was just wondering if you'd seen him yet. I'll catch you later, Leeya." And she was off.

Curious.

Peach scones? L.J. and I exchanged glances at the thought of tomorrow's scrumptious breakfast.

L.J. wiped the last of the bit of purple juice from his mouth with the back of his hand and left me with an empty cup and an expression of regret.

"S'awright," I chuckled. "There are so many more out there. I'll just go get Grand'Mere's picking bucket."

The soft strands started again and L.J. winked as I walked away. "Thanks, m'lady," he called.

I glanced back and waved. "You are most welcome, Mr. Minstrel."

L.J. likes when I call him that. I can tell, because whenever I do, tiny crinkly lines jettison from the corners of his old-man eyes, and his broad, cowboy smile reveals a missing eye tooth. One missing tooth. One missing eye. One big heart. What a dear old man.

The past couple of days I've been thinking about how much the backdrop of his music adds to my life. Of all the challenges in my life since I've arrived, his music is one thing that has not been hard to deal with at all. I just love it. And of course, when he plays that old Celtic melody my mind can't help but turn to Russa.

Things still aren't quite right between us. When she returned from her quiet retreat she was cordial—even warm—but there was something a little off between us. It's been close to a week and our talkie-walks have yet to resume.

My time is increasingly spent with Viddie, and I am not complaining, it's just that . . . well, I'm not sure how to make things return to normal between us.

The most unusual thing is what happened yesterday, something that might be indirectly a result of the row I had with her.

It came out of the blue, really. A rush of cerebro-spinal fluid seemed to be leaking from the edge of my amygdala into the cerebellum, or at least it seemed so. Now, of course I couldn't feel the flow and I know quite well this is virtually impossible without the help of my PZ/1000, but I felt a sudden spur of disengagement going on inside me, a sensation that is not unlike the letting-down of internal fluids when we milk the goats. When we're getting ready to milk them, those mother goats let their milk down so it becomes easier to express. Funny, what a little time with Liberty can teach a person.

Just about everyone back in my world knows how to manipulate the regions of the brain to protect from emotional hang-over, but we all have help. Our brain extensions enable us to sequester the emotional center of the great gray mass from the rational, processing and memory regions. Without them, we are left to wallow in the callous demands of fickle feelings and the irrational ups and downs of human emotionalism.

Being without my tek all this time, well, I am starting to really feel some backlash. There is tension rising just above my temples and noticeable brain fog that wafts through my system several times a day.

One of the biggest changes I'm dealing with is the fact that I now spend so much time thinking. Thinking. I am thinking about the people here, their motivations, our relationships, and all this thinking—well, it's all so new to me.

It's as if an entire section of my brain had been turned off for years, and now that I'm here I have all this time to reflect. That, along with the seemingly endless hours relating to all of them, I sometimes feel as though they've injected me with a mega-dose of their lifestyle.

My Strength—I am apprehending life in an entirely new way.

Chapter 9

Day 80—The Walk

A fine beige powder covered Viddie's feet as we navigated through the heavy verdant brush on the pebbly mountainous path toward Stone Camp. We were carrying our shoes in order to enjoy the thick grassy carpet of the valley below, but by the time we got to the sandy trail around the west side of the mountain we hit more stone than greenery. Because of it, we were both covered in chalky dust from our feet to our knees. I still have a hard time looking at dirt-caked skin and not feeling a bit anxious.

Rubble Ridge never looked as good as it did this noon. We had been out hiking for nearly three hours and the sun was high. Sweat beaded up on both our foreheads and my feet felt like I was carrying two tons instead of the ten-pound backpack. We stopped to rest there for a few minutes and wiggled our toes, laughing at the way the dust made them match perfectly. Twin feet, ha!

I was sorry I hadn't thought to bring a small container of Marissa's luxurious walnut moisturizing cream in the backpack; my swollen toes were hot and they hurt. We were talking about the fawn we saw a few miles back and the sweet taste of the wild strawberries we enjoyed an hour earlier when out-of-the-blue Viddie placed my foot on his lap and began to gently rub it. His strong thumbs brought relief to the ache that had settled into my arch. After he massaged the other one I told him I could get used to that. He smiled and pointed to the back of his neck.

"I bet you could work some of the same magic on my neck. I could use a little relief from this backpack right about now, too."

As I began rubbing his neck I realized that I haven't been giving much thought to leaving lately. In fact, it's getting really hard to think about leaving at all. I must admit, recently I've been rethinking my plan to go back to Addison Avenue. The plan should be clear-cut and decisive, but on days like this the ambivalence keeps rising against the jagged shore of my heart just the way the waves lap up against the rocky bank of Grand Lake. I can't help it; it's just that this . . . this . . . thing that the two of us have going on here is like, well, it's like nothing I ever imagined. I keep going back in my art book and rereading my notes from the past couple of months and it's the same theme, over and over again. Whenever I write about the days we spend together the same phrases keep popping up: "glorious," "beautiful," and "something I never imagined existed."

And the others are giving me pause to reconsider, too. These folks—uuhhhhhh—just about all of them are getting under my skin and it's beginning to get hard to fathom life without them. Hard to believe, too, that this time last year I didn't even know Russa or Viddie, L.J, Firoella, or—even little Libby. These names meant nothing to me last summer, but today they're as good as family. Clearly, I am accustomed to mining the deep archival chambers of my brain, but the subterranean chambers of the heart? Until now I didn't even know they were there! It's like a door opened inside of me that until now was invisible. Uggghh. So hard to explain.

Aside from this inexplicable enlargement of my heart, these folks in FRANCO have swept me into an entirely new way of being. I'm seeing . . . I'm seeing—well, I can't quite put my finger on what I'm seeing, but—I must say that I'm actually enjoying this crazy cast of characters. Where earlier they were simply befuddling and even annoying, now I am increasingly finding that they are quite spectacular people. The variety of personality profiles here is much wider than I ever supposed, but perhaps the most interesting thing about these folks is that none of them fit into any sort of mold. Intelligent, boisterous, highly skilled, hard-working, charming, even a bit erratic at times—just when I think I've got them figured out someone does something uncharacteristic. I never seem to be able to predict how a thing is going to go down.

Take Harold-in-the-camper, for instance. What a character. He's the former trucker from "back-in-the-day" who always keeps to himself, and like my mother, uses that phrase every time I hear him speaking with someone. I've taken to thinking of him as 'back-in-the-day Harold' whenever he comes to mind. Well, he totally surprised us yesterday with an unsolicited visit. Even though he never fails to tip his floppy suede hat and gives me a friendly nod each time we pass, we haven't shared more than one or two words since I arrived. Then yesterday he showed up in Grand'Mere's kitchen, asking for me.

She quickly put up the kettle and brought out her big blue tin of sweet biscuits, but when he sat down to enjoy the snack, his face turned squarely toward me. With little expression and no words, he opened his tattered messenger bag and pulled out a sleek new pair of dark deer hide moccasins. Each shoe had an intricate tan, black, and brown pattern, sewn around the top and all along the edges with thick strands of leather. Along the sides a couple of pretty red beads hung from the tie straps on top of the tongue. Then, on the lip coming up over the back heel there were about two inches or so of smaller strips of leather dangling loosely like fringe, putting me in mind of Libby's wispy brown bangs.

"For you," he said, pushing them across the table toward me.

"Me?" I was really taken by surprise.

"Yeah, 'course they're fer you. Ya need some new shoes, don'tcha Missy? The ones you came in with aren't gunna last forever."

I was completely taken back. "They're . . . they're really lovely Harold. I . . . I don't know what to say. How did you know my size?"

"You do have family here, Missy. A wee bit of stealth inquiry can provide jest what a fellar needs to get the job done. I do hope ya fancy 'em."

Harold-in-the-camper's faded red sweater was layered with a number of different types of material all over the front of it. Rarely have I seen the man without it. It was a rare woolen type of clothing—a cable knit, they called it. Grand'Mere says it was handmade by his wife, Elyse, before she died—back when they were first married in the 2020's. It seems it makes him feel close to her though she's been gone for so many years. Leather patches that once were affixed to each elbow were coming apart, and the pocket material was separating from the wool. A wide zipper with a leather pulley hanging from it kept the whole thing together. Clearly, Harold had no intentions of retiring the thing.

The old man's bright eyes shone through a short, compacted face that was heavily lined with wrinkles, showing the wear and tear of his nearly 80 years. His laid back demeanor and deeply creviced face reminds me a little of a pug dog, much like the loose-jointed stuffed animal that Libby has had since she was a baby. Ha! He really does look quite a bit like her Toby Dog. But there is something so, so—I don't know—crystalline about Harold-in-the-camper. I never noticed it until the conversation we had at Grand'Mere's table, but when as we sat there for those few minutes, it's as if the eyes of a child were staring back at me instead of someone who had been born last century.

I also never noticed until today that Harold's left hand was wrapped up, concealing what should have been three of his fingers. Later Grand'Mere told me that those fingers were gone from knuckle down. He lost them during the D-Day exodus. How on earth does he do any tanning at all with missing fingers? These people are incredible! He broke my daydream with a start.

"Well, I do hope you'll use 'em, Miss Emilya. You'll be needin' a change before very long, especially when it starts to get chilly."

"I will! I need them. I'll use them, Mr. Harold. Thank you so much, really. That was very thoughtful. I didn't realize you knew how to tan hide and all."

"Oh, I din't do the tannin' ba' myself, Missy; never do. Justin set aside a couple of matchin' pieces for me last month. I jes wanted you to have them as a little welcome gift. Sure as shootin' FRANCO is better off fer havin' ya here little lady. I hope ya know that."

The pale green of his eyes disappeared into narrow slits as he offered a quick smile, blinked, and then, well, then he grabbed his biscuit and was gone. Never in twelve lifetimes would I have expected Harold-in-the-camper to think about my need for shoes, nor would I anticipate generosity like that. They're just all full of surprises.

And then there's that other thing they've got going here. It's something else, really. Another social anomaly—I can't quite put my finger on it. The whole lot of them are so thoroughly integrated in each other's lives it seems they are more like extended family than the motley crew of disparate and countercultural sojourners from all across the globe. It's almost as if they have customized a FRANCO dose of vitamin B or some other unifying element that they've got flowing through their blood. Crazy, but that's what it seems like— there's something about their bond that is more than just surviving out here off the grid.

Among all the other colorful characters here none is quite as captivating as Belevedere Florencia. Have I mentioned that? Ha ha ha. He's such a treasure.

Viddie is part of the Italian family at FRANCO, all of whom are just lovely, lovely people. I do wonder each time I see them how it was possible that they stayed together, when my parents say they had no choice but to leave me. While Grand'Mere has taken pains to assure me that ADMIN felt mother was too much of a security risk to simply let her walk away, and that they would never have allowed our entire family to simply choose to live a simpler, alternative life in the mountains, I still grapple with their choices. Marissa and I have had several intense discussions about the matter and they always end with her in tears. She has tried to explain "the severity of the situation, my darh-ling," but I can't quite buy in to her rationale. What she imagines they might have done to us all, I cannot fathom. It's not as though we're living under a dictator—for Strength's sake; "we the people" govern this fine nation. We are the survivors, the remnant who have learned how to rise above the rubble and make life more livable for everyone, insuring a future, inhabiting the promise of tomorrow!

What Marissa and the others don't realize is the extent to which our government is committed to having a civil society— one that is free of war, violence, and heartache. The longer I walk with them here, the more I understand the complexity of their own sense of purpose, but I still don't know how the Florencia's were able to make the change with their family intact. Once I get to know her better, I may gather the courage to ask Fiorella myself.

In any case, I'm intent on writing about the entire kaleidoscope of people living here, partly because they are such an oddly impressive study in human motivation but partly, as well, because I have grown fond of so many of them and I do want to understand them better. Also, the writing—what an odd surprise; I find the writing is really doing much to help me process everything. I'm sure it will also help with recollection once I finally do get back home, but I hadn't realized I would enjoy the actual writing! Storing all this information makes me feel much more secure. Knowing that I've got in this archaic little writing book it is a safe feeling. It's made me think a bit about the actual process of writing and how it's adding something significant to my life.

Funny, but the ability to write has been there all the time and I just never realized I could take the time to do it—gosh, nobody back at the Lab writes. Our communication system is so sophisticated; there is simply no need to write. But here I am, continuing to fill page after page of this art book and it's close to getting filled up. Each morning before chores I take time to collect my thoughts from the day before; sometimes I don't get to it for a few days, and other days I write in the evening about what happened earlier; it just depends. There's certainly enough time up here in these mountains to write for as long as I like each day.

Perhaps the thing I want to note most is the marked difference in my relationships.

What Jude and Zeejay and I shared was nothing like the depth of affection that has emerged in my short time getting to know Viddie. Rake and Jarrow, Paty and Sam—all the crew back at the Lab are good guys but there's not a one who compares with the depth and authenticity of Belevedere Florencia. And, and . . . it never really dawned on me before coming to FRANCO that there was a dearth of friendship with women, but I've never had a female friend. The one that has blossomed with Russa is deep, but it's not just deep. I'm learning that friendship is so much more complicated than anything I've experienced before. It's a powerful force! I mean, just a couple of weeks ago—what was it, three?—she and I were at odds over some silly sentimentalism she was experiencing. We disagreed sharply about the worth of emotions and actually argued over differences of opinion, but now—here we are—it's as if that never happened. What's more, she approached me with an apology and asked to take time to talk it out. That is just not normal, but I like it.

Now my friendship with Russa is even stronger, not in spite of the words that transpired between us but almost because of them! And as we have gotten closer she's told me more about her wild teenage years, her short stint of being homeless after the Devastation, and even some of the secrets surrounding a long lost love at some old shore town in central New Jersey.

So much of the new dimension of life that I am experiencing started with her. She is the one who walked me through every crazy moment in the last few months, especially with my unfurling and out-of-control feelings for Belvedere. She listens to me, prods me to share my thoughts and reflects on what I say. It's all so new, this sharing! It's really delightful— she even remembers things I've mentioned just in passing, and is always looking out for me. To top it all off, she tells me that this is the normal way friendship is experienced. Now, if only I could connect with my parents like that. Unfortunately, each time Marissa approaches me with hopes of a serious conversation, she starts to tear up. It's so annoying. It seems to me like she doesn't really want to explain anything, she just wants to cry. UGH.

In any case, those earliest, bewildering days of life in FRANCO are starting to fade. It's been only a few months here, but it feels like I've taken quantum leaps into what appears to be an ocean of love and kindness. All around is the goodness and simplicity of these people—a community where hope resides as if it were a person.

And what a lively bunch of human beings they are! Oh my Strength—Viddie's mother, Fiorella is a fireball. She is tiny, but feisty and charming. Fiorella is just a bit younger than my mother; her rather exotic looks are captivating, but I must say, she is just as beautiful inside as she is on the outside, and the way this woman speaks—so much with her hands—to watch her is entertaining.

I like Fiorella a lot. She is a true pleasure to be with and there are a few funny things that I appreciate about her. Along with the firsthand knowledge of my extended family, I like the fact that she still has a subtle southern Italian lilt in her voice. The accent is quaint and light—a leftover from the days prior to the Devastation. I also like the fact that she and her husband (Carlo) taught Viddie and Alessa to speak Italian in spite of the fact that they have absolutely no use for it.

Fiorella is friendly with everyone, and that's one of the things I like about her. Actually, well—there are quite a few things. First, she has been a good friend to Marissa, and Mother needs a friend because she is difficult to listen to for very long. The other interesting thing about Fiorella is that she knew my Aunt Emma when she was younger, that is, my actual grandmother. She spent quite a bit of time with her at FRANCO's sister community in Switzerland before the family came here, which, unbeknownst to me, was in operation long before my parents left the Lab to help begin this hideaway.

Quite often Fiorella stops in at Grand'Mere's for tea, and there so often holds me captive with fascinating stories of Aunt Emma and John, always referring to their nurturing, hospitable ways in the kindest of terms. What a strange thing to consider—the idea that my grandparents might be alive somewhere on the other side of the globe, and that I have no way of ever meeting them.

"They taught-a me zo much, LEEya." Her emphasis on my name always falls on the first syllable and she pronounces it as if there's an "a" there instead of two "e's" and lifts up the last syllable quickly at the very end. "Lay-ya"—she says it in such a remarkable and entertaining way, it never fails to bring a smile to my face.

Whatever she says, her tone is always tender, encircled with her rich, Mediterranean accent, but once in a while I find myself distracted from what she is actually saying because her eyes are so full of light. Sometimes when she speaks to me I become engrossed in those smoky blue eyes of hers—so much like her son's. Oh . . . I can just imagine his eyes as they . . .

XXXXXXXXXXXXXXXXLKELNFJXMMMMMMM MMMMMVHNLSJD   MC<XMN   BKJDRM XXXXXXKDM<0-vjw- evojbdllwwwwwwwwwwwwwwwxxxoxxxxxxxxxxxxxxxxxxx xxxxxxxxxxxxojojvoielklalbopa;ssssssssssssssssssssssssjiopknke v psp=====================

Enough about Viddie.

I can't chance this ever being read by him so that's my excuse for the scribbled mess on this page.

In any case, Fiorella seems to take special care to tell me about my grandparents and when she does, I am transfixed. I wonder if she knows how much I appreciate the effort to fill me in on my life.

Yesterday she brought honey-sweetened buns to Grand'Mere's earth shelter and made a point to tell me a story about Aunt Emma's culinary expertise, and how she learned to make them by watching her. I'm sure Jude and Zeejay have never even considered the reality of these delicacies, let alone tasted them.

"Your grandmother is a gift to this world; she certainly is a gift to me."

"You speak of her as if she is alive, Fiorella, yet do you really think it's true?"

"*Si, si, dear dolce* LEEya. I do speak of her that way. *Mi sorella, mi sorella*. Emmah es very dear to my heart and it gives me good comforts to think of your nonna as living somewhere out there—much like we do here in these holy mountains. *Lei è una bella donna*"

I turned my head and gave her a quizzical look. There she goes again interspersing Italian into the conversation. I don't understand a word of it, but I'm sure she means well.

As if she could read my mind, Fiorella repeated her Italian babble. *"Si, si—una bella donna.* A fine, fine woman." And you are jess like her, dolce LEEya—jess, jess like her, *bella.* This, she said all the while pinching my cheek. Ouch. I'm glad Aunt Vee was nowhere in sight or else I would have had both of them pulling at the sides of my face.

What a funny lady.

"Thank you, Fiorella." I reached across the table and gave her hand a little squeeze. "You are so kind to me. Thank you."

"Si, si. And there ess no reason to assume Emmeh has passed on, Dolcelaya. The seestor community was even more fully sooply than we are here when we made dee exodus. More likely eet ess that they are all there, doing so well, working their daily days in de midst of a loving people, no?"

I smiled at her, enjoying the little bit of leftover Italian that hangs so visibly in her voice, and her sentiment as well— the hopeful message she was communicating. But once Fiorella gets going it's hard to stop her. I think that must be why she and mother are so close. Two of kind, for sure. What does Russa always say? Birds of a feather . . . yeah, that's it.

"Oh *mio prezioso,* your presence here has done much to sustain my hope. If you could find your way to us after twenty three years of absentia, perhaps Emmeh and Jahn are indeed leeving and will somehow, one day make it back to our arms. Yet they remain so strong een our hearts."

Fiorella's eyes always get glassy when she speaks of Switzerland—the same sort of reaction I have seen in Grand'Mere on so many occasions. Second to Russa, I enjoy speaking with her the most, even when she lapses into her mother tongue and I can't quite follow.

Unfortunately Firoella is living in a dream when it comes to Switzerland. Everyone knows there's no life beyond the tiniest sliver of the Amalfi coast. It was obliterated. I dare not mention that to her. There's no use in bringing more sadness her way.

If all this is not enough I must say that perhaps the most remarkable thing about Viddie's mother is what the woman does to food! Fiorella has the reputation sewn up for being the best cook in the community; somehow, somehow she creates the most remarkable rustic Italian specialties with half the ingredients necessary. Truth be told, Italian food has become one of the many incredible surprises in my life. Frittatas! Mmmmm. Potatoes and Sausage. Mmmm! Mushroom and leek soup sprinkled generously with Alton's pecorino romano cheese. Oh—so good. There's not a person in FRANCO who doesn't love to greet Fiorella with her favorite statement each day—*mangia*! She always laughs when she hears it and calls back the dish she is making for the day. My absolute favorite of all is the crusty bread with herbs and oil that she serves with tender, braised escarole, a leafy vegetable that I never even heard of before coming to FRANCO. Saturated in a pungent mixture of fresh garlic and onions, and sprinkled with more of Alton's extravagant cheese—my-oh-my, the elaborate feasts we have are such a treat—and always accompanied by music and dancing!

Since the earliest of my childhood memories our main foodstuff consisted of provisio-bars and water. Twice a week or so we'd have hydroponic vegetables like squash, beans, and tomatoes, but by and large our subsistence consisted of perfectly apportioned nutrition bars. They are extremely efficient and they taste pretty good, too. The great variety of flavors and textures kept me from getting bored and the protein in them is an important safeguard against becoming skin and bones. Provisio nutrition also pretty much solved the obesity problem by the middle of the century. But gosh, everyone's so lean at the Lab. I guess you could call the guys "featherweights." Hmmm. The food we have at FRANCO though—wow; I never imagined the act of eating to be something so elegant. It's more like the art of eating here.

Grand'Mere is quick to remind me that food grown from the earth and cooked fresh was the kind of nutrition she grew up on, but my Strength—it's been so many years since then, and I never imagined eating could be anything more than fueling up.

In the midst of it all I'm finding that I'm starting to feel more a part of them, too.

Daily glitches and annoyances are still a part of my days, but I've decided there's absolutely nothing I can do about any of that. On the other hand, there's life to be lived here, and there's something quite special about the way they share life together. I'm liking it quite much. And my own life seems to be spreading out with much more inner reflection than I am accustomed to. Take Belvedere Florencia, for instance. I think about him all the time. That man is the most glorious specimen of male beauty I have ever laid eyes on. (Oh, I guess I've mentioned that before!)

Well, there's more to him than meets the eye, much more. Now that we're getting to know one another better, I notice his unique and nuanced thought patterns. He's not exactly what one could call "the strong silent type," but he isn't quick with a response, nor is he especially witty. He is a thoughtful guy and loves to laugh, and he's very much interested in nature. As wonderful as our conversations are, very often he is content to sit on a rock and watch the birds fly by.

Truth is, not since mastering my early education (E.E.) files and study of classic Greek culture had I ever seen a man of such . . . stature. In fact, the only time I ever saw such a sight was in those images curated for me by my E.E. monitors, none of which matched the rugged, genuine handsomeness of this man. If Viddie had been living back then he could easily have been inspiration for the Adonis. And to think of all the files I scanned later on looking for inspiration at Travelite Global Associates while developing one virtual vacation after the other, well I surely would've used his image. There's definitely nothing to compare him to back home. The skinny muscle-less frames of my co-workers is the norm. Of all the men I know in my age group there's not a one of them that is not pale, lanky, and physically delicate, but here, the men are quite the opposite. They are sturdy and strong—and tan! Viddie, especially. And when he comes around I can usually tell [when he's nearby, I usually know it] before I see him because he's almost always whistling a happy little melody, none of which is familiar to me, but I can always tell it's him. My Strength, this man is impossible to ignore. Especially now, since he has started coming by Grand'Mere's everyday asking if I need help with anything.   :-) At first as I scrutinized my attraction to him I thought it was primarily about his looks or perhaps it was my own lack of romantic experience with men that was caused me to tilt a bit overboard, but now I am sure it's much more than that. Just how much more, I still don't know but our times together have increased in regularity and people are starting to notice.

Long walks, great talks—holding hands and warm affection—Oh, he has made me feel so welcome and wanted, and it's—ah, it's just such a remarkable feeling . . . but really so many other people in FRANCO have made me feel welcome too.

Of course there's Russa—a sister more than a friend. Knowing her has made me realize that I've never had a friend before (not even one), and that is another crazy notion. But Russa, for all her unusual views, is someone who has done nothing less than totally redefine the word "friend" for me.

Could I have missed the joy of friendship all of my life until now? It's mind-boggling. Yet, sometimes I fear I am becoming too dependent upon her; mostly, however, I'm just in awe of the fact that there is a person here who is happy to give that much of her time to someone she hardly knows. Our morning walks often turn into two or three hour jaunts; up and around the mountain bend we go, along Taylor Falls, deep into the craggy woods—like last week at Grand Lake.

Since the swimming incident with Viddie a while back, Russa and I have taken several walks up that way too. Our deep conversation has returned full force, and I am glad—so glad about it. All the while we talk and talk, discussing philosophy and food and, well, life, in general . . . like characters in an old movie. It's the most unusual thing I've ever experienced. In spite of her emotive vulnerability she makes too much sense for me to ignore. And actually because of that same emotionalism she understands what's happening between me and Viddie, usually much better than I do. It's helping to talk about it. Unfortunately, she is a woman who really knows nothing of all the enhancements at our disposal, so how can I help but defend our tek when she starts talking about the high costs. Heck, it costs nothing to try it and the only thing there is to gain is . . . well, everything!

Anyway, the folks in this camp never cease to amaze me. I can't help but mention Russa's dear cousin Alton, who came with her to FRANCO almost twenty years ago. He's a top-notch herbalist and cheese maker, which doesn't surprise me. Before FRANCO he worked in an agricultural corporation pairing remnant tomato seeds with their genetically modified ones— says he remembers the hydroponic manufacturing plants, too. Many others here are part of my amazement, as well.

For example, Earl—whom I rarely see, is almost always off doing something of import. He's the man who found me half frozen in my car back in March; what a fine man he is! His salty-hued beard and matching demeanor really display the tenderness and courage that I know reside in him. He's kind of quiet, but recently I learned that aside from being the one who is constantly scoping FRANCO's borders, he regularly goes out into the deep woods to hunt with my father and Hux. Russa says that Earl's not much of a marksman, but the guys find him invaluable because he's got such a positive way about him. He goes to keep them company and help them with the haul.

Earl is also the king of fixing things. Mother had a broken churn last week and before she could even tell him about it, Earl was there adjusting the level and pulley. It worked good as new when he left. The man is so helpful to everyone; if he doesn't know how to do something, he plunges in and tries anyway. I like that about him.

There are several others who have taken special care to make me feel welcome; L.J. is one of them. Not a day goes by when the old man doesn't ask if he can play me a song. I've really grown to look forward to it. Most of the songs he plays are completely foreign to me, and some of them are way out there—stuff that's totally last century. He's got this thing about old music, music from his childhood that was old even back when he was a kid. He's always strumming on that guitar of his, singing or humming songs by bands called The Beatles, The Association, and some people named Herman's Hermits. Crazy names. I didn't say it, but I find the name of one of his favorite musical groups a bit ironic. Herman's hermits? How 'bout FRANCO'S HERMITS?

Anyway, yesterday as we were walking back from Rubble Ridge, Russa and I heard singing coming from the covered entrance to his earth-shelter. "There's a kind of hushhhhhhhh. . . all over the world, tonight, all over the world. . ."

We giggled and clapped as he turned to see that he had an audience.

"Come on in lady friends; come in!" he greeted us with his big bear smile.

"Have a seat. Let's get some harmonies going, yeah?"

L.J.'s voice is always inviting whether he's singing or speaking; it's like . . . almost like his voice is part of his personality. There's a bit of refinement in it, something that tells me he's studied or just very polite. I mean, he's a mimic, for sure, with a different accent or play on words for everyone he meets. When he sees me, it's a funny cockney—milady this and milady that. With Libby, he pretends he's a clown. His looks remind me just a bit of old Mr. Roland back at the Lab. Everything except the eye patch, of course; Rolly doesn't have a patch, but both he and L.J. have round faces and a snowy crop of hair. They both seem a bit like sentinels to me. L.J.'s soft strumming is somehow such a comfort to me. It's funny but it seems as though L.J. is always somewhere close by, or at least he's never terribly far away. More often than not he is at Stone Camp strumming on that guitar of his—oh and so beautifully— the strands of music that spark forth from his fingers are like nothing I've ever heard before. He's got this special way of picking the strings that makes the instrument sound as if it is speaking. An hour goes by as I sit and just listen to him play, and it feels as though not more than five minutes has passed.

As I get to know him better I find that he is another of FRANCO's generous souls, often taking the time to show me how each song he plays has a different tuning, or the beauty of the wood grain finish on his guitar, a special chord change— something different every day, like he's not satisfied to simply soothe us all with the songs, but he's gotta pass on the love for it. On top of it all, I've gotta admit, hearing him say: "Greetings, milady, and how might thou be today?" is something I have begun to look forward to and welcome with much delight.

Russa tells me my experience with it is part of the magic of music. Imagine that? The magic of music. It's amazing the kinds of ideas I have come to accept these days. What's more, she tells me that this "magic" springs from a place of purity in L's soul. Purity. Soul. Imagination. What a jumble of irrational, indefinable ideas swirling around in their heads. I sure never have associated purity with music, let alone soul. All this soul talk—sheesh!

When I wondered aloud what she meant by that, Russa explained to me that none of his own tunes were written from an impulse to sell them, nor were they competing for attention with anyone else, nor written as a means to gain recognition; They simply—purely—came forth from a place of love within him. Now, talk like that really mystifies me, but at the same time, I can't help but marvel. How can people exist on this planet and think so differently about so many things?

Thinking about strange things, the absolute strangest feeling I get is when I'm near L.J. and it's not a bad sort of strange, but a very warm one. It's as though he is more my father than Liam. Somehow I feel safe around him. He brings so much to all of us. He's open and full of good humor and always has a story. I love his stories, they reveal so much. Funnily, we never really hear stories about his past. I would never pry, but it does make me wonder a bit.

Ah—Liam. Liam, Liam. Another case of mystery and marvel. I know, I know, I know—he contributes much to this community, just as mother said. He brings in the game each week or two and provides that steady rhythm to the ongoing travail of life here in FRANCO. People count on him. He's a bulwark; he's a strength, so giving, so generous; I know, I know....la la la la. I am aware. But still, this soft-spoken moose-of-a-man is sweet, but terribly quiet, and his quietness creeps me out.

His demeanor is a little ominous. Yeah, yeah, he's got a terrific smile, but I wish he wouldn't keep it to himself so often. I still don't quite get him, but I see how he fits into this place and I understand what he brings. Unfortunately, like Marissa—they both seem a bit like they've had partial lobotomies; it's like they've both just turned off a part of their brains. I really do so feel really badly writing this down on paper, but it's true—I can't seem to have a conversation with my father that makes sense for more than two minutes. With mother it's a bit less drastic, but we still can't really converse with total coherence. Russa, Fiorella, L.J., Grand'Mere, even Alessa—we get along so well. Why does it have to be so tense with Marissa and Liam?

There is something, though—something about my mother that, I don't know; she not only stirs me up, but she intrigues me so. Marissa's ways are much more intuitive than I first thought and from time to time she exhibits unexpected insight. I've learned to get past her over-arched eyebrows and excessively expressive face. Our conversations are situated in everyday activities of eating and working side by side, but once in a while we've had a more serious discussion and in the short time we've had together these last month's it's clear that her intelligence quotient is extremely high. I mean, really high.

Other oddballs are here too, but it's hard not to like them. There's Viddie's twin sister, Alessa, for one. She is quite the anomaly. Obviously, they are the same age but she seems as young as he does old. Looking at them, I'd swear he was 30 and she was 15. Not only is she much more reserved than her brother, she looks up to him as if he is the elder, but they're twins! She is hardly as outgoing as he is, and although very polite, she always seems to be only half with you. Kind, sweet, soft-spoken—all these words describe her demeanor, but so often I find her looking out to the distance, and it makes me wonder what she's thinking.

The first time I noticed the faraway look in her eye was the day we met. Fiorella came by Grand'Mere's place with a bunch of little flowers and some small blueberry cakes. (When they're in season everyone makes blueberry everything!) Alessa was with her and made a first impression that hasn't changed much since then: Straight-faced, no words, eyes diverted from the conversation; she said hello, but that was it. As looks go, the funny thing is, her brother and I look more like each other than the two of them do (and lately our thoughts seem to be matching up, as well). :-)

Aside from me, Alessa's the youngest woman here and, well, I do hope to get to know her better. It's possible that I'm projecting a bit of the strangeness because whenever I see her I can't help but think of my boss back at the Lab. Alessandro was instrumental in forcing me to take a "holiday" from work. It's possible I could be projecting my ill feelings on Alessa— their names are so similar, it's hard not to connect the two. When I see her I can't help associating her with him more than with her brother, and it always makes me wonder. . . . Does Alessandro even notice that I am gone? Have they sent out a search party to find me? Have they had a funeral? Thankfully, the flat is completely paid off and it's highly unlikely that anyone has come to visit, but—Strength—I would hope that they've tried to contact me to check in.

Oh, and then of course there's Belvedere. Did I already mention him? :-)

Shortly after I met him, Marissa was in the midst of another of her very direct, disconcerting rants and he poked his head into Grand'Mere's hovel and rescued me.

"I thought I've give you another lesson in gardening, Emi. You have a few minutes to spare?"

My heart sprang at the invitation, but I didn't let on how excited I was to see him again. It was there we began what has now become a nearly daily ritual. Each day he shows up to inquire about something else. Whether it's teaching me to ride a horse, milking a goat, or pruning the apple trees—we seem to be doing so much together.

One day shortly after that he premised his visit without the ruse of helping me do anything.

"How 'bout a walk today, Emi? Just you, me, and the tiger lilies; are you up for a trek around the back lake?"

Every time I think about the way it started, a broad smile spreads across my face. There's no hiding my feelings any longer. That particular afternoon was a double delight. When he popped in, Grand'Mere and I were just finishing up preparing the last of the zucchini pickles. (zucchini pickles! Never in my life have I had occasion to use either of those two words, and now I'm not only using the words together, I am making them!) We have such a bumper crop of green squash this summer that she had to can for three days longer than she usually does. We were just cleaning up when Viddie stopped in. I did a double take because he looked quite a bit less shabby than normal and had a bunch of tiger lilies behind his back.

"To the two most beautiful women in this community," Viddie bowed and presented himself like a fine English gentleman from the nineteenth century. Grand'Mere raised her eyebrows and blushed as she received a handful of the flowers. I just squirmed and felt like I was twelve.

"Where on earth did you find these, Vid? They are unbelievably gorgeous!" I felt a rush of heat racing up my neck as Viddie handed me the rest of the bouquet. My ebullience must have egged him on because with that he embarked on a heady description of their emergence this time of year, the type of soil these wildflowers prefer, and how long they last once they're cut.

"They grow tall very quickly and then all at once they explode into the purest shade of orange you'll ever see. C'mon—let me show you the field where I found them, and on the way I'll show you something even more orange than these."

I looked up at Grand'Mere; her blue eyes sparkled as she motioned for me to put down the pickle jar I had been drying. She is so dear.

The two of us set out together at about 11 o'clock and spent the greater part of the afternoon exploring the woods on the other side of Grand Lake, and even though I don't usually venture out that far I felt completely safe. I mean, aside from his muscles and landscape savvy, the man knows his herbs and vegetation—that's for sure. He also knows critter tracks when he sees them, too.

As usual, I was typically a bit fidgety whenever a squirrel or raccoon scuttled past us, and—as usual—he had a good chuckle over it, but winked to let me know I was just fine. The thing I remember most about that venture into the unknown is that he didn't make me feel like an idiot about being nervous there. I realized right then that he's just a big tease.

Perhaps the most significant thing that happened that day was when we sat down on a huge felled tree trunk to feast on some wild raspberries; I learned some things I did not know about the woods.

"That thing is dead," Viddie pointed to the day-glow-orange-toned fungi firmly attached to the fallen tree.

"Its vibrancy may trick you into thinking it is alive, but it's totally dead. Weird, isn't it, that something so pretty could be so void of life?"

The scent of lilacs wafted through the woods and was rapturous. My head was full of intense sensations and I began to feel a little dizzy, but as our conversation continued it took a different turn. We began talking about what is real and what is not real and Viddie surprised me by asking if there was anything in particular that I missed—anything at all from my old life.

I started to nod in the negative and he smiled and took my hand. "C'mon. You can trust me, Emi. I'm not a bad listener and I'll tell you this—if I were plunged into an utterly foreign environment, you can be sure that there would be plenty that I'd be missing from my life here."

His sweet, unassuming smile melts my heart every time I see it. What a gentle soul, this man is. How can I resist Viddie Florencia? Is it possible that I didn't even know he existed a mere three months ago?

At this point, I had to decide whether or not to tell him about the Lab and the people there. Would he understand that they are important to me? Would he like the life I describe? It was still so early in our relationship I knew I would be taking a risk, but I couldn't help wondering even then—perhaps he'd be willing to come back with me—to leave this place and start a new, more civilized life.

It was worth the risk.

I told him about my team and the importance of my position there, and the way ADMIN used Travelite Global Associates to help inspire hope in a future for the country. I explained how ADMIN governed the entire coast from Nova Scotia to the Florida Keys, and recounted the early post-D history concerning social order and government protocols. I told him about the sad state of the rest of the land—with everything beyond Ohio and Virginia a barren plain. Many of the images of the land prior to the Devastation have become the foundation of all TGA products. Because we no longer have the means to visit America's once flourishing Midwest and Pacific Coast, expanding the vacation software has become something akin to our national purpose. It's funny but as much as he was eager to hear all about the civilized world, the thing that fascinated him most in our discussion was my patent of the P/Z and the particulars of the device. I even told him about the random fragment of messages I have been receiving. He was especially intrigued by the messages and determined to help me find a way to uncover what it meant.

That was the first time I saw his interest in technology. I think he has a mind for software development, I really do. He just about begged me for details about the coding of the P/Z 1000 and seemed especially interested in the "why" behind our use of it.

"If you already have a brain to delve into, why not just think deeply, Emi? That's the part I don't really get. Why develop something to embed into your brain for clean mental focus if you can just approach another person and discuss an idea until greater insight is found?"

Hmmm. I never thought about that question when I was developing the P/Z.

In any case, afternoon turned to evening and we stayed out there far longer than we intended. The rest of the community had already retired for the evening when we got back. I'm not sure exactly what hour I went to bed, but when we returned to Stone Camp and I snuggled under Grand'Mere's thick duck down comforter I couldn't fall asleep for a very long time.

Where this was all leading, I hadn't a clue.

Chapter 10

Day 88—The Rollercoaster

If there is a God I would thank him today for the privacy of the caves and only ask that we each could have our own. GOD HELP US—every one! There is NO getting away from people here. One word, one misspoken word and we've got to have an entire conversation about it. If someone gets sick everybody knows about it. Try going for a walk by yourself. No way—there's always someone wanting to tag along. The more I try and acclimate to FRANCO the more I find frustrating moments like these biting at my ankles like the nasty black flies that dominate this mountain every time the wind blows just a certain way.

Strength!

Fiorella, the food angel, made me some small cheese turnovers with jam today. She made them for me; but instead of being able to enjoy even a few morsels of these tiny treasures, everyone and his brother found their way to the aroma and gobbled up the lion's share of them!

All I wanted was to find a quiet spot outside the center of Stone Camp, take in the fantastic fragrance these little gems and write in my journal. Instead, everywhere I set my feet down someone else greeted me and ended up taking just-a-tiny-piece of my cheese pies. Bit by bit—they devoured them and now the basket is empty!

And another thing—between adjusting to sleeping so many more hours than I'm used to and eating so much more food than I'm used to, I barely know how to organize myself. Some days one day feels like two. Other times a day feels like a week and the sun hasn't even set yet! Strength, so much weirdness. On top of that, just as I find myself adjusting to this crazy new living situation, and the, well—just the entire reconfiguring of my sense of reality—I've started having more and more bizarro dreams. I thought the first one with cougars chasing me was an anomaly, but they're starting to come more regularly now.

Like last night, for instance, it seemed so real! Vibrant colors swirled in my dreams and faces surrounded me from all sides—faces of people I know from back at the Lab and faces of others that I didn't know at all. The first time I woke up I remembered the dream vividly. I was startled by the face of my old mentor from years ago, Dr. Marc. In the dream Dr. Marc seemed to be calling to me. Then I found myself hiding in his office—under an old fashioned desk. While hiding, my eyes fell upon a strange sequence of numbers and somehow, it seemed by magic, I was able to decode the numbers and hack into his research files. To my horror, I discovered that his research was corrupt—that he was corrupt. Uhhhhhhhh, so impossible. There is no one more respected—even revered—than Dr. Marc. He's like the granddaddy of our entire project! I woke up and shook myself and fell right back to sleep but then immediately found myself in that nasty dream again! The strangest thing is that the dream picked up exactly where it left off, as if it were a movie or sequential story of some sort. When I heard footsteps coming down the hall in rapid succession I tried to hide, but some people I've never met came and found me and tied me down. I started to scream and was patently out of control. They looked at each other, nodded, and placed a flimsy white jacket on me with straps around the shoulders and waist. I was yelling, yelling, yelling so loudly but it seemed that no sound could come from my mouth.

Although I didn't really know why I was being held there, it was clear that his corruption was even more egregious than what went on with Marissa and Liam when they worked at the Lab. I screamed that I would tell the world about what they were doing and then bugs came out of the walls and the people surrounding me morphed into furry creatures that started clawing at the gurney. One was a squirrel and when he opened his mouth to talk it sounded like squirrel talk but I understood it!! The little creature held a walnut in both its hands and told me that The Lab was using me. It was all so vivid! It seemed like the squirrel was going to help me but then three or four creepy little animals forcibly held me down and I began to fear for my life. All this took place in the very center of the Design and Development Department but Triple D hardly looked the same. Then, all at once a mask came out of nowhere and was slipped over my face. I heard them making noises that were frightful but indiscernible and I began moving in and out of consciousness. Whatever was being said didn't make sense. It seemed they were trying to use me as a control specimen in their ongoing OLSM research and dear Strength of my life—it shook me right out of a deep sleep.

When I awoke my pillow was drenched. I don't know if it was more tears or sweat, but I was shaken.

It took me quite a while but when I finally fell back to sleep it wasn't long before I had another bizarre dream, this time about Aunt Emma. It was super strange because I thought I had accepted the fact that Grand'Mere is really my aunt and that my true grandmother might be alive stuck somewhere on the other side of the globe, but I guess my brain hasn't processed it yet. Throughout the rest of the night I had all kinds of piecemeal dreams of Aunt Emma. First she was caught in some craggy rock in the Alps crying out for help. Then she was out on a ship with sharks circling. Every time I reached my hand out to her, she got farther away instead of closer. Ugh. I hate this dreaming! I really detest it!! Where is my predictable and efficient micro-sleep?

If that's not enough, my stomach seemed to talk to me half the night with gurgles and gas cramps—pain like I've never experienced before! When I tried to switch over my thinking to the delightful things that are happening between me and Viddie a terrifying thought emerged:

What if he won't come away with me to the Lab?

What if I can't convince him?

What if I never see him again?

Dear Strength! Strength of my blood, bowel, and body—I hate these dreams!!!!

The feelings this man evokes in me are not the sort that I had ever anticipated, and lately they are getting stronger and I am unable to detach. I'm afraid they are beginning to usurp my logic, for surely it hasn't escaped my notice that I am falling into an illusional pattern of thinking, here. Authors like Charlotte Bronte, Victor Hugo, J.D. Salinger and others that I learned about in my E.E. files are archaic and certainly anachronistic. The romantic ideas that they depicted were completely detached from reality. Well, I certainly never took any of them seriously. Just stories, stories, of course; tales of the way the Victorians and the Postmoderns managed their emotions in light of their many cognitive limitations. E.E. files aside, as for the possibility of the two of us having any real hope for a future—well, I know in my heart-of-hearts, it's ludicrous. I simply need to stop giving myself over to such fantasy. His place is here; my place is home. As for why it won't work, Strength, the list goes on and on.

First off, Viddie and I have no efficient way of communicating on a regular basis. Except for the odd chance of running into each other during chores, or intentionally going to find one another at our respective residences, there are no screens, walls, or gadgets that might connect us; we are here completely without the possibly of any tek. Secondly, he is obviously much younger. Seven years is seven years. It's a long time. Lastly, I'm not staying here for long. There's no use in getting further involved or even considering it.

"Time for a walk, Em?"

Oh dear. There he is, right in front of me. The most handsome male specimen on the planet out his hand as I look up from what I am writing. I can't help but smiling inwardly. It's one of those intentional times, I guess. Viddie came to find me!

"Hold on a minute, my friend," I say. "I'll just be a second; let me finish this up."

Even though I smiled he must have picked up on my hesitance. I was right in the middle of writing the final paragraph in yesterday's journal entry.

"C'mon—the woods are calling. That's not too dangerous for you, now, is it?" There was that crooked little smile again.

I gave him my hand and let him pull me up from the grassy knoll where I was sitting.

"Sure, Vid. You know I always love a walk. You'll help me navigate the dangers, won't you?" I said with a wink.

We traipsed past L.J.'s post at the fire pit and then found our stride heading up the hill to the ridge. Settling onto a nice, flat rock, I found a comfortable spot and opened up my journal while he strode off to pick us a few berries.

When he returned we soon settled into our favorite position on Rubble Ridge and sat back-to-back, leaning on each other. It's a little game we started a few weeks back where he would describe something he was seeing and I'd have to guess what it was. Then it would be my turn and I could do the describing. If I guessed correctly, he'd slip me a berry; if he guessed my description, he'd be the recipient of juicy blackberry. It started out as a way to make the berries last more than two minutes but has gone on to be something of a ritual for us.

We chomped through most of the berries and I had my sights set on a couple of bright red cardinals zipping playfully between a few spruce trees, but never got back to my turn because as soon as I said, "squirrel eating a nut" he stood to his feet, turned, and scooped me up. Clasping his strong arms around my middle, he looked at me squarely.

I almost lost my balance, and laughed a little. "Now what is this all about, Mr. Florencia?"

"What? What's what?" he said with a tinge of feigned innocence.

He was holding me closer than he ever had before and I could feel his breath on my ear when he whispered his response. I closed my eyes momentarily to savor the sensation.

"This." I broke our hold slightly and pointed back and forth first to him then to me, returning his gaze with equal intensity.

"This?" He replied, drawing me right back to his chest and squeezing me with just the perfect amount of strength. "This, my lovely lady, is whatcha call real."

Oh dear. My previous resolve to keep my heart in check floated up and out to the stratosphere.

"Emi, do you ever wonder what might have happened had we not met?"

My jaw must have dropped a mile because a smile flashed across his face as soon as he looked at me and he immediately cupped his hands around my face. "I ask only because I've been thinking lately that if you hadn't come here I might never have found the woman I have always dreamed of."

His words pierced me in the most beautiful way possible as his lips melted onto my own.

I didn't move an inch.

Chapter 11

Day 89—The Food

A rustic aroma drew me out of a dead sleep.

The sweet smell of cinnamon and apples wafted across the open pathways of Grand'Mere's kitchen enclosure and as I looked up, there was Russa, standing in the narrow archway with a wide smile and a plate of something Fiorella just took off her stone hearth.

"Yum!" Russa mouthed the word as she offered her outstretched hand to help me up.

Mmmm. The aroma was out of this world.

"Is Grand'Mere up Roos? I don't hear her stirring. If not, we should be quiet."

"No, she's up, Leeya. She's outside chatting with Fi."

Rubbing the sleep from my eyes, I let my friend pull me up from the lumpy mattress and we nearly tumbled over together. Thankfully, her steady grip on Fiorella's dish saved us from landing in a crumbled mess.

Russa's rollicking laughter made me wonder how I could ever have gotten along without her as my friend. What sheer happiness to know that there is someone on the planet who really knows me and cares about my life.

The feelings of friendship that engross me these days are grand but they are vastly different from the flood of feeling I experience when Belevedere looks my way, That whole . . .

well, that's next on my agenda. I really must explore the layers of feelings that are found in friendship against the more intense feelings that pound through my body and cause me to melt in that man's presence. Russa will help me figure it out; she always does. She's so good at nuance and never seems to mind how much I talk about him. Wait till I tell her about what happened yesterday—the kiss, the conversation, all of it. She'll have a good laugh when I tell her how his left palm turned completely purple from holding onto to those three juicy berries that we never finished eating.

Grand'Mere appeared with her favorite wooden spoon in hand and scooped out a serving of the cooked apple and sweet potato casserole, placing a generous bowl of it on the small bedside table that stood between my room and the kitchen. She sprinkled it with some crunchy walnuts and a bit of caramelized honey comb. What a way to begin a day!

"I hope we didn't disturb you Madremia; I know it's early." Russa winked at Grand'Mere, kissing her on the cheek as is the custom in FRANCO, and addressing her with the affectionate nickname that everyone uses interchangeably when speaking to Grand'Mere.

Mmmmm. Apples. Apples are everywhere this week. There's a gigantic crop of 'em and we are really starting to enjoy them. Russa's apple-ey wakeup call was a delightful way to ease out of the night. It was such a fine, toasty feeling that wrapped itself around me this morning, but most interesting was that a day starting out with such warmth and earthy pleasures could end on such opposite terms.

It started with a walk.

After breakfast Russa and I embarked on our regular trek around the south side of the mountain and headed up to Rubble Ridge, the site that had quickly become our place to hang out. Thankfully, the black flies weren't out. We thought we might head toward the juniper and birch groves just beyond the ridge because the flies steer clear of them, but the breeze was stronger than normal and we found the day pleasantly free of those little pests.

Grassy hills dotted with purple buddleia and forsythia swallow up the spaces between the jagged terrain and the clearing. Trekking through the hillside is lovely on a cool day, and today was just such a one. I brought the cozy sweater Grand'Mere made me just in case the breeze kicked up even further.

Rubble Ridge works well for our hangout because it's just far enough from the center of activity to give us space to enjoy long, pensive talks of self-discovery and poetry, but not too far to put us more than twenty minutes from the rest of the community.

Even when we don't end up talking much, our walks are almost always voyages of exploration and adventure.

When we sat down, Russa opened the little book of sayings and notes that she's been compiling for . . . well, decades. Its well-worn cover is still intact and the pages are a combination of pre-digital typeface and hand-written scribble. I'm glad she can read her writing, because I sure can't!

Over the years Roos has gathered numerous snippets of old books and axioms and developed the practice of reading and memorizing the ones that she holds most dear. She tells me, "These precious gems are safer in my heart than they are on the paper, Lee. What if the book got lost or we ran out of paper?"

It's so Russa—my pragmatic, poetic friend whose joy is often tempered with a little vinegar thrown in for good measure. Whenever I see fresh water streaming over huge gray boulders (which is quite often up here), I think of her. She's complexity of contrasts, that woman is.

Anyway, as often happens, when we settle down to talk, these sayings spark our discussion, leading us into deep dialogue about everything from politics and world religion to love and of course, my current favorite topic—friendship. Our time together is usually vastly enriching, and categorically different from any other kind of conversation I ever had back home. Some days we just laugh and look at flowers; other times it's almost like school for me. I learn so much from our talks! Today, it was heartier than usual.

As we began our chat, she asked if there was a particular body of literature that I enjoyed, something, she said "that spoke to" me. For starters, it was her question that startled me. I opened my mouth to say something intelligent, but for the life of me couldn't think of one bit of literature that I knew deeply enough to say that it spoke to me.

She, unsurprisingly, seemed to have a million quotes and passages from all kinds of sources, each "speaking to her" in ways that had never occurred to me. From Ellul and Buber to Emerson and Einstein, she could quote them all.

I remember the first day we walked by Rubble Ridge. That's when I became aware of her fascination with literature. At first, we didn't even stop to sit on the thick slabs of granite; we just kept walking as she shared something written by a man of the past named Sertillanges. It was an interesting passage full of metaphor and laced with nuanced meaning; she likes it so much that under her influence, of course, I have since committed it to memory. It goes like this:

Friendship is an obstetric art; it draws out our richest and deepest resources; it unfolds the wings of our dreams and hidden indeterminate thoughts; it serves as a check on our judgments, tries out our new ideas, keeps up our ardor, and inflames our enthusiasm. 2

"The wings of our dreams . . ." what a statement. For days we had been talking about that passage, and with each morning walk more insight followed. Never before had the idea of friendship struck me in the way we have been discussing it, nor in the way we've been experiencing it. Prior to Russa, I thought of my friends as basically . . . people, just people that I know.

It's only recently that I have thought of friendship as something that draws out what is on the inside of a person. An obstetric art. Wow—what a picture. I can't imagine giving birth, but the idea that there is something (or someone!) that grows in a woman and will eventually have a life of its own—whew; it's just too much to contemplate. But the more I think about it, the more I am finally starting to get what Russa meant a few weeks ago when we had that blow up.

It's odd, but our very way of life at the Lab is the complete opposite of this idea. There is really no need to draw anything out when it's all there and accessible. I mean, social protocols make it impolite to hack into someone else's gray matter, and of course, there are more secure locks on our deep archives, but everyone I know plucks information from everyone they know—fairly indiscriminately. We really don't have to wait for an invitation. Waiting for nine months until a child is ready to be born, drawn out by nature—well, it's quite the opposite. And to liken this process to friendship. Hmmm. I can't stop thinking about it.

Our "best practices" training back in the Lab teaches us clearly that we are not to use this unfettered access to another's mind against them, but—well, only if it's a case of being more productive or—or if it's going to be used toward our own perfection. We live in pretty much an open society. We all avail ourselves of everything that's out there whether it's really necessary or not; and it's usually not. Everything we need to know for life and success is so easily accessed within our own very personal, customized information systems. It's extremely efficient—works like a charm, so, so . . . friendship, well, it's just not something that is necessary.

But that day, that first day walking with Roos, I did begin to think about it.

Since then it feels as though the inner workings of my mind are being mapped out in strange, indefinable ways, almost as though my neural pathways are bending or branching out in new directions. Truth be told that is quite likely exactly what's happening.

Still tethered to the clean lines and exacting formulations provided by the Principles of Global Citizenship, I find myself simultaneously pushing away from the emotional overload associated with friendship, but also pulling toward the messy, impractical bonds of love and friendship. What a strange dichotomy. Even stranger to admit!

Unfortunately, this morning my conversation with Russa took a different turn. One would think we might have a meeting of the minds, especially about friendship, but it wasn't to be.

It seems that Russa thinks people who don't live in a shared, community-style life live in stark, sheet metal walls that cramp and stifle—walls that keep us from each other, walls of utter loneliness—and she is determined to make me understand that "they weren't born for that!" Whew . . .

She must have said the same thing three different times. "We were born to share life with others, Lee. Anything less leads to delusion."

Well, it seemed simple enough to disagree, but unfortunately we moved a bit past that.

Today, as we trekked up past the rustic earth-shelters and quiet caverns of Stone Camp, past the worn-out trailers and meticulously-kept garden plots, and once again ventured up to Rubble Ridge, we found ourselves in somewhat unknown territory. Instead of sitting down, we continued walking up around the goat's grazing area toward the Friendly Wood, and came to the narrows—the mountain pass that looks over the exquisitely verdant hillside that leads to a gorgeous rushing stream. Beyond it is an area dense with trees and wildlife and no definitive path. I'm not sure how I let the danger of heading up this way without Viddie slip past me.

The buzzing swarm of distractions that engulfed me just a few months before is mostly gone, but more often than not, managing all the nuance of emotion continues to throw me off kilter. That must be it, because when we got up there the wind swept across my face and I felt a bit of a chill. I inched the sleeves of my toffee-colored sweater a bit further down my arms and thought about how the scene might look with my P/Z 1000 to enhance it. There, brightened by the density of my software I could just imagine this magnificent gorge encircling my entire system of walls. Surround scope. Beautiful. Mesmerizing. But no, there's no hope for that anymore, not unless I get back to Addison Avenue.

The breeze blew in my face again and felt as though it carried me with it all way to never-never land. Ha! Never-never land. Some things just stick with a girl, I guess. Ha ha ha. I remember always wanting to fly like Tinker bell and thinking one day when I was about eight that I might just open my window and do it! There it is—perhaps that's why creating my virtual vacation packages has always thrilled me so. It's that feeling of freedom—getting somewhere instantly, without any hassle and enjoying the free fall that sends you into a totally new situation in the blink of an eye—oh, how I do miss the adventure.

It's a mystery to me how some of the most obscure details of these ancient fairy tales stick with me and I don't even have access to my Deep Archives. It's probably because of Grand'Mere's frequent retelling of these stories that I do remember them at all. Her nightly recitation of the childhood classics has long stayed with me, and it seems the more I experience life outside the protective walls of our virtual travel business, more comes back to me.

"Lee? Knock, knock, are you there?"

Russa pretended to knock on my skull and drew me out of my reverie.

So, there we were, walking and talking, making our way through the lavish greenery and delicious blackberry bushes of the mountain and our conversation turned to my life back at

Addison Ave. It started because she asked me what I was dreaming about and then, no doubt, that led to questions about my life at the Lab. Then she asked me to explain in more detail how the features of my OLSM are truly a benefit to us. Before I describe our conversation, I must note that I find it unusually and wonderfully inspiring that both she and Viddie have questions about the stupendous worth of our Ongoing Life Sustaining Membrane, especially that they want to understand how the membrane is used with the P/Z to manage more effective and efficient communication with others. This gives me pause to smile. Even if they're the only ones who are interested in new-world tek, at least they are here and they are curious. They are not dinosaurs like my parents.

I told her flatly that it makes me sad to think about all the loss of my tek, but that I would take the time to unpack the story if she really wanted to hear. She really wanted to hear. :-) So we began with the P/Z. I explained that in order to properly access my own Deep Archive I needed the P/Z 1000. At first the network system was a clunky pocket top, but in the past decade we reworked the design to make it cleaner, smaller, and virtually invisible. Currently, it works transparently and is embedded on a person's left index finger, held in place by a non-sticky adhesive—a substance we call diamond dust. The emergence of this latest version revolutionized the micro-com business.

I explained, "The beauty of it is that its energy source is maintained so effectively. All we really need is clear mental focus, an embedded wireless router chip activated by the diamond dust (which is really an amalgam of several super cheap metals with just the smallest touch of genuine diamonds), and it fits easily and undetectably on top of one's fingernail. The dust makes the digi-flap glitter in the sunlight, but that's about the extent of its visibility. The coolest part of the device is that it allows us to access information from multiple sources at one time, as well as interact with ourselves and each other on ever-deepening levels of memory. Using it is the way I've been able to design truly interactive Xtreme vacation packages, tapping into the collective consciousness of the survivors of the Devastation, drawing images from their recollection and experience."

She was listening, but also hunting in the immediate vicinity for more blackberries, so I just continued and joined her in the picking spree.

"It's a sad, sad day when people have to go on their own cognitive steam, Roos. Working together on this mission is part of what has spurred on hope and inspired many in Post-D days, Roos. It gives me pride and much satisfaction to know that I am part of it—actually, in the inner circle of development. Life would be rather blasé and dim without the benefit of productivity, you know?"

Russa stood and popped a couple of the juicy berries into her mouth. When she spoke her teeth were stained with a tint of berries. "You are so dispiritingly melancholic at times, Leeya, do you know that?" Russa chuckled affectionately as she ribbed me with a bit of her unrelenting opinion wrapped up in a bluish smile. These are so sweet today—here, try some from the bush I just picked."

Mmmm. They were good. "Should we try and bring some back for Grand'Mere to make jam?" I wondered aloud.

Russa pulled open her pockets and I saw that they were brimming with berries. "I thought the same thing for a minute, but we'll need to come back with buckets. There's enough on these bushes to fill several buckets. Let's remember the spot and come back tomorrow. Maybe we'll even bring Libby with us to get a third bucket. She'll be thrilled."

I didn't care; she seemed interested enough in my invention today and I was going to take advantage of it. I quickly agreed, but couldn't resist plunging back into the conversation right where we left off. "So, Miss Sanguine, what do you want to talk about today? I may be moody and creative but you are always ready for some philosophical banter. How 'bout forgetting the blackberry bush over there and really thinking deeply at what I'm talking about. C'mon; I listen to you about all your literary greats and scholarly authors!"

She was game, and it was going alright for a while, but then she challenged me with my feelings about the Lab and made a statement that really gave me a gut punch.

It all started as I shared my observations about the differences in values and principles between ADMIN and FRANCO, and when I tried to explain to her the meaning of the Golden Triangle, she didn't get it. Not at all! It was clear that Russa wasn't grasping the ingenious beauty of the Golden Triangle of Belief, so I offered to recite the new world's mantra; perhaps it would spur on a bit of enthusiasm for the civilized world. She nodded, but listened with furrowed brow as I spoke:

"Surround yourself with things that make you happy.
Cast off all that makes you sad.
Surround yourself with just a few; too many people will weigh you down.
Submerge yourself in things that matter—your needs, your work, your life.
Make your own meaning.
Create your story on your walls.
Cast off the restraints of the past.
Live for pride.
Live for progress.
Live for perfection—Holla!"

When I finished, a deep sense of pride welled within me, knowing that I was part of the great new society and a member of the global citizenry; but instead of praise, she looked at me quizzically and shook her head in disapproving motion.

Wow. Russa's reaction was nothing that I expected. I knew I had to be careful not to offend her again because I sure didn't want to deal with another spat, or for that matter risk losing her friendship. But then she tore into me!

"Pride? This is a value? Lee, I'm sorry, but I don't get it; I don't get it at all. How could you be bamboozled into believing that there is any such thing as human perfection? Do you really think that perfection is attainable? Is it truly a goal that individual's strive for back there in that poor excuse for a government—what, what do you call it, ADMIN?"

The tiny hairs on the back of my neck seemed to stand up straight, but I contained my emotions, of course.

"Back there?" I raised my eyebrows and continued calmly. "Roos—my friend, back there is civilization. Back there is the real world. There is where hope exists and the promise of progress is alive."

I could feel my dander starting to get up, but keeping my emotions firmly in check, I paused for her response. Not being familiar with the sophistication of life outside of FRANCO, I thought I'd give her the benefit of the doubt, but it was there, at that precise moment that she freaked.

"Progress?" She countered. "Progress toward what? Where is it taking you, this Triangle of Belief? Is there any evidence that the human race is progressing, Leeya? From my vantage point it seems to me that we are on a trajectory moving backward trajectory, falling farther and farther away from all that is sane, human, and sublime."

Backward? I can't believe she said BACKWARD? Is she crazy? I know Russa's not actually insane, but I can't figure out why she got so upset. It's impossible that she really thinks the world is going backwards. I mean, they're all about belief here. Granted, I haven't heard explicitly about it, but on occasion it is clearly obvious that Belief drives them. They have faith . . . I guess in another way of life. Faith, that this FRANCO world is the right way to do things. I just don't get the level of disparagement and disdain I saw this morning in Russa. I tried to give it another shot.

"You know about the Hoffman-Bows Circle of Achievement, Russa, right? The Golden Triangle is simply part of the entire proposal for a better world. That's all—that's its strength. The principles structure that proposal. That's all.

They teach us to rely on ourselves, to believe in our strength and then to draw from it. Don't you understand that these brilliant ideas are the very things that brought our world out of chaos? They are the principles that sustain our society. Without them, we never would have been able to rebuild after the Devastation."

Russa responded to me with quiet, penetrating eyes. Calmer, she looked directly at me and picked up my hand. "Leeya, the 'Golden Triangle' once was something that we all believed in. It had nothing to do with progress or perfection, but the very foundations of old America. The Golden Triangle once was all about freedom, serving as a symbol of what is required in order to truly be free people."

"I'm not sure I understand what you're talking about, Russa. Are you saying that the Golden Triangle was something that once inspired you . . . all of you?"

She answered tentatively, repeating the words but going into a bit more depth.

"Leeya, once upon a time Freedom was the primary value in this beautiful land. In spite of the tumultuous 2030's, the country maintained freedom and liberty for all as the highest priority, and these social goods were firmly situated in open debate, discussion and public oratory. There were brutal disagreements about policy, etc., but everyone knew that if freedom was to be preserved, we needed to be able to disagree. It may seem counterintuitive, but it's important to give full flower to differing ideas. It takes many voices. Debate is good. Dialogue is important! Safety, security, comfort—back then, these were important, but not primary values."

Surely, it has been too long since my friend has experienced the reality of the city. She's been living under a rock for far too long. The only way to quell violence and avoid terrorism is to control the flow of information and make sure everyone is on the same page. I felt my eyes start to bulge as she barreled on.

"We lost our freedom in small increments, Leeya, and with it much virtue. You see, to truly walk in freedom requires virtue and faith. I remember reading an author named Guiness who really unpacked the idea so simply, explaining that these three feed into each other. Freedom requires virtue and virtue requires faith and faith demands freedom. They all go together; part of a cycle that propels a culture into stability and strength— true strength. But once digital communication morphed into digital fabrication and the rearranging of human genes became commonplace, the meaning of the Golden Triangle shifted. Instead of personal responsibility and a collective understanding of our social responsibility, people started to go off the deep end, printing everything and anything they desired. Manufacturing came to a screeching halt, jobs disappeared, there was no work, etc., Freedom does not work unless is it coupled with virtue and faith."

Russa's knee seemed to be bothering her so we stopped briefly to lean on a smooth granite ridge nearby. I scooted up a few feet above the ground and she just leaned against the rocks, but our conversation didn't miss a beat.

"Roos. You weren't even old enough to understand what was happening in the thirties. How do you know that wasn't just old fashioned propaganda?"

All I did was pose a question and our conversation went far south from there. Her words, stilted and measured, struck me as condescending. Her tone was wooden.

"Is your mind open at all, Emilya Hoffman-Bowes Brown? Do you think there is anything you might learn as a result of being plucked out of your environment and cast into this foreign field of FRANCO? I love you, my friend. I am learning from you, but you seem as closed to new ideas as the resort is to new customers."

As far as I can tell, this is the divide. I notice it every once in a while, speaking to Russa especially, but even with Viddie, there seems to be this undying nostalgia for the old days. Mother uses the words outright, but Russa clings to them as well even though she doesn't opine about them the way Marissa does.

I am tentative about sharing my patriotism because my own sense of pride is so important to me and I am tired of feeling like the odd one. Even back home, I kept it quiet because I didn't want my colleagues to be jealous or think I was too passionate about it. But Russa's response was . . . so degrading. She just doesn't understand. Nonetheless, she is my friend, and my only aim was to inspire her, so I tried once again, this time from a different angle.

"Russa, do you know the story of my mother's involvement in helping to create our new society? Do you know that she was the innovator? Her research was the primary tool used to help advance OLSM technology. Did you know that?"

She tapped her walking stick sharply on the ground as she shook her head with tiny movements. Then, she breathed deeply and after a tight-lipped pause, she returned my question with one of her own. "Of course I know, my friend, but did you know that this is not something your parents are proud of, that it is something they wish never happened?"

I gasped at her words. "Russa, how can you say that? The Circle of Achievement is in my family line. It has only been awarded twice since my Great Grandmother's time and it continues to set the bar for all achievement. It is the highest honor, recognizing innovation that not only uncovers genetic anomalies that prohibit life extension, but advances that strike at the core of the new world's foundational principles and highest values—*Superbia, progressio, absolutio.*"

Instead of showing awe, Russa chuckled. She laughed at me.

"Leeya, darling, I sincerely don't mean to be rude, but you should hear how silly that sounds. Do you really think that progress is a value? I mean, you just don't realize how paltry the principles are compared to life, liberty, and the pursuit of happiness. The American way is truth and justice, not the paltry abstraction of progress."

Every muscle in my body tensed up as I looked at her in disbelief.

She continued without pause. "Pursuing and lauding the Pride, Progress and Perfection of the human race is precisely what put the world in such dire standing. Lee—it wasn't the wreck of the land and elimination of most of the population of the earth that has had the most significant effect on us all. As horrible as the Devastation was, it's actually been the substitution of true values of—goodness, kindness, love, peace, and patience—all these, for false, flimsy ones. This has had the most deleterious effect on society, more than anything else. If you open your eyes you will see the effects of this switch everywhere, and it's especially so in regard to relationships. Think of it, really: The very hope of community is pretty much null and void when we seek perfection. People will never be perfect. We are all flawed."

"Roos, you can't be serious. These principles are the only thing that we have to cling to. So much is at stake. If we don't hang on to our values, where will we be; what will come of us? There will be anarchy and dissolution of civilization. We will be no better than the animals!"

At that, Russa politely changed the subject. She questioned me instead about mother's previous life at the lab and wondered aloud if Marissa told me everything.

"Everything?" I was quizzical.

"Yes." Russa rambled forward. "There is much that went on at the Lab and I just wondered if you've heard it all from Liam and Marissa or if any one of your people back there bothered to clue you in."

I knew she was angling about something, and her tone made me nervous, but I also knew that I could count on her to be truthful. At the moment I wasn't sure what she was inferring but I sensed her evasiveness meant there was something more. UGH . . . here we go again?

"If you're talking about the inordinate use of mother's neural mitosis code or the way the Lab used her womb in a research trial—yeah; I know all about that, Roos. I know it must have been awful. I know . . . I know. What those at the helm did was egregious and it pushed Liam and Marissa to the limit. But here's the thing—using her research to help the next generation sequester our brain's emotional headquarters is nothing new. The Lab had been teaching the military to quash their emotions for decades prior so that it might help them endure torture in enemy camps. Previously, it had been a military anti-terror strategy. The OLSM fix just made all that a bit easier and ADMIN spread it across the entire population—to help us all deal with the immense emotional overload of the nuclear holocaust."

My highly opinionated friend glanced down at her hands and didn't respond immediately. By now our walk had taken us back around toward Stone Camp. I'm not sure if it was more physically or emotionally draining but the walk was wearing us out, so we took a short rest on the jagged slabs of granite that jutted out from the earth. Russa's feet dangled from the second tier of a part of the rock formation that looked like a ladder, while I sat just one level higher than her. She fiddled with a purple bloom that was growing in-between the rocks. I pressed her to continue.

"Is that what you mean by 'everything,' Roos?"

She didn't look up, but silently nodded and swallowed hard.

"Russa—you've got something to say, don't you? If so, please say it. You've got to know that by this time, I can take it."

Haltingly, the words began to tumble out of her mouth. "You know they were hoping the research they were doing would lead to breakthroughs in healing for the new brain cancers and the many other diseases that developed as a direct result of the Devastation, but. . . . Well, did you know that the Lab tricked your parents into giving over the codes that enabled them to access your OLSM?"

"Tricked them?" my reply was quick. "I hadn't heard that part of the story. What do you mean, tricked them?"

Her reply was parsed in uneasy syllables.

"She . . . uh . . . Marissa used a particle accelerator, Lee . . . to . . . uh . . . expand the work of your great-grandmother."

I climbed down from my place on the ridge and sat next to her. "I know about the accelerator, Roos. That's the point from which my own research and development embarked. Without the particle accelerator I would never have been able to build the P/Z. What are you talking about . . . ?"

"Leeya. Listen to me." Russa grabbed both of my forearms and looked at me squarely. "When Marissa first used the accelerator a perturbation somewhere in the system created a neural anomalism—a condition she couldn't control; she wrote it out of the code and created systemic locks that would prohibit any further cognitive brain research to be done using the particle accelerator. She thought it was too risky."

"But this is fine. I mean, my mother did what was right. We never use the accelerator in communication. It's part of policy. She did well, so I don't think. . ."

"Lee, wait. Listen. This is the terrible tragedy of Liam and Marisa. Her knowledge and caution were used massively against her. In spite of all their efforts for privacy protection and the ethical use of her research findings; in spite of the extreme measures she took to develop safe, ethical practices in the Lab; in spite of all the precautions, uh, it . . . uh . . . ."

"Spit it out, Russa! Please. I am sick of secrets and if you don't tell me exactly what you're trying to tell me immediately I will, I will just. . ."

"Your hippocampus, Leeya. It's different. The Lab used your brain membrane to access the locked codes, in vitro. They messed with your embryonic neural cells before implanting your mother. Lee, they used you against your parents for their own purposes. Your parents didn't discover this until late in her pregnancy, and the only thing they could have done to prohibit the misuse of that information was . . . well, was, a late-term abortion."

She looked at me with those penetrating eyes of hers and said, "ADMIN knew that your parents would not compromise their only child's life, which is precisely why they put them in the unconscionable position of having to choose between your life or allowing the rest of society to be enslaved by their cognitive encroachments. They wouldn't consider aborting you or doing anything to hamper your development, so they had to endure ADMIN's strangulating manipulation and did so for several years so that you could have a chance at a normal life. It was outright criminal what the Lab did to them."

I gasped again at her outrage and the revelation of this layer of pain. "Russa! How do you know all this? What on earth do you mean by manipulation? Have my parents told you all of this?"

"Yes, yes! And Grand'Mere has corroborated it completely. You'll have to discuss the details with Marissa and Liam—you need to know! Lee, your parents are heroes. Without flinching they continued raging against ADMIN trying to effectuate change. They worked for justice and truth, but faced a fusillade of lies and propaganda every day until they left to help build FRANCO. They were forced to live with the knowledge that they were not only responsible for advancing research in the field, they were party to an unethical use of the findings in population control.

I looked at her quizzically. "Roos. What are you getting at? How does their research in any way affect the population? And me . . . personally? I don't see the connection. She's a particle physicist. He's a math genius. Mother's work dealt primarily with superconducting magnets and smashing atoms to rearrange energy. In the end, they helped the world, but one small, part of it went bad. The Lab betrayed my parents' trust and went ahead and messed with me in vitro, but what does it have to do with their greater contribution to the universe? Look—just look at my life: it set me up for excellence and productivity at a much younger age. Look at me! What's the problem here? Why the secret?"

Russa blinked and offered a strangely calm, half-smile, but didn't say anything. I was still fired up and thought I'd continue on my anti-worrying campaign. She was really beginning to sound like an alarmist.

"Roos, we can't guarantee people will always do the right thing. ADMIN made a mistake. Can we leave it at that? And Russa—Strength, my part in the whole thing is really rather insignificant. I'd rather just let it go, okay?"

She took my hand.

"My friend, Marissa's particle acceleration research allowed them to create a break between the neurotransmitters that produce serotonin and dopamine, introducing an optimal climate for procreation. You know about these brain chemicals much better than I do. But now you need to know one other thing that I thought would have been an early conversation between you and your parents, but I see now that it was never discussed."

"What. . . what is it, Roos? I can't imagine that there's some deep, dark issue that I'm not privy to."

"The thing is this, Lee. You see . . . the Lab took Marissa's findings and used it to reroute some of the neuro-transmitters inside your brain while you were still in her womb; they created an environment that . . . well, it's an environment that malfunctions in one particular area of your physiology."

I blinked, still not quite sure what she was saying. Then the question tumbled out of my mouth almost as if I was speaking without the choice of remaining silent. "And that area?"

Russa swallowed hard again and started chewing her lower lip. "It's the area of the brain that connects with your reproductive hormones, Lee. You . . . you won't; what I mean is: if you ever hoped to have children, um . . . that will not be possible."

Dead silence ensued.

Chapter 12

Day 93—The Clouds

A few days have passed and I've tried to process what Russa told me.

Bottom line: I never thought I'd have children anyway. It's all in the past and there's nothing I can do about it, but I know that eventually I'll want to talk about this with Marissa. Right now, however, I can't even imagine talking with her. The entire episode leading up to their departure from the Lab is still so incomprehensible and unsettling—I've just decided to put off dealing with it for the time being. Russa and I haven't even discussed it since then.

Our morning walk was short today. Russa needed to set up her canning project with Fiorella—the plums are all ripening at once—so I spent the most of the morning through noon taking in the sights and sounds of the deeply greening earth by myself. It's still hard to believe that all this bounty is free and not dangerous.

When I got back to Stone Camp everyone was busily working on their own projects and I decided to take even more time to just hang around and give myself to the beauty of the day. This is as foreign to me as the thought of living on Jupiter, but I'm finding the leisurely time to think about everything that has happened is somewhat helpful. Part of me feels lame, like an unproductive wonk whose been set out to pasture, but frankly, another part feels quite good to lull around a bit.

Clearly, something significant has changed inside me. Somehow I am coming to enjoy the dubiously ennobling privilege of being Emilya Hoffman-Bowes Brown, the sought after. The lost, now found. The wearer of the amethyst ring. The one they've been waiting for.

I no longer feel that my life is nothing more than a five foot, seven inch frame weighing one hundred twenty pounds, and loaded up with a super-brain that can help save the world from boredom. There is something different about me these last few weeks, and although I'm not sure what it is, it's clear that the ideas at FRANCO are no longer a jumble of disconnected dots, completely alien and riddled with fault. I am starting to see that something more than "connection" is an essential element in the complex mix of what it means to be human.

So much of what I'm learning comes from Russa, not primarily through what she says, but just mostly by watching and observing her, and by, well—just being a part of everything that's going on here.

Yes, it's definitely changing me. The early, bewildering days of finding myself here in a lifestyle of such primitive means and with people whom the world seems to have forgotten, well, those days are over. The anxiety and annoyance seem to be fading and, I don't know, I'm not sure any more about when I'll return to Addison Avenue. Perhaps I'll stay just a bit longer. It's going to be more difficult to leave then I thought.

Not sure why I come back so often to the subject of friendship when I settle down to write, but it seems like I can hardly help it; I am so grateful for these friendships. They're so . . . real—yes, real; they don't keep the truth from me, but are honest even when it's not convenient. Russa, Fiorella—all of them—they are teaching me how to better handle the rough stuff—the things that are just absolutely inexplicable; the emotional stuff; the stuff I still don't get.

What a contrast to my last encounters with Zeejay and Jude. I thought they visited my flat last winter to see how I was doing and maybe talk a bit about the latest things happening at the LAB, but no. Not at all. It almost seemed they were doing

Allesandro's bidding and mildly threatening me. When they left I felt more confused than ever. And Paty—he didn't even look up at me the last time I stopped into the department. Some faithful assistant he is! I don't think I put these ideas together until seeing the opposite in action. Relating to everybody here makes me feel like maybe I do have a place at FRANCO.

Just as much as with friends, perhaps the most significant way I am learning is by observing and spending time with Belevedere. After chores this morning he came around and found me on my favorite flat rock at Rubble Ridge and we had the longest talk—about the clouds! The funny thing is, he didn't want to talk about the different categories of clouds, or about the density and difference between them, nor about why they are important in sustaining the earth's climate. He wanted to twirl me around underneath them! What a clown, this man. Who would ever have known that this dashing, muscular, he-man-of-a-person, could be so childlike; or, that I could possibly find his childlike behavior some so tirelessly delightful?

We laughed and laughed and spoke of the inexplicable beauty of the canopy of clouds under which we danced. Venturing a bit west of the Ridge, we came upon a quiet expanse where the clearing almost seemed like it was once a homestead, but it no longer had even a remnant of a building. It was a lovely day, the bluest of blue skies and a dazzling display of puffy white cumulus clouds. There we staked our claim to this woodless acreage and he named it "Cloudland."

"Yeah—that's what we're calling it and we're not telling anybody, clear? It's our own little sphere of reality, right Emi?"

I shot him a look of uncertainty, mostly because I couldn't believe he would suggest such a lovely idea, but also mixed with incredulity at my own ability to accept such silliness.

"C'mon," he said as he twirled me around, "Why can't we create our own little world? Just you and me; we'll dance under the stars and talk and laugh 'til the cows come home."

"Cows?"

He spoke with such playful intention, and in spite of his idealism I couldn't help but play along and promised to call it Cloudland, too.

As I ponder our time together today I am just overtaken by the beauty I find in this place. It's this crazy, big-sky landscape that is just so . . . so dazzling. Here, in the low mountains of eastern Pennsylvania I have become literally enthralled in the ways these white, puffy spheres waft across the sky and hang like globes between the peaks. Their evanescence is remarkable, morphing into faces and animals one moment and the next they are trees or flowers floating across the blue. Some of them are so close I actually walk through them. It's amazing—as if I'd never seen a cloud before—uhhh; like I have new eyes.

But it's not just the beauty of Viddie's handsome face or the magnificent blueness of the mid-summer sky; I am quite in awe of these inexplicable feelings. Viddie and I are experiencing a beauty in our relationship that I cannot account for—something so earthy and delicious it's hard to bring myself to admit that we have no such comparable thing back home. Yet, with the way it's going, I can't help wondering why he has not tried to get more physical. He says I'm the woman he's always dreamed of; well, if that's true, why isn't it progressing? There was that one delectable kiss back at the ridge last week and those few kisses on my forehead weeks before, some hand-holding, a few hugs, but now—what? Nothing, for days. I do hope I'm not misreading him.

Is it my inexorable fate to be single my entire life?

The dancing, the clouds, "our stake in the world, UGGGH—what does all of this mean?!?!?

A thick layer of pine needles covered the ground as we made our way beyond Cloudland into the woods. As we did, some of the branches were in my way and as I tried to push through them I got a little scratched up. I'm noticing a few slice-like red marks on my left shoulder and neck. Nature is dangerous.

Once we got through the wood into the clearing, we stopped along a small grassy knoll to rest. Viddie took the small pouch of sweetened, toasted oats, walnuts, and dried grapes out of his satchel. We munched for a while and took a short break before we set out again.

When we continued back into the woods we came upon a lovely spectacle—two rows of trees that grew into each other at the top, their upper branches forming an arch. They formed a green canopy over a path. As we walked through them it seemed as though we were entering a regal, new country.

Then, out of nowhere, Viddie scooped me up and carried me through the archway, shouting out to the wind and whatever animal life that might be within earshot: "Hear ye, hear ye—the noble princess Emilya is now ready to grace this foreign land with her presence. Go, and ye and prepare her castle."

I laughed and laughed, and when he put me down I chased him through the trees until we fell over each other onto a thick bed of pine needles. I didn't even feel silly.

He's got me.

The guy's got me, hook, line and sinker.

(Hook, line, and sinker? Ugh. Where did that come from? Now I'm talking like them! What does that mean, anyway? I'll have to ask L.J; He knows everything).

Several shades of green threaded through the thick underbrush as we settled onto the thin woolen blanket Viddie stashed in his backpack. It was super cozy. I couldn't believe we ventured so far past the tree line.

The grove of tall pines beyond the lake was the farthest I had ever traversed into the woods, but there's something about being with him makes me feel braver than I really am. Today, he held me close to him again and looked into my eyes and said something in Italian that sounded ravishing.

At first I thought he was trying to teach me his family's language of origin, but then I remembered how much Belvedere Florencia loves to tease.

Try as I might to get it out of him, he's not letting me in on much of the meaning, and in the meantime, had a good go at teasing me to death. Cupping my face in his hands he shook his head as if in disbelief and repeated the words,"*tu sei la mia donna dei sogni.*"

Twice he repeated the phrase; each time chuckling a little bit more because I couldn't translate. Exasperated, I only recognized one word, so the third time he said it I stood up on my knees and demanded, "Who's Donna?"

With that, he roared, laughing until there were tears in his eyes.

I stood akimbo, waiting for an answer, my head held high, my very dignity at stake, and I tried not to smile. "Okay big guy, so you think this is very funny, I can see that. Keeping me in the dark again, eh? This is now the second time you are torturing me through a lesson in Italian and if you continue to hold out on me I swear. . I swear, I will revert to computer language and speak to you only in numeric code!

I must have started to pout because he quickly caught his breath and looked at me squarely, and said. "Okay Emi-girl, I'll give you a really big hint: Read my eyes and you will know what I am trying to say."

Ah, those eyes. They do speak! At this point I was melting all over the place, and the emo-overload seems to be happening more and more often. If I'm not careful this man will own my every thought. I keep thinking my feelings are as strong as they can get, but each time it seems we go another level deeper and I find myself more and more drenched in this man's whole personality.

I really do want to know what those Italian words mean, but I dare not investigate. If I ask Grand'Mere or Fiorella . . . what if it's something personal? Well, it's definitely very private. Hmmm. I may just have to learn the language!

An unexpected afternoon fog moved in so we wrapped up our picnic foods and used the blanket to keep us warm. We snuggled close and enjoyed a few minutes of quiet reflection before packing up and heading back.

As I write about the day I continue to savor each moment. I wish I could make a print of each one and store it all in my D.A. Without my tek these moments are just fading memories, evaporating with the morning dew. Never before have I experienced such depth of feeling; it's truly indescribable, and what it's doing to me has much deeper implications. I have so much to think about now, so much to consider. My feelings for Viddie have made me increasingly more comfortable with being here. And, the funny thing is—I am finding that as I grow more comfortable with being at FRANCO I find myself looking upon all its entangled alliances with quite a bit more charity than I had the first few weeks. The people who populate this small community are all by and large very normal human beings, but not one of them is average and strangely, not a one is a world citizen.

I keep noticing things that I've never noticed before, too; not just about the people here, but things like the birds and the squirrels and—cloudland, :-) for instance. It's strange, I know, but a little less strange with each passing day.

Perhaps it's odd to notice the clouds, but maybe not. Sometimes when I sit by the brook and watch them waft by I wonder if they look the same from my flat. It's almost as if I could get lost in their billowy softness; they look so different from this vantage point. I know better than to think the clouds actually change. It must be me. I am changing. I am changing so much.

Chapter 13

Day 99—The Desire

Aurorean light spilled splendidly through the open space where there once was a window in cabin number 707 of the old resort. The coziness of the small fire Viddie built in the room's dilapidated hearth kept us warm for hours. Or, maybe it was because I never moved from his embrace.

We didn't plan on spending the night together and the way it worked out surprised us both. After an early dinner of venison stew at Stone Camp, Viddie suggested we take a walk to gather from the new supply of chamomile flowers we found for his mother's tea obsession. We still had a couple hours of daylight to enjoy, so he packed a collapsible container to carry the flowers back and a snack for us, and we were off.

Forty-five minutes later that patch of chamomile was nowhere to be found. He swore it was just east of the Ridge, but we couldn't find it so we kept walking until with got to the old resort. By that time I was exhausted so we scouted around and found one of the smaller cottages that was largely intact.

The otherwise balmy July air turned a bit colder when the sun went down and the mountainous cool of the evening might have even been uncomfortable had he not brought the blanket along. Instead, it was toasty and so cozy. In fact, we might have been too cozy because somehow, in the midst of our marathon discussion about the problems of the universe and idiosyncrasies of each personality present in FRANCO, our words faded into the night and sleep overtook.

When we awoke there were only embers in the pit and the sun was still hours from rising. A chill filled the mountain air; we got up on our elbows and looked around.

A tiny smile began to curl upward around Viddie's cheeks. He ducked down below the blanket and began to tickle me until I could no longer resist. Roaring with laughter I could hardly breathe.

We quickly bundled up and set out on the two-mile trek back to Stone Camp. When we arrived, a quiet, pinkish hue was rising above the treetops. It probably wasn't less than 50 degrees but I felt a bitter cold right to my bones. Where was the sun when you needed it?

He walked me to Grand'Mere's without a word and waited until I tiptoed into her earth-shelter. Thankfully, my little straw bed and duck-down comforter were waiting.

So was Grand'Mere.

Chapter 14

Day 102—The Vacuum

"She's adorable, but I'm not sure why she's always so eager to be around me. Sometimes I turn around and she's just standing there, Vid, as if she's following me."

My annoyance meter was once again cranked up. Liberty, sweet as she was, would not leave us alone.

I've stopped trying to sequester my emotions from my language and cognition center. Without my tek, all the effort is to no avail.

Viddie scrunched his nose as he stretched his arms. His bulging biceps were nicely tanned and I couldn't help noticing them in the sleeveless t-shirt he was wearing.

"Emi, do you know how long it's been since someone new has come to FRANCO? I'm sure she is just being an inquisitive, curious kid."

"Do you think that's all it is, Vid? Her curiosity? What's it been, three months? I'm not so new anymore."

"Actually," it's probably that she looks up to you, too. In fact, I'm sure that's part of it. She wants to be like you, Emi— Yeah, I'll betcha that's it. I mean, look at this long silky nut-colored hair, these dazzling hazel eyes sparkling like sunlit gems on Grand Lake in the morning."

"Oh my, my . . . aren't you quite the poet this morning. Gems on Grand Lake, eh? That's pretty funny, Vid!"

"I'm not trying to be funny, love. I look at you and think in poetry. Do you know the work of Whitman? "

"Walt Whitman? Uh, why, yes, I do; a little. All those sappy old poets from the 19th and twentieth centuries were uploaded into my early education files when I was seven. I detested memorizing them, but Grand'Mere insisted."

"Oh really? So you probably know that he wrote this little couplet: 'What is that you express in your eyes? It seems to me more than all the words I have read in my life.'"

Oh my Strength. He is such a clown. "You are funny, Mr. Florencia. So funny."

"Funny, eh? I don't think so. I couldn't be more serious. And as far as Libby goes, I'm telling you, she wants to be just like you when she grows up. Just look at her eyes the next time you're speaking with her. She stares so deeply at you; it's as if she wants to get inside your head and memorize every detail of your incredibly wonderful personality."

"Stop. Enough! You are just too much, Viddie Florencia. Stop teasing me." He pulled me close and feigned sadness. "What? Teasing you? No way. You know it's true because I haven't been able to take my eyes off you since the moment you set foot in this camp, and you know it. Come here."

We walked back to Stone Camp hand-in-hand, looking forward to the Friday night shout-out. It's nice to have a common area to gather. No appointments need to be made. Whoever is there is there. Whoever isn't, is fine wherever they are. No pressure, no problem; it's just a nice feature of this little life here up in the mountains. While it's still something I'm getting used to, there's much to like about sharing the same space together. Oh—and the value of hugs; who knew? From the gruffy, cumbersome arms of Harold-in-the-camper and little Libby's slender little-girl arms to Marissa's bear hugs and Liam's lingering pat-pat-pat, I find myself enjoying the human touch and the affection it brings.

Once back at FRANCO, there were already a few friendly faces gathered at Stone Camp. When Viddie and I arrived it made eight of us—and unexpectedly, I found myself sharing some of the weirdness of my experiences back at Addison Avenue. Up till now I've kept most of my confusion and chaos private, only sharing bits and scraps with Viddie or Roos. I don't know what got into me, but today I told them all about the vacuum.

It all started quite innocently and came on the heels of Fiorella's story about some of the most frightening moments of her journey from her home port town just outside of Sorrento to New York City harbor. She was waxing poetic about her verdant, sea-bound homeland, the high cliffs overlooking the water, and the majesty of the countryside, and winced as she recalled the harrowing night she and her family left their home just prior to the Devastation.

Prior to their vacation they were living in a small village on the Amalfi coast called Positano, one of the most gorgeous stretches of coastline on the Italian peninsula. Fiorella pines for it at times, but she knows that the quaint, colorful shops and enchanting town square no longer exist. It seems that the big family vacation they planned just returned to port. It was as they disembarked from the cruise liner that the first explosions began. Fiorella started to cry when she began explaining what they saw and heard in those first few moments. Within minutes the captain hurried them all back on ship, fueled up, and spent the next the seven days crossing the Atlantic in hopes to find refuge in New York.

I think I must have gotten a bit lost in the simultaneous tragedy and loveliness of her description because little Liberty picked up on my wordless horror and aimed her question directly toward me. She point-blanked me asking if there was anything super scary like that for me. It definitely caught me off guard.

At that precise moment I felt so safe next to Viddie and so unencumbered that all I could think about was how to avoid revealing the fear I deal with daily about getting stuck on this mountain forever and never seeing my home again. That little piece of information would never do, so instead of the truth I blurted out the story of the devilish sound that used to hound me.

I told them all about its harrowing vacuum-like whirr and the way it hawked me for the better part of this last year, and even though it had been some time since I felt it's monstrous presence, once in a while I get a sense of its pending rumble. I told them that my colleagues at the Lab thought I was mad and explained how they pressured me to take a furlough from work.

Everyone seemed genuinely interested my story and several had something to say. Dr. Salingwa took me aside later to say that there are numerous psychological anomalies that could be at the root of the vacuum's whirr. He was sure to tell me that psychology is not his primary area of expertise, but that he did have training in the subject in his thirties, and he offered to talk more with me about it if I so desired. That was the first real conversation I've had with the man; he seems nice. Perhaps I'll take him up on it.

Marissa glanced at me with a sheepish expression but surprisingly did not comment.

Viddie's father, Carlos, who is normally very quiet, mentioned that some of the men he knew from his youthful days in the military described similar problems. Fiorella, sitting by his side, motioned to me and said something about coming to her place for a visit with scones and tea.

I felt a little too exposed, but it was better than letting everyone in on my real feelings. If they knew that getting home occupied so much of my thought life, I dare say they'd all be on my case night and day.

Although it has been mostly at bay these last months, I can't help but wonder why the vacuous machine-like sound ever started in the first place, where it came from, and why it has since subsided. The thought occurred to me that perhaps I simply had an excess of the norepinepherine neurotransmitter sloshing around in the baso-lateral area of my brain. Brain chemicals can create malfunctions of all sorts. I don't know. I could see ADMIN'S point; maybe it all was in my head. If it was outside my brain, why couldn't anyone else hear it?

The sloping grasses of eastern PA courted my attention as I shared the vagaries of my story and my heart wandered home even as I spoke convincingly of the harrowing vacuum. My eyes drifted to the loveliness of the magnificent blue larkspur that dots the craggy mountainous rock formation a short distance from Stone Camp. Spurting up from the lavish green hills, they looked like sentinels waiting for orders. I was there, but somehow, I was not.

Chapter 15

Day 103—The Talk

"Hello, Hello in there?"

A lilting, upbeat voice beckoned me and I sat up, startled. It was Marissa knocking on Grand'Mere's cutting board—the one that hung on the wall rack inside her hearth room. Marissa, who could clearly see that I was sitting on my mat busily writing in the tiny alcove of Grand'Mere's inmost cavern, was pretending to inquire whether or not I was there. <<sigh>> We are so un-alike. As usual, her gestures are often more symbolic than actual, but I've come to expect that of Marissa, for there she was, once again making a grand entrance to my space for whatever reason it was that brought her here today.

She sat at the edge of my mat and sighed. I couldn't help picturing us sitting in a London café as she spoke. Everything was brilliant and lovely.

"My darling, Emilya. What you said last night. I wonder if we might have a chat about it. Won't you take a short break from all that journaling please?"

"That's rather blunt, mother. Can it wait; I'm right in the middle of a sentence. Yesterday was a monumental day."

Marissa reached out her hand to me as if to say, "no it can't," so I begrudgingly put my art book down and let her help me to my feet. Her long brown hair still had a luster that many people her age have long since lost. Her earrings—opaque, aqua-colored stones hanging from silver hoops—framed her oval face nicely. Mother always wore earrings. Everyday a different style.

She suggested we go for a walk in the sunshine: "The day is just lovely," she said.

Oh mother.

L.J. tipped his hat as we past him strumming his guitar at the center stump in Stone Camp. He winked at me with his good eye. Marissa was already chirping away. Something about setting things right once and for all.

"Darling, would you be so kind as to tell me why you are keeping your distance? Your father and I devised an immensely complicated plan to help you make your way here to us, and now you are here, but it's been more than three months and frankly, my daughter dear, you are not letting us in to your heart. Please tell me what I can do to change that."

Her words sounded blunt, honest, and raw, but I simply could not accept their authenticity. I answered with a diversion: "I thought you said you wanted to talk with me about last night."

"Oh, yes. The vacuum. Brilliant. Yes, I want to talk with you about that. I believe I know what that beastly sound is all about, but first we really must get to the bottom of these unresolved concerns. Please answer my question, would you darling?"

I stopped short and shook my head with quiet incredulity. Running my feet over the pebbles on the dusty mountain path, I considered telling her how I really felt. I so much wanted to tear into her with all of my questions and really just blurt out the one piece of confusion that keeps me from embracing her fully. Mother, mother, how could you leave me? But no. I don't want to know the answer. To be true, there isn't really any answer that would satisfy me. I was speechless. She was still waiting.

"Leeya—my beautiful girl—I fear all this aggro is much ado about nothing. I've told you thrice and again, we had little choice. I've recounted the story, over and over. Grand'Mere has told you the truth, as well. Could you possibly want to hear the details again and again? Darling, I have asked your forgiveness; I've wept; I've groveled . . . Leeya, why will you not see it? You were not the only one devastated by our departure!"

"Mother! Stop. Stop it right now. I don't understand your devastation; all I know is that you lied to me. You left ME; I did not leave you! And now you're calling it 'nothing?' Please, please stop with the questions. Just let it be."

We were far into the woods, in both the heavily treed landscape surrounding Stone Camp and the backwater acreage of our uncharted emotions. She went wild.

"It's rubbish, pure rubbish, Leeya . . . I love you; your father loves you more than life itself, and I have been driven to the brink of my sanity just to make a way for you to be safe and have a chance at a normal life."

Things started to break down in both our hearts at that precise moment. I'm not quite sure what it was that prompted me to let my guard down, but Mother started to sob and I gestured toward her. I looked at her, for the first time ready to try and understand. When she calmed down, her words were warmer, slower, and broken up by rocky, tumultuous breaths.

"I have told you that ADMIN'S treatment of our family was far worse than dodgy and that their indiscriminate behavior toward our work not only put you in harm's way, but worked to create an entirely alternative ethos in this grand country. We saw it coming. We tried to stop it. We were ignored, then outlawed, and threatened. I was afraid. I was lost. What if they hurt you or stole you or . . . worse. Oh, I could never explain the depths of my heart to you dear daughter, and our reasoning may never make sense, but I beg you—I beg you, truly—please forgive me!"

My heart felt like it was exploding in a million tiny pieces, but for the first time it seemed like a beautiful mosaic might just be possible.

Mother and I walked back to camp with our wounds dressed and at last the hope of healing filled the air.

Chapter 16

Day 110—The Pondering

It's Saturday morning and it's a slow go here at Franco, incredibly slower than life at the Lab, but on the whole, I think I am adjusting well.

The hunger for my office and P/Z is not as prominent these days and I've not thought about my cozy bed back home for at least a week. Although I have not stopped questioning, a day doesn't go by when I don't at least ponder my life at Addison Avenue, the Lab, and wondering still if they are tracking my steps or have created some sort of virtual environment that looks like . . . this mountainous terrain. Sure, some days I hanker for them, but mostly I just sit and think about the complexity of life outside the walls. In the midst of the beauty, there is so much dysfunction. The digital symbiosis I have experienced since the day I was born has not died quietly.

More often than I let on, I find myself confused, thinking about my tools as part of who I am, and then questioning my identity because my tools are gone. But life without my PZ/1000 isn't all that bad. In fact, it's quite a bit better than I initially thought it would be. I actually feel content most days. It's a strange kind of contentment, not without curiosity or conundrum, but contentment nonetheless. What I have noticed is that the connection I share with this community is not just stronger or deeper than that which I experienced back home. No. There's more, and it's hard to put my finger on exactly what that more actually means. Suffice it to say, there is a qualitative difference in relationships. Back in the days of Travelite Global and my life within the walls I could not even conceive of spending the kind of time I presently spend listening to others and . . . especially disclosing my thoughts the way I have begun to do. In fact, so much about me has changed I almost feel as though I am a completely different person.

Here there are no walls or screens to mediate our thoughts, no images toggling in the space between us, no icons to use as markers of space and time—just eyeball-to-eyeball, voice-to-voice, person-to-person. That's the most significant change, I think. There's nothing to hide behind, no way to edit my responses, so, it's . . . well, it's sort of raw and scary. Everyone around me picks up immediately on my mood; there's no way to hide what I'm feeling. Well, fact is, I still do hide some things. They can't hack my D.A., or my own secret scenarios, that's for sure. I have given this much thought, but still do not have it completely clear. Whatever the reasons, our conversations are much deeper here in FRANCO than anything I had with anyone at the Lab.

Yet, as I anticipate another morning in the garden, picking the weeds and tending to the burgeoning bean plants, I cannot help but to ponder the life I left behind at the Lab. What new upgrades are being implemented at TGA? Is Jude working happily with a new director? Has Paty been promoted? I sure don't miss the intrigue and confusion, but I do wonder what has happened to my life there. Is Rolly still at his post? How about Paty, Charm, and Zeej? Are they still working on exercise eleven in the 8000 series? They must have completed it by now. I hope the ski simulation for the Great Gorge package is flawless. Have they replaced my marker icon? Have my passwords been changed? Are my walls still live? There are just way more questions than I can handle at the moment.

Nearly four months have passed in FRANCO, and for all the lack of strategic planning the community thrives and is teaming with life. There is life in the streams, life in the sky, the trees, and the hearts of its residents; it's all here. By no means is it what I would call a well-oiled organization, but everything works in a sort of symbiotic way, everyone with the other. The kind of built-in mutuality that is here is evident in everything they do, but—it's funny—I never hear it being discussed. Everyone knows that the community they experience is not possible without the participation of every individual and the very intentional piece they each bring, so everyone brings something, every day.

All in all, they continue to fascinate me. The more I get to know them the more I see that they all seem to reflect so easily on whatever conversation or event is happening. Even when their discomfort is obvious; they talk! It's like they just ebb and flow like the little waves on the lake, happily turning back and forth on each other in a pattern that seems so natural and unplanned. Viddie tells me they're just being conversational—it's natural! Yeah, right. Maybe for you, Viddie Florencia, but it doesn't seem terribly natural to me. Every conversation is a stretch.

In any case, I find this conversational dynamic rather amazing. It really does seem to happen as naturally as breathing for them. They'll strike up a conversation—about nothing. No matter where they are or what's going on, a conversation seems as desirable and important as eating. I definitely don't have that down yet, and I'm not sure if I ever will; it's a lot to get used to.

This carries over to everything here—the cooking, preparing the fields, hunting, mending, everything—and is especially true in regard to the friendships. Take, for instance, the development of friendship between me and Roos.

When I first started walking with her the readiness of her warm smile and open heart was immediately evident. Admittedly though, it took me a while to see that she wanted the same kind of talking from me that she was offering, but now that I understand a bit more about the importance of mutuality, our friendship seems much more like a sisterhood. And for all the riffs we've experienced in these last few months, what I think of most when her face comes to mind is the joy . . . the sheer joy of just laughing and walking and—I don't know—sharing life together.

She is the one who showed up that first day when Earl first brought me to the mountain; she—with a faded red kerchief tied around three round, flakey scones—sat down, spread the cloth over the rock we use as a makeshift table, and invited Grand'Mere and I to partake.

My head was a bit in a fog that day and I could hardly track what was happening, but—well—I know that I liked her immediately.

Then, as our walks became more regular I learned that this Devastation Day orphan and I have quite a bit in common. We discovered that we are more like each other than not; me, with my lost parents and her, with the very sad loss of her own family.

I find it terribly intriguing that she and Alton were originally from FRANCO's sister community in Switzerland; they came to America shortly before air travel stopped. She was just a toddler at the time, and Alton, her cousin, was five when their families were visiting with their longtime friends—the Florencias. They were vacationing along the Mediterranean and hurried back to sea once the terror started. It wasn't until the second conflagration that their parents died, which is why Carlos and Fiorella stepped in to care for them.

So many people died that year. Most of the 6 billion that populated the earth were just gone; vaporized. The bulk of those who survived live on a skinny ribbon of coastal land along the north American and Canadian borders, but the survivors also include a few million in western Europe, also along the coast.

When Fiorella and Carlos settled in Philadelphia they kept Alton and Russa safe by spending nearly three weeks in a bunker underneath one of their cousin's homes just outside the city. My parents, living in New Jersey at the time were with

Grand'Mere in the Lab's secure underground facility where the original R&D department was housed. Of course, air travel came to a striking halt, but at the time no one imagined it would never resume.

So, Roos and Alton essentially grew up together, which is why they consider each other more as brother and sister than cousins.

After the Florencia's settled into life in the United States they got stuck on this side of the globe. It was unintended, and quite unfortunate to be separated from everyone and everything they knew, but at least they had Russa and Alton. Years later when their children were born Russa changed diapers, helped feed them, and became like an aunt to both Viddie and Alessa. It's still a touchy subject for her, but one of these days I'm going to get up the courage to ask Roos if she remembers anything more about her parents.

In the meantime, I'm learning more about L.J.'s history, too.

At least once a day or so I find myself wandering toward his favorite sitting spot, over there between Grand'Mere's earth shelter and the small grove of walnut trees next to Stone Camp. He doesn't seem to mind my company and lets me just sit there without forcing conversation, but the sort of sideways talks we often have in between songs are what I look forward to most. Sitting back against the nearby stoop, closing my eyes, and letting the music wash over me—ah, it is an unexpected delight!

The thing about it is his guitar emits such a lovely variety of tones and sounds. It is so very different from the transendzz back home. There, every public space is filled with the lulling music to provide better insulation from hackers. Music is a very important tool, composed and recorded with one objective in mind: keep the brain power sequestered. L.J.'s guitar playing is so different; it makes me want to sing, and while singing is not something I'm very good at, he seems to have a way of drawing me out. There was that song again; his "go to" song. I recognized it immediately, sat up straight and smiled at my musician friend. I got up from the stoop and made my way over to him.

"L.J., you are so sweet to play your music over and over again, and I just drink it in. And you are very kind to always take time to ask me how I feel and about my family. How selfish of me to think only about myself. How about your people, near and far? Do you have family outside of FRANCO?"

"Oh no, milady, not me; not like you. They are all gone. My entire family lived here in the states when the Devastation began. We had a massive log home that my father and I built in Wisconsin—you know, up by the big Mit, right on the lake—and when the fires started Sierra and I just happened to be visiting New York's Adirondacks. We were celebrating empty nest. It was our first time in 25 years away from the homestead. Yeah, we lost everyone—our parents, our grown kids, the house—everything but the RV we drove out here. But that's not a subject that you really want to hear about, Milady. Look at you—what a blessing your life is! You fair child—you are surrounded with your family and people who love you all over the population points."

At the time it didn't hit me, but when I went to sleep last night I started thinking about what he said. People all over the population points. Hmmm. Just what was he talking about? I couldn't help but think about my parent's outlandish behavior and crazy stories. The dubious origins of their own story sent my head swirling in directions that reminded me of last winter at the Lab, when Alessandro began questioning my reliability, when everything seemed upside down. It was an unpleasant thought, but what if all the information they had been feeding me was a lie? What if I really wasn't their daughter at all? Heck—the fact that they could leave me at age 6 would make sense. I still haven't had a straight answer from her regarding the details of their departure. If they really had such a problem conceiving a child, maybe they actually adopted me. Maybe I belong to a totally different family. What else are they hiding from me? Maybe . . . well, maybe my entire life is a lie.

I took a deep breath and determined to get to the bottom of this once and for all. A vexing feeling seemed like it was beginning to seep through my pores. Oh, where is L.J. and his guitar when you need him?!?!?

Trying to quell the angst I was feeling did not work, but when I stopped to remember L.J.'s elegant, soothing chords and gentle finger-picking melodies, the familiar strands of his guitar filled my head and helped ease my growing anxiety. I began to quietly hum his go-to song.

It's funny: he's not around this morning, but sometimes I can almost hear him, just as if he is there, three feet away. It's a sort-of inexplicable thing that happens when I listen to L's music; there is a theme to it, and although I'm not sure what it is all the songs seem to resolve the same way so when I get one in my head it just seems to fold into the next. The chords aren't the same, neither are the tempos, but it's as if a particular theme drives every song.

His playing is serene and comforting, and then other times it is celebratory and just . . . plain old fun. The music is such a splendid surprise to my life and adds so much to FRANCO.

In fact, I've found that it even helps me recall the splendid mantra of The Principles.

Surround yourself with things that make you happy.

Cast off those things that make you sad.

Ah . . . I am refreshed. It's quite amazing how focusing on something better can really help a person's state of mind. Letting that music wash over me really has set my day off to a better place than where it started.

I am growing accustomed to doing just that and today is no exception. The music has eased my mind and helped me to think more clearly about setting a time to go back home. At this precise moment, however, I am simply unprepared to think about life without Russa and Viddie, so I simply . . . so, well, I will just not think about it at all.

Chapter 17

Day 111—The Surprise

Just as I was finishing up yesterday's log entry, Viddie showed up unexpectedly.

There I was, legs dangling over one of the many old railroad irons that helped us create a sitting space on Rubble Ridge; my back was to the wind and an intermittent stream of lilac petals danced past me. I was minding my own business, pen to paper, lost in my thoughts, when all at once he scooped me up from behind, turned me around and held me tightly. There he was; his delightfully rugged face greeting with me intensity and playfulness, topped off by a smile I never tire of seeing.

We started out with a good laugh as he shared what was happening back at Stone Camp. When he left, it seems Libby was bombarding L.J. with questions about his guitar playing, one after the other—non-stop. He said L. J.'s face looked like a question mark. I can just picture it—bushy grey eyebrows nearly touching each other in the middle of his large, jowly face, the familiar black patch over one eye, and his big burly mouth dropped open to a fine little "o." Viddie said that every time he tried to answer one of her questions she bolted in with another before he could even answer the last one. We had a hearty chuckle over our dear effervescent Miss Liberty Martin, but all at once our conversation landed in more serious, personal territory.

I'm not exactly sure what prompted it, but Viddie does have a unique way of disarming my self-protective tendencies. His mention of Libby and another stray comment about L.J. provoked me to admit several things to him that had been knocking around in my head for a few weeks.

It started with a funny comment that came from L.J.'s lips last week when I was sitting on the smooth gray stone that doubles as a chair in Stone Camp. It's such a delightful rock because it curves backward at just the right spot to allow me to lean back, close my eyes, and drink in the sun while listening to the quiet strands of our minstrel's finger-picking goodness. I was quietly humming the melody as he finished playing his "go to" song. When he stopped, I opened my eyes and he was looking directly at me, smiling, and shaking his head while saying something like, "all your people near and far should have the opportunity to know you, Miss Leah. You are a gem indeed, a gem indeed."

That really surprised me. Why did he say that? I wonder what people L.J. could be referring to, and—Strength—could he really think such kind thoughts about me? Although they're frequent, our conversations are not especially content-laden, mostly a lot of niceties, some encouragement, and always, a bit of laughter. Over the months we've gotten to know one another quite well and it's helped me to see how some older folks really have something special to offer us. They sort of ooze a particular kind of knowledge that I don't remember getting from my studies. My own E.E. files are so expansive, but this . . . this life wisdom is something I never learned about. L.J.'s sure got it, and Grand'Mere's got it too, of course. I see some of it in Russa, as well, but she's still fairly young.

So . . . so I was telling Viddie about how easy it is to talk with L and he stopped me cold, put his index finger over my lips, and looked at me intensely. I stopped talking, but I'm sure I looked surprised.

"You are a gem, fair lady. A gem indeed. Mr. L. J. Morehouse knows a diamond when he sees one, but I wonder . .

. can we continue this conversation about L and all that happened yesterday while we walk? I'm itching to get out to the woods, and I haven't seen you for days. Plus, I want to go out to Cloudland. Will you come with me fair princess?"

I could not help giggling. "Strength, Viddie, I just saw you last night; our families had dinner together around the pit to celebrate your birthday!"

"Yes, yes, but I haven't seen you alone in days, and I miss you."

He just makes me laugh.

So we were off, headed toward Cloudland, and with a quick reminder he prompted me to take up where I left off.

"Mmmm. I'm not sure I know how to explain it, Vid, but it's something about L.J. that makes me feel very safe, like the way I felt when I was very little, when my father was still alive . . . I mean when he was still around."

"Didn't you tell me that L. J. was Grand'Mere's friend, and lived in the flat next to you when you were very little? Surely, there's some sort of emotional connection there, Emi. Maybe it's just that strong tie with your past that is . . . I dunno, warming. . . welcoming?"

Pine needles and old leaves crunched beneath our feet as we walked and talked our way through the woods. He continued with his insightful observations.

"Emi, you had major trauma, more than most, in fact. The switching of your grandmothers, the secrecy, the two vastly different cultures—it can't be easy. It must be like you're in a time warp or something; everything has changed for you. Living out here is just normal for me—it's all I've ever known, but I can imagine it must feel like your world is upside down these days. It's okay; it's really okay to care about L.J. I can tell you feel daughterly toward him, and he obviously feels something paternal toward you. Fact is, there's something about him that makes us all feel safe. It's like he's an anchor—

the man's got wisdom. He's lived a long time; what is he? Eighty?"

Knowing that Viddie understood and didn't think me silly just felt so good. It felt good just being next to him. I feel . . . I feel . . . I don't know, somehow more anchored myself. Just knowing that someone understands me and realizes what a roller coaster ride this past four months is a help. It truly is.

Viddie didn't stop there but continued to probe my inner thoughts.

"I don't think that caring about him and feeling close to him is the thing you're grappling with most, though. You know . . . Emi . . . you need to reconcile with Liam. You are a Brown; Liam's daughter. He loves you, girl. He made choices years ago with your best interests in mind and it hurt; it stills hurts, I know it does."

"Am I? Am I really a Brown, Viddie? I hardly know what to believe anymore. Mother's so evasive about parts of the story, and even though she has spent hours trying to explain the intricacies of their reasons for leaving, I still don't know what to think. I'm wary. I just don't trust them! Tell me, don't you think that closeness is more about how a person treats another person, not just their name or blood ties? Liam's never shown me that he truly cares. How can I change that? What if all of this is a dream or a . . . or . . . or a virtual environment created by the Lab to test my loyalty?"

Oh dear, it just popped out! How did I let that happen? My guard is down and I'm just not thinking straight! I've got to cover myself!!!

Viddie's quizzical look lingered in the air between us. I immediately tried to back pedal but the man dug in and wouldn't let it go. He leaned in and looked at me squarely, seeming to pin my back to an invisible wall.

"A virtual environment? Is that what you think is going on here? Emi, look at me. Touch me. Tell me seriously, is there any question in your heart that what's going on between us is not real?

Viddie had no way of knowing how much I have struggled with these indiscernible message fragments since the day I arrived. He didn't have a clue that I have felt literally tortured some nights, wondering if I'm being tracked or if the Lab has involved me in some subversive plan or experiment. Strength—I don't trust anyone!!!! How could he really know? The look on his face was so forlorn that I had to tell him the truth. He had to know that my struggle was not about our relationship but about all these unresolved projections.

Once I told him the strangest thing happened. Without hesitation he offered a solution!

"Look at your hand, Emi. Did you forget that those small stones surrounding the amethyst are diamonds? I couldn't forget because I have heard about that ring my whole life. Why don't we remove one of those little stones and work some dust into your . . . what is it, the mechanism or device. You still have it, right? We could maybe tap into your prefrontal to get the full message or see if there's any more that you've missed. No, no my darling—this is not dream. You are here, and we are together."

Something like a weight seemed to fall off my shoulders. I felt so light and hopeful for the first time in months.

Sun streamed through the trees as we trekked toward Cloudland. On the way, he helped me devise a plan to extract the stone and after that Viddie went right back to the discussion we were having about Marissa and Liam. The man is amazing!

"Emi, I think you're only looking at him from one vantage point. Think about it: When Liam returned from the hunt and found you here, what happened the very next day? We had a party. The whole community came together, roasting the venison he brought with him and bringing every kind of confection you might imagine. We celebrated with instruments and song and feasting—and dancing! We've never had a celebration that was as elaborate. I remember you didn't say much, and we hadn't even spoken to each other yet, but tell me it wasn't a super time watching everyone dance that evening around the fire? We ate delicacies that are usually only saved for Christmas and Easter. We reveled and feasted and laughed until it was late into the night. Who do you think initiated that special time? It was your father. He organized everything. He had L.J. and Alton put together that blazing bonfire; he asked Grand'Mere to rally the women to bring out their best jams and preserved fruit; the man was beside himself with joy. He loves you, Emi, and you must know by now . . . we all do, especially yours truly."

What? Did he really say that? He did. I gasped; I'm sure I heard it. Didn't I? I really didn't know what to say so I just smiled. He slipped his hand in mine and we continued walking.

By now we were far beyond the ridge and had come upon our Cloudland. That lovely archway of trees was just up ahead.

"C'mere. I've want to show you something.

I looked at him quizzically.

"It's something a bit beyond the arbor arch, this way. C'mon. Trust me, Emi, you'll like it. I'm sure there aren't any bears or snakes; just come."

"Is this the way Earl brought me into Stone Camp? I don't think I've ever been out this far, Viddie."

"No, you haven't. When you came in it was the opposite way from Rubble Ridge—up beyond the goat herd. C'mon. You're gonna like this, I'm sure of it. It's like nothing you've ever seen, I'm sure."

The sun was hot; I was happy for the dense trees that helped shade us. After about 15 more minutes we came upon what appeared to have once been a lavish estate. A large cement fountain was situated in the middle of a mass of tangled greenery just beyond old, crackled pavement. English ivy crawled up the sides and over the top of the fountain and at each corner—perhaps 50 feet away from each other—stood four massive oak trees. Little rivulets of cement led neatly away from the center, all intact and lined with giant juniper bushes. Beyond the main fountain area, the place was littered with statuary in various degrees of disrepair. There was one of Plato pointing to the sky with his hand cut off. Another piece looked like David, the young Jewish shepherd boy, holding a sling shot. Several statues were turned completely over, some in many small pieces, others in large chunks lying on the ground. Surely, it once was a grand, grand place.

The grass surrounding the courtyard was completely covered with buttercups. Outside of the impressively large wrought iron gate and to the left was what looked like a giant roll of paper towels curled up and twisted in odd disfigurement. Upon closer inspection I saw that it was just aluminum mesh fencing that must have been ripped up by a tornado or hurricane. All along the fence were lilac bushes—huge, loping bushes, brimming with white and lavender flowers.

"This is just the courtyard, Emi. Wait 'til you see the house."

I detected a bit of awe and mystique in Viddie's voice. His mischievous smile tenderized my heart and dampened a bit of the anxiety I was feeling as we began to explore this unknown part of the mountain.

Pointing straight ahead his eager voice edged up in volume. "See—just ahead, look past those trees. Do you see it?"

He was right. Just ahead was a massive stone building mostly hidden by so many trees that it looked like it was in the woods.

"That's a pretty steep driveway, sir, and it's certainly not a house beyond that grove; more like a castle. What was this place anyway? My Strength, it's huge! And it's at the very top of the hill. What's in there? Have you ever seen the inside?"

"Oh, Miss Libby, Miss Libby, don't worry, there are no bears inside; I promise."

He got a punch in the arm for that one!

That sweet, side-winding smile of his countered the feigned mockery coming in my direction. I just shook my head and held my tongue, but he was on a roll and continued with a deep and dastardly cartoonish voice that sounded like some alien monster. What a crack-up!

"Ah, my dear, this is what I wanted to show you. Look just ahead—this is FRANCO'S closet. We use it as our storage area, a place to keep our supply of food for the winter. Wait 'til you see the inside—C'mon!"

A few feet before the front gate I stopped to catch my breath and noticed a large oblong plank hanging on a post. It was exquisitely carved around the border with leaf-like filigree and two words were burned into the wood: "Holly Hill." Seeing it provoked me to break my silence.

"I wonder who made this," I said aloud as I ran my hand over the intricate carvings that framed the words.

"Actually, we did." Viddie smiled and raised his brows with a look that let me know he was proud of his workmanship. "Yeah. Liam took me out here about seven years ago after a major community meeting about our contingencies. Once it was decided, the work was divided up so we all could have a share in it. You father and I worked on the sign back at Stone Camp—he did the lettering and I carved the leaves—so when we got here all I had to do is hold the post steady while your father hammered it in. Then we hung it through the opening here with some chain we found in the house.

"Viddie, this is astonishing. You never told me you could sculpt like this. This is a work of art! And this place—it's gorgeous, a surprise indeed. My, my, my—you are just full of surprises today!"

"You bet I am, and there's more. C'mon!"

We stepped over mangled pieces of gate and miscellaneous tree limbs as we walked hand-in-hand, occasionally brushing against each other's shoulders. As much as my heart throbbed with desire for him, I was also intensely interested in the grounds and building.

"This part definitely looks newer than all the rest of this dilapidated old estate, especially the drive up and courtyard. What an overgrown, broken down mess."

My breath was just short of panting. The elevation was much higher than Stone Camp. I could barely get the words out with any sort of a flow.

"What's this all about, Viddie? What. Whew. What. . .What do you mean, 'contingencies'?"

"This mansion is our back-up. In case any of us ever get separated from the community, or we have to flee for any reason, or if there's some sort of emergency that we haven't even thought of yet, Holly Hill is our hideaway. It's the secret that FRANCO keeps for our own safety and wellbeing. Everyone knows about it and has been here at one time or another."

"Everyone? Even Justin and Liberty?"

"Oh yeah; definitely. Especially them. I mean, they need to know where to go if there's trouble. In fact, we do drills regularly. The whole community treks out here a couple times a year so everyone knows how to find it, what supplies are here, how to utilize them; especially the kiddos. We're about due again—probably September is the next jaunt out here. We like to make a day of it."

"Well, it's good to know you all have a contingency plan because, well . . . it's not just those over-the-top snow storms or deep freeze days that worry me. You're really not terribly far from City Centre and who knows what could happen; the authorities could find you and try to meddle or . . . or even disperse the group!"

He was clear, focused, and obviously nonplused when he answered, but looking ahead to the front entrance of the building, he pressed forward.

"Right. Yeah, that's part of it too. Definitely. So . . . it's our "go-to" place where we'll meet if there if there is ever a problem or breech in security at Stone Camp."

"That's so good to hear, Viddie. I should have imagined there would be some back-up security plan, but honestly, I thought you all just walked around without a thought of the future. I mean—no offense—but it just seems that the community flows so naturally together each day, sort of mindlessly going on without a thought of trouble. Actually, it's smartest thing I've seen FRANCO do yet!"

Then it was my turn to receive a playful punch in the arm.

"I was just a teenager when they discovered this place," he said. "Truth is, I just came along for the ride. Liam, L.J., your mother, my parents—everyone in FRANCO brainstormed about all the potential problems we could face and decided to take on the estate as our own. But come on, Emi; there's more marvel to be seen. Let's check out the inside."

Overgrown holly bushes lined the soft grey stone walls of the building's sturdy facade. The wooden door was immense and looked like something right out of the French Renaissance. It was completely intact with burnished wrought iron hinges and a huge ring in the center. I swear, it was big enough for a couple of horses to gallop right through it.

A lump arose in my throat as we approached. I do hate adventure.

When we passed through the entrance way, however, I was pleasantly surprised. The room did not appear to have the same level of deterioration of everything else I've seen around the mountain. In fact, its grandeur took my breath away.

A dark, burnished banister circling upward toward a second floor led to a mural of Plato's Academy on the landing wall. It was amazing. The stairs and the foyer floor matched in deep brown wood that looked to me like walnut; Viddie thought it was mahogany.

The early afternoon sun poured in through a large window, washing over the contents of the great room with a stream of white light. It felt like another world completely.

I closed my eyes and looked down, wanting to savor the moment but it wasn't to last very long because my handsome escort thought it was time to explore.

"There are many rooms throughout this place, Emi, and it'll be fun to explore some other time, but today I want you to see the basement."

"The basement? Why do we have to see the basement?" I asked. Uggh. What if there are bugs down there?

"Come on, now Emi. You've got to trust me. This is something you need to see."

We made our way down the curved stone stairs enclosed by narrow walls on either side. It was pretty dark in the stairway and once we got to the end of it, the darkness turned black.

What little courage I have faded as quickly as the sunlight. I balked. "Viddie, wait. We don't know what's down here. There's no sunlight at all, and it's musty and—what if there are bears or snakes or big bugs—I don't like any of that stuff. Please."

"See this?" He lifted up my hand and held it tightly. I'm not gonna let go of you, Emi. No need to be afraid, I promise you. Do you hear any bears? No. They're not gonna pop in through virtual reality. Besides, oh lovely one—I've been down here countless times. I know my way around. Look, just to my left here is a candle stick with a book of matches. Here, take two steps to your right—just come with me—and let me light this. . . . See? Here, now. You can see. Look around. Do you want to hold the candle?"

"I don't like the dark, Viddie. Please. Yes, let me hold it, please."

He handed me the tiny waxed plume in a little metal holder and took my face in his hand. Looking deeply into my eyes, his words were spoken with an assuredness and confidence that wafted down about my head and shoulders like a fine, gentle breeze. It calmed me. "You can do this, Emi. I know you can. I need show you some things. C'mon, now; you need to know what's here."

I closed my eyes again, obediently following his lead and clinging to the back of his shirt. Courage is something I am still working on.

We were only down there for about five minutes because—frankly—I could hardly breathe, but he was right; the trek to the basement was well worthwhile. There were various piles of goods all covered by expansive bright blue tarps, a mountain of clothes and blankets; a full workbench and tool supply; an entire wall of canned peaches, apples, and green beans to our left, and in front of us was a creaky metal gate that opened outward revealing an incredible number of wine bottles.

Numerous oak barrels in racks were leaning one on top of the other in the far corner. The labels said molasses, honey, vinegar, and a few other things. Thick wax covered numerous large and small wheels of cheese. There were scores of them in corner by the stairs.

"Viddie, where on earth did you get all of this? And, and, my goodness, how do you even know how to use all this antiquated stuff?

"Just call me resourceful, I guess." His raised eyebrows and clownish expression made it clear he was teasing again.

"Oh, come on, Mr. Florencia. We all know you're part superman, part human, but I'd like a real, earthbound answer please."

"Emi, Emi, Emi—you know—of course—it wasn't just me. I mean, we stockpiled some of it, especially what you see here to the left, but much of it was already here. The wine, candles, matches, titanium flash lights, salt, bolts of cloth and yarn, sundry tools—they were all here. After multiple visits when we were sure that the place was abandoned we began storing a good portion of our winter food here, but we're sure to use all of it as sparingly as possible in order to keep it for emergencies—like if our crops fail entirely one year or some other sort of unforeseen problem arises."

"So, uh . . . where are the flash lights you mentioned? Can you reach one? I can barely see one foot in front of myself with this little piece of wax that's passing for a candle."

"Why are you whispering?" Viddie chuckled and leaned back.

"I don't know," I whispered back with a laugh to allay my nerves. "It just seems appropriate. I don't want to wake the dead or bother any mice!"

He was close enough for me to feel the heat of his forearm against mine, and shot me a quick backward glance as if to say, "I'm here," and then reached for one of the flashlights. Old tek, but it still works, and—wow, what a difference. Now I could really see the many layers of supplies; rows of goods on racks and shelves throughout this burgeoning storehouse were packed with boxes of canning jars, stacks of blankets, and pickles of every sort. Viddie grabbed a small waxed cheese from the top of the wooden crates closest to us along with two glasses from a closed box and then told me to pick whatever bottle I wanted from the wine cellar. Racks and racks of wine were lying sideways in small iron sleeves that jutted out of a stone archway. As we made our way over to that side of the cellar I felt like Grand'Mere's proverbial kid in a candy store, mostly because it's fun to be given a choice. What do I really know about wine? Not much, so I chose one with a little picture of some dancing shoes on the label. It said, California, pinot gris, 2021. He grabbed the bottle opener that was close by, glanced at the label and gave me a nod.

"Pinot Gris, huh? Whoa, that is old!—fifty years!"

"Yeah, it's almost as old as Grand'Mere and L.J."

We giggled and gingerly made our way up those steep stone stairs to the great room. I stretched out on the fancy leather lounge while he popped the cork. By now I was accustomed to the feel of leather on my skin, but this piece of furniture was something else. It must have been filled with feathers or some sort of time-resistant materials because it was so soft and comfortable!

"I can't believe all these supplies are here, Viddie. I wonder who did this. Who stockpiled all this stuff?

"I don't really know Emi, but we can get a pretty good idea about the people who lived here from looking at the things surrounding this place. For instance, this biggest hint is through that metal plate that we saw outside between the big bay window and the front door; it tells us that the mansion was built in 1950, and that tells us something about the people who built the place. 'Course, we know that the 1950s was a time of major change in our country. Folks were afraid of impending doom, what with World War II so recently over. And then there was the fear that the atom bomb might find its way into unethical, unwieldy hands. Think about the basement; do you realize how far below the surface it is? It's much deeper than typical basements of the time period and the measure of supply— sheesh—clearly the folks behind this project were creating a bunker. I doubt they were the ones who stocked it, though. Liam and some of the others thought it looked like twenty-first century technology. The seals on the barrels that preserve freshness, the solar-powered tools, the hand-cranked lights, the locks, the wall insulation—they're all relatively new . . . I mean, this century, new.   Perhaps the people who built it were grandparents by then or their heirs did the stockpiling. In any case, though no one would have predicted the degree of mass destruction brought about by the Devastation, I'm glad they had the foresight to prepare so well for disaster. It sure has gotten us through a few rough times."

"You sure have surprised me today Viddie Florencia. I didn't think there was anything new about FRANCO to be discovered, but you proved me wrong."

Sipping my pinot gris I wondered what California might have been like in its vineyard heyday. I savored the oaky blend of grapes that were well aged. Mmmm. It felt good to breathe deeply and be so close to him; luxurious, really. Although the surroundings were totally retro, for a second it almost felt as comfortable as home. I smiled and he continued chatting about the property and its contents.

"We certainly owe a debt of gratitude to whomever it was that took the time to so carefully preserve all these goods. But you know, I often wonder what it was like here too—like, who lived in this exact spot when the country was in full tilt—I mean, what their lives were like? Did they have vegetable gardens, multiple cars—did you see the four car garage when we were entering? We've never been able to figure any of that out, but we are grateful for the supply, that's for sure. It's helped us avoid disaster a couple of times, already."

"Really? What happened? I'd like to hear about that. Pray, tell."

Viddie poured us a second glass of wine and we cozied up even closer on that sofa. He went on to share a couple of the hard winters he remembered—times when snow kept them inside for days on end. One time, when he was a child—before the apple and plum trees were revitalized—he remembers when the winter was bitter cold and forced them inside the caverns.

The rocks kept the wind and snow away but the food supply started to dwindle so they all banned together and hiked to Holly Hill, feasting from the basement supply for nearly a week. That Christmas his mother made a special cheese spread with some of the waxed wheels, and Grand'Mere used the molasses, oats and dried grapes to make a crunchy granola and a warmingly delicious fruit and nut bread.

Funny how he can remember details like that from years ago. I can barely call up my colleague's faces and it's not even been six months since I've seen them.

Anyway, we seemed to talk for hours, nibbling away at the cheese while we shared increasing portions of our deepest thoughts. I felt a bit like I was on an old fashioned movie set, or part of a software developer's story board.

The couch was so comfortable I thought I'd get lost in it! In fact, I don't remember if there has ever been a time in my entire life when I've been as comfortable. It had been at least an hour since I slipped off my shoes and put my feet up on the arm of the sofa. Leaning back against his chest was so comfy, I didn't want to budge. But then our conversation took an unexpected turn. He put down his glass and kissed the back of my neck. He took my glass from my hand and placed it on the floor and turned me toward him. Our eyes locked and he brushed the hair away from my forehead, just the way he did that day up at the lake.

I just about lost consciousness when he drew me into his arms. The tenderness of his touch against my skin was almost too much to bear. My senses were going crazy. In a dazzling dalliance of sheer delight he drew me so close I felt his breath, hot against my cheek. Then, in a single, glorious moment his lips melted into mine and we lost ourselves in a thousand kisses. Our hearts raced with passion and I felt a burning desire to be one with him. I know he felt it too.

His wavy locks were tousled and for the first time he looked his age. Vulnerable, young, searching. His boyish smile was shy as he whispered in my ear, "This feeling. . . this depth of emotion . . . I didn't know it could be like this, Emi. Your kisses make me want to never move from this spot." His words were as gentle as the fragrance of the lilac bushes surrounding the house.

His whisper caressed my cheek as my sensory supervisor exploded within me. I drew closer and snuggled next to his chest. An other-worldly evanescence flowed through me that was unlike anything I have ever known. If this moment could last forever, it would be fine by me. Surely my words fell short of the magnitude of my emotion. "Me too, Viddie. This is all new for me, too."

"Emi, have you ever been in love before?"

"Oh dear. Love? I've imagined it, but . . . oh Viddie. . . not like this."

I tried to gain some composure but my skin felt hot and I didn't have the presence of mind to hold back any of my most private thoughts from him.

"I guess you could say I've gone through the motions and sort of 'played love' like we see Libby play house with her dolls. But this? Nothing like this, Viddie. This is a first for me.

That smile once again melted my heart. Our lips met again, burning into one another with intensity and gentleness that felt like the floor was literally moving beneath us. We were there, locked in each other's arms for the better part of the day with few words passing between us, just warmth, kisses, and long, lavish hugs.

Engulfed in the splendor of his embrace Viddie finally broke the silence before we got up to leave. With words that pierced me to the very core, I felt as though I had been transported to another planet.

"I never imagined," he said, "that falling for someone could feel this way; never. I want to know every part of you,

Emi—every bit—and I need to know if you feel the same way as I do, or is this all just a dream?"

He pulled slightly back and looked at me squarely, his face declaring in no uncertain terms what he wanted to hear.

"You've gotta know by now Viddie that I am just wild about you. You have drawn me out and helped me to make sense of my feelings and . . . and, I don't want to spend one day of life without you."

After that, more kissing engulfed us and my head felt a bit like it was spinning, but the day was growing short and we were nearly an hour's walk from Stone Camp.

We packed up the remainder of the cheese in his backpack and got ready to head back but I couldn't help lingering for a moment to take in the lavish décor and lovely design touch in the great room. I wanted to imprint the scene on my memory forever.

This was the day.

This was the moment when my life changed forever.

Viddie loves me.

I am his.

He is mine.

The entire day was remarkable, but the hours in his embrace felt almost surreal, as though my heart was glistening on a lake of diamond crystals, shimmering in the bright noon sun. With every kiss I felt him drawing me closer and closer; I yearned to touch the water, to make sure it was real. Never, ever, do I want to forget these splendid moments.

As we made our way back out of the woods, it felt as though we were walking on the clouds rather than watching them float above us. I know he felt it too. His eyes completely captured me and spoke with wordless affection.

We held hands the whole way back and our conversation took on quite a different cast then it ever had before. Anticipating each other's thoughts, finishing each other's sentences, we laughed like children nearly the entire walk back. Then he asked me a funny question about my habit of calling on my Strength. How odd, but I guess there are just as many oddities in the way he speaks as there are in mine. For Strength's sake, I need my Strength. My Strength is all I've got to help me in this world. What else could I ever call upon? I deflected, as is my default mode of operation, and laughingly reminded him that he constantly peppers his sentences with two words I've heard—gosh—hundreds of times from his lips and for no apparent reason. "I mean this and I mean that . . . I mean, I mean, I mean."

"Why do you preface so much of what you say with the words 'I mean?' Huh, Vid, huh, huh?"

For that I got tickled until I could barely breathe! We continued to talk the rest of the way back to camp and I listened intently as he bemoaned leaving the woods, explaining how significant his quiet walks out here have been throughout all his younger years. Seems the woods were formative for him much the same way my early education files have been for me.

"Yeah, in a way it's like the trees were my teachers. I love these woods, Emi. I hear the Voice of God most clearly out here."

At first I thought he was kidding. In ten seconds I knew better.

"God? I never heard you talk about God before, Viddie. Where on earth is that coming from?"

He gently squeezed my hand. "It's coming from my heart, Emi. Right from my heart."

We stopped walking for a second and he tapped his chest. The quiet here comes from spending hours walking with our Maker in these majestic woodlands. His Voice is still and small, but I hear it plainly when I take time to hear it, and I am always deeply, deeply enriched."

I was simultaneously mesmerized and terrified by this unexpected declaration of faith.

"Don't you think that if God's Voice was real other people could hear it too, Viddie?"

He looked surprised at my question but nodded confidently. "Well, yeah. I sure do."

My tone was soft, I'm sure of it, but still, I know he's not accustomed to any antagonism coming from me so I nearly whispered it: "So—how do you suppose you can hear Him if I can't?"

"I don't know that, my love. Could it be you just haven't been listening?"

He leaned over and kissed me on the forehead as we stood in the shade of two of the tallest pine trees I'd ever seen. Hmmm. How could I respond to him with anything but admiration? I didn't know how to respond so I kept silent.

L.J. was standing by the stump at Stone Camp in the distance. I could see the outline of his hat and guitar strapped across his back. We were just about there when he launched onto the subject of his fascination with the library at Holly Hill. While there, we took a scant glimpse at the many shelves of books in the second room beyond the foyer, but didn't take the time to really dig in. I hadn't realized he enjoyed reading so much.

"There's a book I read that I found there when I was 16. It's by a Frenchman who lived four centuries ago. His name was Francois Fenelon and he wrote something that I like a lot, so much so that I committed to memory.

"Oh my gosh, I was sure you were going to say Jacques Ellul!" I laughed aloud.

"See what happens when you're so sure of yourself, Miss Emi-love!" His wink took the sting out of his statement, but I'm still not sure I liked it, so I came back with my own minor dig.

"Russa loves that philosopher and has committed some of his writings to memory as well. What's with you all and the French people, eh?"

He stopped in his tracks and smiled wryly. Picking up a piece of my hair, he wound one of the curls around his finger and responded to me with a look that seemed to say, you win for now, then answered more seriously with his thoughts on the author's work.

"No, no. Ellul was the twentieth century, my dear. Fenelon lived in the 1600s. Listen, and tell me if you think it makes sense:

> 'God does not cease speaking, but the noise of the creatures without, and of our passion within, deafens us, and stops our hearing.
> We must silence every creature, we must silence ourselves to hear in the deep hush of the whole soul the ineffable voice of the spouse.
> We must bend the ear, because it is a gentle and delicate voice, only heard by those who no longer hear anything else.' " [3]

Was that a glisten in his eye? Our hearts were so in sync at that moment it's nearly as if the distance between us disappeared, but I scarcely knew what to say. Here he was talking to me twice in five minutes about God.

"The deep hush of the woods is beautiful, Viddie. I feel it too. And, the soul . . . the mention of the soul, well, that's such a mystery to me. I don't believe in such a thing but . . . I'm starting to understand that there is something deeper inside me . . . uh, under my skin that I can't . . ."

"A soul, my love. It's a soul." He spoke it lightly as he drew me close and just held me tightly without a word.

Finally, I felt I had to be honest, so—much as I hated to—I pulled away and spoke up.

"You know—I'm sorry, I really am—but I simply do not understand the notion of bending the ear to an unseen Creator-Spirit. You are such a poet and . . . oh, Viddie, you are irresistible, and as much as I'd like to just pretend that I agree, I know I only my own strength to draw from, and my own voice is the only voice I hear in my head."

The man was nonplused—it was like my retort didn't even faze him. A soft smile of acceptance spread across his face as he looked at me with a depth of feeling that was nearly as tangible as the grass beneath our feet. Then he took my hand and we made our way back to the others in quiet peace.

Funny that he proclaims his love for me and immediately begins invoking God. What an odd pairing of feelings. Even though his background is nothing like mine and he really hasn't more than a clue about neuroscience, nanotechnology, or brain chemicals, his eyes told me everything.

I do love this man.

Chapter 18

Day 125—The Grief

We found her three days ago drifting into the dimness. It's still unbelievable to me that one tiny insect—a gross, despicable spider could drain the life out of a vibrant, life-loving, beautiful human being. Even stranger is that L.J. found the bug right behind her. It was caught between the ivy leaves that were creeping up the tree behind her, dead; seemingly paralyzed in its own web. L.J. is sure it is the rarest of rare—a Brazilian Wandering spider. He was shocked to see the species in North America.

Oh, I miss her. I miss her so!!!!

It seems impossible that Russa is not here. My Strength, she just went out to see if some of the apples from the old grove were ripe enough to pick. Libby was with her and when they saw the crop, she sent her back to get a second bucket. They hadn't planned on picking so many that day but . . .well, they found so many ripe ones they could hardly help gathering them. When Libby got back she found Russa slouching under one of the apple trees, barely breathing. Her hands and feet were swollen and her eyes were little slits. She tried to rouse her and help her walk back to camp but Russa couldn't move. That's when Libby came yelping back to the camp, raving like a mad dog. It couldn't have been more than forty-five minutes that the whole ordeal took place, but we couldn't revive her . . . she was gone.

My heart has all but collapsed within me.

I can't imagine waking up again tomorrow to a world without Russa in it. It seems so impossible. I really have no desire to write a thing in this old art book, but I don't know what else to do!

Marissa came by to comfort me this morning. She brought me a new, empty art book, made from her secret stash of non-renewables. I've known about the large trunk of treasures she keeps at her bedside, but I've never seen what's inside; I guess paper is part of her treasure; it's a rare commodity here. When she appeared in the archway with the thick, leather-bound book I knew she thought it might make me smile, but . . . oh my Str . . . oh, there's no strength, and there is no comfort. Russa's never coming back.

Mother drew me near to her and spoke in hushed tones. "I've been saving this for a special time, my darling, hoping one day to present it to you. I am so sorry, so very sorry that it is on this very sad occasion, but I do hope it will cheer you, even just a bit."

She released me from her wobbly embrace and knelt by my bedside and handed me a large wad of paper loosely bound by swaths of deer hide, threaded with smaller shreds of the leather to hold it together. The cover, so beautifully decorated with grey, black, and white threads depict a mountainous pattern. It would have appealed so to Russa. Yes, she would have loved it.

Thinking of my dear departed friend again, my anger erupted.

"She wouldn't be gone if we were living like every other normal human being left on this planet, Marissa! Surely, the Lab would have a solution." I turned toward the wall.

"Stop. You know Charlie could've saved her if we had just an hour more, Leeya. He can make the serum. He has the stock of necessary ingredients. We just . . . we just didn't find her in time, love."

I continued with my face to the wall as Marissa stood to leave. She touched my elbow.

I'm sure I forgot to thank her for the book, but she left it at the foot of my straw mattress and turned to go.

"Heal, sweet daughter." She blew me a kiss and was gone.

Heal?

Ugh.

Right.

All I am is numb.

What to do?

I have no idea.

Viddie has been by several times a day throughout the last two weeks and when he comes, he holds me in his arms and I do feel slightly better but . . . but . . . he can't hold me close all day. Today, he held my hand and tried to talk to me about our plan with the diamond. I have no energy for that. Can't even think about it.

Besides, just seeing him reminds me that there was once a reason for getting up in the morning. Seeing him is a reminder of all that I have lost.

Yesterday Liberty came by with something called apple brown betty and fresh whipped crème. She coaxed me to take a bite but it seemed that my taste buds shriveled up and died along with Roos.

Nothing is appealing.

How is it possible that the others are just going on? Liam's out hunting. Marissa is weeding. Grand'Mere is staying busy canning. But when I wake there's a shallow, motionless feeling that's following me around, almost like it has a life of its own. Bhaw—these emotions! I am a fool for letting my control slip away!

Chapter 19

Day 130—The Nothing

Right after the burial Liam came to see me. It was the first time he had made such an overture in a long time. He brought with him a fancy leather bracelet—it had tiny shells woven through the top—the workmanship is exquisite, all the colors Russa loved. <<sigh>>

Seen through her beauty-loving eyes I can no more despise the work of my father or the distance he created between us then I can stop breathing. What I cannot fathom, however, is that she is never coming back.

Like a continent that has drifted far from its original land mass, my emotions are so vastly removed from my present reality that I am completely, utterly, unimaginably . . .

Undone.

We will have no more talks, no more arguments or tea or scones—she is gone, gone forever.

Russa always found reasons for grace and mercy, which is such an anomaly because the more I knew her, the more I realized that her life was not without pain, nor was it without loneliness. My goodness, the void of romance in her life lapsed on for the better part of twenty years, yet she loved life and loved me and she loved my romance with Viddie. She is the one who was always rooting for us, shoring up my weak knees and cheering on the dubious dance I've had with my emotions.

Since she arrived at Franco there seemed no possibility to find a new love of her own, yet, yet . . . she rejoiced with me in the affection Viddie and I have found—she rejoiced over every detail with never a moment of jealously, just kindness. Just generosity. What sort of person is that? How could I ever be so lucky to have a sister like that? And now that sister is gone! How can she be gone? But adulation aside, I know Russa was just a person—just like me—and we all die. One day, we all must leave this world. Today, however, I cannot cope with that reality.

My heart feels like it has been drawn and quartered and whoever is pulling the chassis has no mercy at all.

Chapter 20

Day 137—The Empty

What are words when grief does not subside?

Like a mouthful of sawdust, I cannot wash the gritty specks out of my mind's eye. I keep seeing her laughing in the sunshine, bursting into Grand'Mere's with a basketful of muffins, or chiding me with one of her many affectionate admonitions.

There are no words.

Words are not worthy.

No words.

No. No. No.

Nothing.

Day 142—The Sorrow

It's been nearly three weeks since the loss of my friend. My eyelids feel like thick, smooth stones, lying flat against my eyeballs. Every blink brings the pain of salty tears.

I am washed out.

I am lost and it's getting chilly.

Grand'Mere keeps trying to serve me soup. I don't want chicken soup. I don't want anything.

Chapter 21

Day 144—The Remembering

Today the sun was shining brightly. I peered outside and the breezy air seemed to call my name. Before I could get myself together to get out for a walk it started to rain so back to the old straw mat again.

I keep going over the things she told me, the deep, private things about Russa's life that nobody else knows, and I wince inwardly every time I think of her being in the ground underneath that old birch by the Ridge. I just can't understand why she had to die. Why so young? Why now? When I think of the rough breaks she had it makes me even sadder. She didn't deserve the life she had.

Mother thinks she knew Russa, but she had secrets that she only shared with me. She told me so. Surely Fiorella must know about Jeremy, having spent so many of those early years with her, but we never discussed it. It's likely Fiorella knows about him, but I'm certain she does not know the depth of their relationship, and I know for a fact she doesn't know about Judson.

The way Russa told it, Jeremy came into her life when she was 'the prodigal,' out on her own in New York City at 17. He was older, but not by much. I think he was 20 or 21. After two years of seeing each other, an unexpected pregnancy coaxed them to marry but a month before the date, Jeremy disappeared. It was a mysterious departure because there was no disharmony, conflict or discussion about breaking up. He was at the scene of a terrible terrorist bombing in the city and never came back to the apartment. The ordeal left Russa dazed and in shock. Her own personal Devastation, she said—and she was sure that he perished in the blast because he would never have left her. He was looking forward to the baby!

She was too ashamed to go back to New Jersey to find the Florencia's—and once Judson was born she had no way to feed him anything but mother's milk. When it came time for her to go back to work there was no one to care for him or help her in any way. Her decision to give the little one up for adoption was probably a good one, but I know she ached for him and regretted ever walking through the doors of Single View Child Services. She was such a wreck that she lost her job, and ultimately found her way back to Fiorella in New Jersey. That was just a short time before they all came to FRANCO. I know she never stopped thinking about Jeremy or little Judd. I do wonder what happened to the baby? Oh, I can hardly bear thinking about it all.

There are several things that amaze me about Russa's life and one of them is that the short season of true love seemed to sustain her for more than twenty years. It's also beyond comprehension that she could have amassed the amount of knowledge and information that she did without a formal education. Fiorella pretty much home-schooled her until she ran off. She didn't have the benefit of E.E. files or any of the downloads I've received; how crazy is that? The woman could run circles around me with her knowledge of literature and philosophy, and all with access to no more than just books and conversation! Further, it's beyond me how could she have been deprived of so much and yet continued to give and give to others, pouring out her life and wisdom on the likes of me!

Oh how I miss my friend.

It's been a few weeks now and each day since we buried her L.J. has come by to play quietly at my bedside. Over and over, he plays the songs he knows I most enjoy and generally stays for at least an hour, sometimes a bit longer. It's been something of a comfort, but then again—not really. I don't think anything will ever assuage the pain that rips through my heart every time I think about going for a walk without her.

I hate this. I really hate it! My heart feels like it has tumbled to my feet and is dragging along behind me. The torrents of this brackish water flow over and take me down. Every day, every night, there's hardly a moment when the weight of this loss doesn't sink my heart and break me in two. It is horrible, really horrible, and it's the perfect example of why controlling human emotions with technological means is the only reasonable, sane thing to do.

Day 145—The Weather

We had another very cold day this week. Grand'Mere gave me an orange-colored sweater she just finished knitting. Russa would have liked it.

Day 147—The Path

Coming from a place where virtual but maximum connectedness is the ideal, it's still hard to see why anyone would give up global citizenship and disconnect from the world—unless of course, you were my parents who had experienced such a devastating breech of confidence with the powers that be. Even then, it's hardly rational.

Yet everyone here definitely has their own perfectly legitimate (but quite various) reason for disconnecting from the global network. Everyone, that is, except me.

At first, seeing the disconnect up close was annoying, but then I became a bit more acclimated. Lately, though, I find it just plain uninteresting to listen to their stories. I want to be alone.

The feeling of being known and seen and—yeah, maybe loved—whatever—is more than it's cracked up to be; It's downright dangerous.

I feel unprotected.

Oh.

Yeah.

Well.

Viddie continues to come by.

Yesterday he sat by my cot and was quiet the entire time he was here. He smiled but didn't say much. Before he left he brushed the hair away from my face and held my hands in his hands, the way he often does.

Then he sat without a word for at least a half hour, bowing his head; silent.

The day before he was quite talkative. He asked me to remember our fun times at Holly Hill and at the resort. He tried to make me smile. I have no patience for happiness.

Then he brought up "my strength," and told me I needed to draw from it, to dig down deep and stand in the knowledge that there's a purpose for my life. He said,

"You're strong, Emi. Don't you forget it. You have strength, don't let it go."

Ha! Like I have any anymore, right?

This life is just not fair.

I did not ask for love.

I did not ask for friendship.

Taking up either one is far too dangerous a journey to ever embark upon again.

Chapter 22

Day 150—The Strength

A brooding sky eclipsed the few shining rays of sun peeking out from behind the clouds. I wasn't sure which way to go so I just continued, walking, walking, walking until my legs could carry me no farther.

It's the first full day on the road. I hope I won't need more than two.

I was up most of the night, walking until at least 3 and then took a short break. Who knows if I'll ever find my car.

I don't recognize a thing out here.

The quilt in my backpack is the one Grand'Mere made me; It's thin, but it is made from duck down so I was able to sleep in quasi-comfort for a few hours until the sun rose and I was on my way again. Plus, I've got her sweater.

Nothing looks familiar.

I am running again. Is it a dream? This time I can't tell. This time there really are dangers that are hawking me. The first problem was brought on by my own carelessness.

My troubles began with the ferocious clatter of an unwelcome acquaintance, the vacuum; it struck up again and came on strong—worse than ever! When I first heard it the sound shocked me. Why now? I panicked and started to run. I didn't realize that I left my shoes on the floor.

Uhhhhhhhhhhhh. The pebbles felt like glass against my skin. It was so bad I had to double back and retrieve my stupid shoes.

I can't let this pain take me out.

It must have been somewhere just before midnight that I got past Rubble Ridge and found myself at the old resort; By now I think I'm probably about eight hours past it, unless I've been walking in circles.

The water and berries I brought along have sustained me thus far, but I do feel a bit dizzy. Taking this short break to eat is an unwanted necessity. The soles of my feet hurt, and all I want is to find my way back to the old roads.

Sitting here against this shady pine, my attempts to flee the vacuum's terror prove useless. Beads of sweat bubble up on my forehead. As tired as I am, there's a strength surging through me, just like Viddie said. There's a way out of these woods, I'm sure of it. Even if a vacuous, haranguing sound is nipping at my heels, even if it is somewhere within me and I am forced to live forever with this unforgiving nemesis, I will not stop. I will not give in. I am strong.

Is this my soul? Is this the place they all talk about—the Emilya inside me? This, this place within that is being hammered with taunting anticipation—is this the true me? I'd prefer to think it is only a hallucination, but unfortunately the regularity and recurrence of this vengeful opponent prompts me to think it is me, just me. If so, I will conquer it—this plight that feels like a consuming vacuum, this empty caldron that echoes with sputtering snippets of desperation and glee. In spite of my inability to engage my tek and straighten all this out, I'm glad I know that my feelings cannot ultimately control me. I must be strong.

Just like before, I haven't a clue where that hellish sound is coming from, so the only thing I can think to do is run. Ugghhhhhhh, my feet are bleeding—flesh sticking to the leather bottoms of these awful, make-shift shoes.

I am panting.

My thoughts swirl and now the sun is up and strong. The field before me has a few shade trees, and I've come out of the woods.

If I stop I may never get up, but . . . oh dear, a short break is needed.

Strength, where am I?!?!

My emotions are out of control. The vacuum's roar is so loud I begin to hold my ears. It's much worse than last winter at home. Where is this coming from? Why is it harassing me? Why now?

Right now my heart is as raw as my feet.

It was so much easier when I didn't know there was anything more to my existence than succeeding at work. But now I want to do more; I want to be more; My thoughts careen as I jog down the side of the foothill.

I don't know how to get there or exactly what it all means, but something's not right and this machine feels like it's getting ready to plow me down in my tracks.

There's a walnut tree just a few yards ahead. I . . . I need to stop, lean against it and catch my breath.

Finally, a moment of rest.

So here I sit, pen in hand, swatting the echo of voices from Stone Camp as if they were mosquitoes ready to suck my blood.

"Where is she?"

"Oh, my little girl; my beautiful little girl!"

"Leeya, Leeya—where are you?"

Ugggggh, my head is blaring!

Oh dear, just a few more pieces of Grand'Mere's crisp granola chunks at the bottom of the pouch. Not too much water left either.

I try to take stock. It's got to be close to evening but the sun is still up at about 3 o'clock.

I don't think I can walk anymore. . .

A short nap and I'm ready to run again. Maybe if I head down to the left in the opposite direction of the woods.

I'm running and my mind races to the possibility of seeing my workmates again.

Where once I heard them loud and clear using the P/Z 1000, today they are just fading memories in my ear. Is Paty's hair blonde or light brown? He is such a good designer. I wonder what he's developed in my absence. And Jude . . . Zeejay and Alessandro, what are they doing? Are they wondering about me?

Not that I ever felt terribly close to Jude or Zeejay, but it's hard not to wonder how they are doing, what they are working on, or if they even think of me. Have they tried to visit me at Addison Avenue? I wonder if they've tried to leave messages on my interior wall?

Dusk has set in I think I am on the right track.

Jotting down a few landmarks here under an old overpass, a soft rain falls. The road looks like it leads somewhere so I scribble it down to remember in case I start going in circles.

My pace has slowed considerably and now that I am out of water, things could get dire.

Wait, there's a dusty old road and a bended sign. I run.

I hobble.

There's a small grove of trees.

Oh my Strength, is that a car behind the branches?

Am I seeing things?

Strength—it's a Trans Am. Oh my Strength, it's my little '70 oxio7200!!!

What? The key is in the car and it turns on. I'm in the back driver's lounge, bleeding, panting, feeling exhilarated.

The extremely luxurious microfiber sofa covering over my backseat lounge is perfect. What a welcome relief.

The GPS works—a lifesaver. I pass my palm over the button that says "home."

City Center can't be more than 30 minutes away.

Could it be I am really here?

Am I dreaming?

My head.

My head.

My head is swirling.

Chapter 23

Day 152—The Arrival

Okay, okay, maybe there is something to miracles. I don't know how it's really possible, but it just must be a miracle that I found my car and that it worked.

It's day two that I am home here, my feet are swollen and the skin is broken and bruised. I can barely move, but . . . but I am here.

Not much has changed in the flat. From the looks of it, no one has come searching for me in all these months away.

My feet are bandaged and raised. My poor head still throbs.

Thankfully, the provisio console is full. I'm glad I remembered to order a new rack last winter. Ah—and a month's supply of bottled water neatly lines my pantry shelves. I am saved!

Ugh—But who feels like eating?

The ache in my heart is so deep that it seems to echo through my walls.

Here I am, almost six months since I left and not a thing is changed. It's as if I've never even been away.

The vacuum has subsided a bit, but periodically continues to taunt. Water, more water. That should take some of the pressure away. My muscles need water. I'm sure I'll be fine before very long.

My mind wanders back to Viddie and then to the Lab. I can't think about him. I've got to check in with ADMIN soon, but when?

The maddening questions of the winter have all been answered but they have led to new ones and they are even more daunting than before.

Without supplies from the department I can't get my P/Z working again and my walls are silent. Should I go to the Lab? What should I tell them? Should I warn Jude and Zeejay about the false campaign regarding the state of things on this planet or go straight to the top and feign innocence? Should I approach Alessandro directly?

If I do get his ear, will he turn on me and interrogate me and make me compromise the people I care about in FRANCO?

What if they find out and go raid Stone Camp?

Oh dear, I hadn't fully thought that out.

I flip through the ragged edges of my new art book and run my hand over the leather threaded mountain scene on the cover.

What is my place?

Is there any place in the world for the likes of me?

Chapter 24

Day 154—The Realization

I'm not dreaming. Four days back and the realization that I am no longer at FRANCO has settled in on me, deeply. My head has finally stopped throbbing.

The lovely sense of aloneness and privacy that I have craved for so long has faded fast and I am acutely aware that I will never be the same.

All I have here is this book and these walls. I can't even run to the Lab to say hello because I don't know how to explain myself. I don't know where to start!

The walls are silent and it's creepy quiet around here. What I wouldn't give for a simple word from my interior messenger right about now! I could certainly benefit from the gentle rhythms of those faithful admonitions ready to calm me down at the slightest rise of blood pressure, but alas—without the diamond dust I can't renew any of my tek. Ughhh.

Oh Strength, strength—I need strength. I need some of that Russa-wisdom and . . . and a taste of Fiorella's scones and even mother's rants and—oh!—I need Viddie's arms. What's wrong with me?

There is a whole world out there that no one knows about; no one even thinks about it.

It was mine and I left it!!

He was mine and I left him.

I want to go outside and see if there are any birds singing, but my feet hurt too much. I am stung with the realization that I may have just made the biggest mistake of my life. I left the little finches along with everyone I care about back on the mountain.

Regret engulfs me.

Russa's gone, but she's not the only person in FRANCO who matters to me.

What did I do?

What's wrong with me?

The urge to run washes over me, but my feet won't carry me, I am sure. I still can barely move them.

Lamenting, I doze a bit, and start to fall into a fitful sleep when a knock at the door startles me.

Surprised, I hobble to the door and hang on the knob before I open it. "Yes? Who is there?"

A voice I clearly recognize answers me.

I fling open the door and two grey-blue eyes, rimmed in red and deeply set greet me with hardly a trace of a smile.

I look back at the chair I had been dozing in to make sure I'm not dreaming.

"How? What? How did you get here? How did you find me?

Stunned is the only word to describe what I am feeling.

The dirty-crusted face and weak posture didn't dampen his humor. "Guess you could just call me resourceful."

With that, Belvedere Florencia falls into my arms.

Chapter 25

Day 155—The Tangle

The events leading to yesterday's reunion with the man I love more than my own breath have become something of a blur. I barely remember much of the last month except for the site of Russa's breathless body beneath the tree and my straw mat at Grand'Mere's. How I even got home is a mystery to me. How it is possible that my car was untouched and still working—uh—it's crazy. If miracles do exist, this is one of them.

He's sleeping now in the vacation room, sprawled out on the travelounger. He'll probably sleep the whole day away, just like I did a few days ago. I wish I could call up an Xtreme vacation package for him, somewhere completely relaxing—the Caribbean, perhaps—and let the pristine waters of the southern sea renew his body and mind. Alas, that will have to wait until I can figure out how to reconnect with the Lab and renew my supplies.

Yesterday was more than a miracle. I truly thought it was a dream. The sight of Belevedere Florencia in my front room shook me to the deepest parts of myself and nearly made me believe there is such thing as a soul because what I felt was inexplicably deeper than anything I can possibly hope to communicate in writing.

When I first saw him he fell into my arms and clung to me so tightly. Then words began to tumble out of his mouth. Words, strung together and all a-jumble, some didn't even make sense. Finally, he was clear.

"How could you leave me? How could you venture out without bringing me into your plans? I thought we were something. I thought . . . we were real."

Regret continued to well up inside me until it began to pour out of my tear ducts. "I'm so sorry, Viddie. I'm a fool. I'm so deeply, deeply sorry."

He kissed the tears off my face and took both my hands in his own. I coaxed him away from the door and made him sit down. His shirt was torn along the sleeve with three parallel rips like something pawed him, and his face was caked with dirt everywhere.

"We belong together, Emi. Tell me you know that now. Please."

On the left side of his head the brown curls were matted down with uneven chunks of mud; his face and arms were streaked with so much dirt it looked like he must have rolled down that mountain.

"You need a shower, Viddie. C'mon. You must feel terribly gritty. Let me show you to the bathroom and get you some soft towels."

"No, no, not yet. I'm not letting you out of my sight, not until we get some things cleared up."

Viddie seemed determined, and although I didn't perceive anger, nor even a hint of a smile, his face was soft; his demeanor, tender.

"Of course." I hobbled from the couch and grabbed him a bottle of water from the rack. "Tell me, how did you find me? How did you even get to City Centre?"

"Shhhhh." He placed his finger over my lips as I handed him the drink and sat close by his side. His voice started to crack as he placed his other hand on my knee. "That's not what we're going to talk about now. I want to know where we stand. Are you with me, Emilya Hoffman-Bowes Brown? Are we together or are you just going to run away from me? Is that what this is all about? Because if it is, I will back off. You don't have to leave everyone who loves you just because you don't want a life with me."

Once again I found myself giving into helpless tears. Talk about emotions being off the chart! Through choked words I could no longer keep back the deepest pantings of my heart.

"Viddie, I am a mess. Look at me! I don't know what's happening to me. Up is down and down is up; black is white; everything I thought I understood my whole lifelong is changed. It's all wrong. Everything here is wrong. I can't make sense of any of it! If love is something good it shouldn't hurt like this. How can I possibly expect to give my heart to you only to know that one day you will be ripped away from me just like my parents, my Grand'Mere, and now Russa? I don't . . . I won't. . . . I don't want that kind of pain! I don't know, I don't know. I'm afraid I don't know anything anymore. Truth is, the only thing I do know is that I love you with every last molecule that is in me and I never want to spend another minute without you, but . . . but . . . there's one . . . ."

He cut me off at the chase. With eyes were wider than I'd ever seen them before Viddie grabbed me to himself and held me closely, then looked at me squarely. Those amazing, sensual eyes beckoned me, drawing me with a depth of emotion that I found impossible to resist, and at that precise moment filled up to the brim with glassy water that seemed just on the verge of spilling over.

"I knew there was a 'but' in there, Emi. There's something wrong. You want me as much as I want you—I can feel it. But what's happened between us? What's stopping you? What made you leave me?"

To try and explain my actions to him was nearly impossible, especially since I can hardly begin to really understand them myself. I wanted to crumble into his arms, lay there against his strong chest and never move another inch, but it needed to be said. He needed to know, and I could see in his eyes that he was not going to let me move from the sofa until I gave him a real answer. It was as good a time as any. I drew a deep breath and plunged right in.

"I'm not from FRANCO, Viddie. There will be things I will miss about the mountain, but I've felt like an alien the entire summer. This is my home."

A lump the size of a peach pit formed in my throat as he searched my face for an answer that I couldn't give him. It felt like I swallowed one of L.J.'s hard honey candies whole, and suddenly I went completely dry. I licked my lips and swallowed hard. As difficult as it was to tell him, I had to continue.

"I have to go back to the Lab. I've got to find my way back into ADMIN'S good graces. If I'm to do any good here at all I've got to figure out how to go back to work without letting on about FRANCO. If they know there's a community that's functioning just a few hours away outside of their authority, well, who knows what might happen to you all? And Viddie, I've got to renew my tek; don't you see? There's so much that needs attention here. There's a life here for me and . . . work for me to do, and Viddie . . . Viddie I can't go back there. I don't belong in FRANCO."

Eyes that pierce the soul—that's what he has. Oh, dear— the concept of the soul is becoming too hard to deny because something so deep inside of me has broken wide open and I have no other explanation as to what it is.

"All you have to do is open your mouth and I'm sure you will pull on my jagged emotions and remind me about Grand'Mere and mother and all the others, but I can't let you sway me and, and, and . . . the fact is, I couldn't bear saying goodbye to you, so I . . . I just left."

As I watched his face, his eyes softened and his tears flowed openly; still he did not turn his gaze from me. The encounter was nearly too much for me to bear but he would not budge until he was satisfied. He stared at me and did not blink;

our eyes locked. To see him in such pain: swollen feet, dirty, smelly, miserable, feeling betrayed—oh, I don't deserve him, but he does deserve more than I've given him thus far, so I continued to dispense with my feeble rationale anyway.

"Feeling everything all the time is too intense, Viddie. It is excruciating and unfair, and that's what you do—you all do it—at FRANCO. You relish your emotions. Allowing oneself to be that vulnerable, why it's torture, sheer torture. So I ran. I ran and I wasn't thinking straight. It wasn't a rational decision, I know that. And I was wrong to run from the problem, I know that now too, but I just didn't see any way around it. Viddie, this . . . this is my home. I belong here."

Total silence ensued. Mere seconds passed. Water still flowed unhindered from my eyes, but his tear-stained face was now dry.

"Are you finished?" He finally spoke and repeated himself almost immediately with greater verve. "Are you finished?"

I shook my head in confusion. "I . . . I don't know. For now, maybe, yes. I'm finished for the moment, but there are a great many things I am feeling and until I can find a way to cap them and control them there's no telling what I'll say. Do you see? Do you see? I am out of control!"

"You may be out of control, but you need to know one thing before we go any further with this conversation." His red rimmed eyes appeared almost steely as he spoke, but then they softened again, just a touch, and seemed to engulf me.

"You are my home, Emilya Hoffman-Bowes Brown. You are where I belong. We will figure out the Lab together, do you hear me? I don't care where I live out the rest of my days, but as long as you are with me I know I will be home."

The End

ENDNOTES

[1] McCartney, Paul, "I Will," by Paul McCartney and originally recorded on the album, The Beatles, 1968, LP

[2] Sertillanges, Antonin, The Intellectual Life: Its Spirit, Conditions, Methods, first published in 1920, translated into English by Mary Ryan in 1946. Current editions published by Catholic University of America Press, Washington DC

[3] Francois Fenelon "God Does not Cease" Christian Perfection. Minneapolis: Bethany House, 1975, pp 155-156.

We hope you have enjoyed *Breaking the Silence*, Book 2 in the Within the Walls trilogy. You can learn more about the author, purchase copies of Books 1 and 2, or find updates about Book 3 in the trilogy online at: **www.wildflowerpress.biz**

The eBbook versions of these books are available on Kindle (at Amazon.com) and Nook (at BarnesandNoble.com).

Like fiction with a message?

Wild Flower Press, Inc. currently offers books by:

Stephanie Bennett

- *Within the Walls* (Book 1 in the trilogy)
- *Breaking the Silence*, (Book 2 in the *Within the Walls* trilogy)
- Book 3 to be launched in 2014

Terry L. Craig

Fellowship of the Mystery trilogy available in paperback or eBook:
- *GATEKEEPER*
- *SOJOURNER*,
- *SWORDSMAN*

AND

- We're happy to announce the launch of the first book of Terry's new fiction series, ***Scions of the Aegean C*** in the spring of 2014.

To learn more about our books or read our articles, visit us on the web at:

www.wildflowerpress.biz